Rustling

A Frank 'Buffalo Robe' Bass Novel, Volume 7

Will Astrike

Published by Will Astrike, 2024.

This is a work of fiction. Similarities to real people, places, or events are entirely coincidental.

RUSTLING

First edition. July 9, 2024.

Copyright © 2024 Will Astrike.

ISBN: 979-8227177827

Written by Will Astrike.

Also by Will Astrike

A Frank 'Buffalo Robe' Bass Novel
The Skills of Ezra Lacey
Rustling
Track Down

Standalone
The Knack
Amos Getting - A Life on the American Frontier
The Joe Neely Files
Slaughter

Watch for more at https://www.westernauthor.net.

Table of Contents

What Readers Are Saying About Will Astrike and the Frank Bass Series

Meet Buffalo Robe Bass, the Crocodile Dundee of Wyoming Territory. But wait...his lady friend, Sally Bloom, is every bit his match. This sleuthing pair brings the Old West back to life, keeps you guessing until the last page, and leaves you hoping that Bass and Bloom and company will soon ride again. –Margaret Coel, New York Times bestselling author of *Winter's Child.*

... As a writer who lives in Wyoming and writes about the West, I can honestly say he nails it: lock, stock, and barrel. Speaking of new heroes, when you think Will Astrike, think early Elmore Leonard. - Gregory Zeigler - Author of The Jake Goddard and Susan Brand Thrillers

I loved the whole book. Characters, plot, and descriptions were all excellent. I especially enjoyed the language—the expressions, idioms, and pace were outstanding. It put you back to the 1880s and how people talked, dressed, and acted. Will read the next book. Thanks, Deputy Marshall Bass, for letting me ride.

... the book was well written, the characters fun, and the story interesting. I have read all of Louis Lamour's books, many two or three times and Will Astrike might be just as good a writer.

This was a great read with outstanding characters and lots of action. Would highly recommend this book to all those that enjoy a great Western story.

Book two of the Frank Bass series by Will Astrike. This story was full of mystery and drama. Enjoyed every page. Thank you.

An excellent read. Keeps you tapping the Kindle. The characters are exciting and believable. I am anxious to read more of Ezra Lacy's adventures. All of you cowboys and cowgirls will enjoy this book. So, "Giddy Up."

... I still think Will Astrike may be the best Western author since Louie L'Amour. I look forward to his next book.

A most wonderful read. Gotta love following Deputy Marshall Bass and Sally around and the messes they get themselves into!

Frank Bass series book Three by Will Astrike. I love the character of Frank Bass. The legendary Marshall of the West. This has been a great series and I've enjoyed reading each book. This story's legacy of the young man who wants to clear his father's name is a good one also.

Another great read. Excellent characters, plot, and description of surroundings. But my favorite thing is the dialog. The idioms and meanings of the day are right online. I had never heard of "consists" used as a noun. Keep 'em coming.

5.0 out of 5 stars[1] **Another winner...**[2]

Reviewed in the United States on May 26, 2023

Verified Purchase[3]

I enjoyed the read... fast-paced...I learned a thing or two about how people lived and survived back then...The descriptions of the city of Austin, the bars, hotels, were great...The characters? AWESOME!!!!...I was never a huge fan of Western novels, but Will Astrike has made me a Frank Bass fan for life...can't wait for Book 6?

Robert F. Thompson[4]

5.0 out of 5 stars **Good read**[5]

---

1. *https://www.amazon.com/gp/customer-reviews/R26H0QCY8Q8LCY/*

   ref=cm_cr_dp_d_rvw_ttl?ie=UTF8&ASIN=B0C46S7751

2. https://www.amazon.com/gp/customer-reviews/R26H0QCY8Q8LCY/

   ref=cm_cr_dp_d_rvw_ttl?ie=UTF8&ASIN=B0C46S7751

3. https://www.amazon.com/gp/help/customer/display.html/

   ref=cm_cr_dp_d_rvw_avp?nodeId=G75XTB7MBMBTXP6W

4. https://www.amazon.com/gp/profile/

   amzn1.account.AGVRXE5V3GWY4MVWOFFG4HQQ3K5A/ref=cm_cr_dp_d_gw_tr?ie=UTF8

5. https://www.amazon.com/gp/customer-reviews/R19QYQOSC6A2ZN/

   ref=cm_cr_dp_d_rvw_ttl?ie=UTF8&ASIN=B0BYMDXKSD

Reviewed in the United States on October 6, 2023

Verified Purchase[6]

I have read Mr. Astride's Frank Bass series also...This one was really good...the colorful characters...the historical figures of the West came alive...The Texas Rangers...The Indian Nations...The Civil War...Custer...Crook...I will read anything else by Mr. Astrike...

Deborah Sue Lacy[7]

5.0 out of 5 stars <u>Great writing</u>[8]

Reviewed in the United States on December 3, 2023

<u>Verified Purchase</u>[9]

You, sir, are an awesome writer, and the story of Amos Getting was the BEST Western I've read in my 75 years, of which the last 65 have been as an avid reader.

---

6. https://www.amazon.com/gp/help/customer/display.html/
ref=cm_cr_dp_d_rvw_avp?nodeId=G75XTB7MBMBTXP6W

7. https://www.amazon.com/gp/profile/amzn1.account.AF453PUPKMFW2CN3CYEP6ZWGA63Q/
ref=cm_cr_dp_d_gw_tr?ie=UTF8

8. https://www.amazon.com/gp/customer-reviews/R394E73STG0YX9/
ref=cm_cr_dp_d_rvw_ttl?ie=UTF8&ASIN=B09SX1JHZW

9. https://www.amazon.com/gp/help/customer/display.html/
ref=cm_cr_dp_d_rvw_avp?nodeId=G75XTB7MBMBTXP6W

Other Books

By Award Winning Author
Will Astrike
The Knack
The Skills of Ezra Lacy
Legacy
Stolen
Amos Getting
A Life on the American Prairie
Slaughter
The Regulator
And Soon to be Released
GUNSLINGER

- Winner of the 2024 International Impact Award for Historical Fiction*

Copywrite Page

Copywrite, 2024

William F. Oesterreich

As

Will Astrike

Rustling

Will Astrike

Prolog

12:15 a.m. October 12th, 1888
  Near Santa Gertrudis Creek
  Wild Horse Desert,
  Nueces Strip, Texas

Six men on horseback, working by the light of a gibbous moon, had encircled a herd of twenty-four Longhorn cattle and were quietly moving them north to the San Fernando Creek. They'd follow the creek to the small town of Aguileras. From there, they'd drive them west to their final destination, the Tierra Blanca Ranch outside of Laredo, a journey of about twenty-five miles. The leader of the group was an outlaw named Dan Bogan, and with him were 'Cherry' Lennox, 'Bloody' Ron Fox, Lonny Dahl, the younger, and two Mexican Vaqueros whose names Bogan didn't care to remember.

They'd stolen the Longhorns from the King Ranch, and the animals all had the Running W brand licensed to that ranch burned into their hips. The Longhorns were an experimental group that Richard King used to improve the breed. As they were, the Longhorn, a hybrid animal of Spanish Retinto stock, was a hearty breed that matured quickly, could eat and thrive on almost any grass, and produced leaner meat than fattier breeds. But its skittish, even aggressive temperament, born of years in the wild, made it difficult to domesticate. The King Ranch had been working on a crossbreed for years that retained all the finer qualities of the breed but produced a more docile animal. These twenty-four cows that Bogan had rustled represented one of the results The King Ranch had produced over three years. It also represented a sizeable investment in dollars as well.

By sunrise, the herd had made twenty miles, and by mid-morning, they'd be within a few miles of Tierra Blanca. The owner of Tierra Blanca was a man named Landon Atwill, who'd won a stake in the ranch in a rigged card game. Over the years, his four partners in the spread had sold out or... disappeared. It was widely assumed that Landon Atwill had arranged the disappearances. He was a tall, thin man of elegant bearing and speech. At forty-five, he owned the second-largest cattle ranch north of Brownsville. Only the King Ranch was larger. To look at him, he was certainly not the type you'd figure for a cattle thief. And yet he waited anxiously for the arrival of the new stock. His foreman, a grizzled older man named Banes, had created a running iron that would change the Running W to look like an A, which was the brand registered to Tierra Blanca. Because the animals were experimental, the King Ranch had tattooed an identifying marking on each animal's left ear. Changing the tattoos on the ear was more complicated and would take longer, but at first blush, the animals would look like they belonged to Atwill.

At daybreak, the herd was eight miles outside of Laredo when they confronted a posse led by U.S. Marshal Harold Gosling. With him were five well-armed deputies, and they'd formed a line blocking the only bridge over the San Ygnacio Creek, which was notorious for being steeply banked and difficult to ford. Marshal Gosling pointed his pistol at Dan Bogan and spoke first.

"Dan? I don't suppose you have a bill of sale for them animals, do ye?" Bogan smiled and looked back at his men.

"No, Harold, we don't, and that's a fact." Gosling swallowed hard then and said,

"Well, you and your boys are under arrest for cattle thieven." At that, Bloody Ron Fox, who was behind Bogan, lifted his saddle gun and shot Gosling through the chest. He then took aim at a deputy and shot him, too. Everyone was shooting by then, and when it ended, Gosling and four deputies lay dead on the ground. The fifth deputy had the presence of mind to turn his horse's head north and spur the animal into a full gallop. Dan Bogan and his three remaining men, one of the Vaqueros had been shot dead, and the other run off, set about rounding up the small herd that had spooked and scattered when the shooting started. They delivered the cows to the Tierra Blanca at 11:00 a.m. that morning. By noon, the four remaining riders had been paid and had lit out to Nuevo Laredo on the Mexican Side of the Rio. Dan Bogan, their leader, stayed behind.

At 1:00 p.m., Landon Atwill was sitting on the veranda of the main house at Tierra Blanca. He had a plate of beefsteak and eggs in front of him and a whiskey and apple juice sitting on his right. Atwill dressed as he usually did when he was about to go riding, in tight-fitting breeches, a white shirt with a black vest, and a red riding jacket. He wore black, knee-high paddock boots in the style of English Gentry and carried a thirty-inch riding crop. Atwill came from a moneyed family in Georgia and took great pride in his personal habits and appearance. The treacherous manner in which he acquired the Tierra Blanca was also a source of pride. He enjoyed the reputation of ruthless cattleman and took every opportunity to enhance that reputation. He was also, however, a pragmatic businessman, and the two personas' were occasionally at odds with him. For example, the killing of a U.S. Marshal was good for his reputation, but he knew it could ultimately be bad for business. That's why he waited for Dan Bogan's arrival to begin his breakfast.

The outlaw sauntered onto the veranda, spurs a-jangle and cutting into the woodwork. Atwill decided to be tolerant. Bogan sat at the chair opposite Atwill without his employer's leave, and Atwill again was tolerant.

"Whatcha got there, boss? Steak and eggs? Sounds good to me, too. Long trail last night." Atwill raised his index finger, and his long-time butler, a mestizo named Mateo, standing nearby, nodded silently and went inside the kitchen. Mateo was more than a manservant to Atwill. He was an accomplished killer who was half Spanish and half Mexican Nahua, a descendant of Aztec blood. He had trained with the Nahua as a sniper and assassin during the

Franco-Mexican war and killed more French Fighters than any one man in that conflict. Benito Juarez had decorated him personally.

He was Atwill's constant companion and saw to the older man's every need. Though he rarely spoke, he understood every nuance of Landon Atwill's behavior, and there was no command, task, or chore that he would not complete for his master. He set a plate similar to Atwill's in front of the rustler and returned to his place at the doorway. Atwill spoke first.

"So, Daniel, you've brought me a very great prize in those heifers. I know that Captain King invested a great deal of time and money in creating the herd. Thank you."

"Hell, don't thank me, Atwill, just pay me what you promised, and we're quits here. I got places to see yet, and I'll need money to spend." Bogan was smiling at Mateo and Atwill while he spoke. As he chewed, a dribble of grease escaped his mouth and ran down his chin. Atwill noted it and moved on.

"Yes, yes, of course. There is, however, the matter of Marshal Gosling and his cohorts. I take it you left them at the bridge to be discovered by passers-by?"

"Hell yeah, I did. Listen, them cattle scattered at the first sound of gunfire and wouldn't cross that damned bridge till the smell of smoke had cleared. ' Had my hands full, see. Didn't have no time to be hidin' no bodies."

"Yes, I'm sure you're right, Daniel, but your actions have put me in an awkward position, you see. By now, the deputy you allowed to escape will have returned with men to retrieve the bodies, and the trail of a small herd of cattle to my land will be easy to follow. Do you take my meaning?"

"Atwill, how the hell did you find out all this so quickly?"

"Mateo here had a conversation with your men while paying them. It was an illuminating discussion." Bogan just shook his head as if none of what happened mattered.

"You got your Longhorn cattle like you wanted. Now, it's time to pay up. And because we had that trouble with Harry Gosling, my fee is doubled." Atwill remained calm and smiled.

"Yes, of course, and just payment you shall have." Atwill glanced away at nothing in particular, and Mateo silently stepped behind the outlaw. In one motion, the Mestizo pulled back Bogan's head and sliced open the man's throat, throwing him into the dirt alongside the veranda. Bogan was still conscious, clutching at his neck, choking as he watched Atwill walk away.

Atwill went to the corral where the Longhorn heifers stood idly gazing about their surroundings and grunting in that breed's peculiar way. He called his foreman to him, an older man wise to the ruses and tricks of cattlemen, and asked. "Mr. Banes, now that you've seen them, are you still certain you can alter the brand?" Willy Banes had been around cattle all his life. There wasn't much about cows he didn't know. As a younger man, he stood mostly honest, the only way for a young cowboy to continue to get work. As he grew older, the trail bosses didn't want him. They assumed that an old cowboy might quit in the middle of a drive or leave at branding season. It was hard work, after all, and older men sometimes didn't measure up. He took the job at the Tierra Blanca because it meant a good living at easy tasks, even if it was a bit dishonest. It was a trade-off old men sometimes had to make. Now, he was charged with the task of altering the 'Running W' to the 'Circle A' brand of Tierra Blanca.

Banes took a long look at the 'Running W' brand of the King Ranch. It wasn't the first time he'd seen it. It had been designed, as most were, to thwart rustling and to heal quickly. The King Ranch was the largest cattle outfit in Texas and pretty much dominated the state's southeastern corner. "Yes sir, the River mark won't be no problem, but that damned W, well, I'm gonna have to use an acid wash and burn the A over it. The earmarks we'll just cut off. After a month or so, you won't be able to tell the difference. In the meantime, we'll run 'em up to Botines. Quiet up there, nothin' but peons and tame Indians." Atwill nodded, pleased that the old man had devised a workable plan.

"Fine, fine, Mr. Banes. How long will they be here, do you think?"

"Should be finished with 'em by day after tomorrow. If you're worried about snoopers after what happened at the bridge, me and the boys can move 'em over toward the Rio, up in the hills, to do the branding. Might be a good idee anyway."

"Indeed. Please see to it, Mr. Banes, move them as soon as possible. I'll be riding for the next hour or so.

Banes touched the brim of his hat, "Yes, sir." And Atwill walked to the barn.

Noon, October 14th, 1888
King Ranch Headquarters
Santa Gertrudis Creek
North of Baffin Bay

In 1853, a riverboat captain named Richard King partnered with a Captain of the Texas Rangers named Gideon K. Lewis to form a cattle ranch in the Santa Gertrudis Creek area. The original ranch was comprised of fifteen thousand five hundred acres in a Spanish Land Grant named Rincon Santa Gertrudis. The brand used for the original herd was the LK for the ranch founders. Gideon Lewis was killed in 1855. A jealous husband did for him, and the ranch ownership fell to King.

The area around Santa Gertrudis Creek was home to several herds of wild mustangs and Longhorn cattle. Over the years and throughout the Civil War, the King Ranch grew through the purchase of additional grants and included not only cattle but horses, too. Captain King was anxious to improve the breeding of his mustangs and the original Longhorn herd.

When Captain King died in 1885, the ownership of the ranch went to his heirs, but the management of the ranch fell to his friend and ranch attorney, Robert J. Kleberg. He and his several foremen were gathered in Kleberg's office in the main ranch house to discuss the recent cattle theft. With Kleberg were Oscar Bale, senior Ranch Foreman, Teddy Kleinhurst, the man who oversaw the cattle operation, and Josiah Boone, the top wrangler, and foreman of horse operations. Kleberg was speaking.

"Oscar, what have you heard? Are we certain it was Atwill's people that stole the animals?"

"Absolutely certain, sir, though they were not regular hands. They were all itinerant gunmen, sir, organized for the job by Dan Bogan. My guess is they'll be found in Nuevo Laredo."

"And the animals stolen were from the San Fernando Creek operation?"

"Yes, sir." Kleberg turned to Teddy Kleinhurst, "Teddy, what can you tell me about the condition of those animals? How many were there?"

"Twenty-four, all Longhorn from the heavily inbred group. The animals, all heifers, were calved from the Red Angus experiment that Captain King began twelve years ago. The stolen animals are third-generation inbred by the same Red Angus bull. All the animals on the San Fernando were a part of the Red Angus project."

"And what success rate should Mr. Atwill expect? Assuming he uses another Angus bull?"

"With a new Angus gene pool, his probable success rate will be 18 to 25 percent. Most of the cows will abort by midterm." Kleberg clasped his hands in front of him, "Well, it's a project that was due for discontinuance anyway. What can any of you tell me about the lawmen who were killed at that bridge? We should do something for them, for their families." Josiah Boone spoke up, "Sir, I knew Harry Gosling, the Deputy U.S. Marshal and one of the deputies that was shot. Harry was a good man. 'Timid at times, but only because I believe he carried the burden of his job heavily. I would not have called him fearless nor yet a coward. I believe he was better suited to the less violent tasks of his profession. And Dan Bogan is a son of a bitch, pardon me, sir."

"No, go on, Boone, speak your mind."

"Sir, I don't believe Harry Gosling had an evil bone in his body. He was well-liked in Laredo, I know. He was real friendly with the rancher I worked for before landing here. I remember the foreman there saying that Harry was too nice a fella for his job."

"I see. Well, we must encourage justice to take its course here. The world can't come to know the King Ranch as being shy in its pursuit of rustlers. Bad precedent. Any idea who will replace Marshal Gosling?" Boone again,

"Well, the Town Marshal in Laredo, Matt Cole, is known to be a hardnose, but he's also known for his greasy palms. He'll look the other way if the price is right. As to the Marshal Service? It may be a while, sir, before a replacement is named."

Kleberg thought for a moment and stood from his chair. "Boys, we must do something. I'm disinclined to undertake vigilantism, as it is counter to the laws of Texas. Do any of you have a suggestion?" Again, Boone nodded his head and spoke.

"Yes, sir, I may have. U.S. Marshals don't have any jurisdictional restrictions, ones as likely to shoot a bandit as another. Don't matter where he's standing."

"I like the sound of that, Boone. How do we get one to help out?"

"I believe a wire to the Governor requesting help would do it."

"Oh? You got a Marshal in mind, Boone?"

"Well, sir, there's this fella up in El Paso..."

One

8:15 a.m. October 18th, 1888
Sheriff's Office
St. Louis Street
El Paso, Texas

Sheriff Bart Mariany had just finished re-lighting the stove in the small front office and was cleaning the porcelain coffee pot when Greg Vale, the newest deputy sheriff of El Paso County, walked in to start his day. Vale had been hired last spring while Deputy Marshal Frank Bass was heavily involved with a serial murder case in Austin. Then, shortly after returning from that ordeal, while Bass was on an overdue vacation to visit his sister in Colorado, the Marshal became embroiled in a range conflict wherein his own and his sister's family barely escaped serious injury.

As a result of these demands on Marshal Bass's time, Vale had no real occasion to get to know the famous and recently decorated lawman. When Bart Mariany hired him, he looked forward to a relationship with the Marshal. Still, since his return from Colorado, Marshal Bass had taken an extended leave and concerned himself more with his young family and the workings of his own cattle ranch than the day-to-day activities of law and order in EL Paso.

Mariany, who knew Frank Bass better than anyone, attributed Bass's leave more to the intense rigors of his recent involvements and the threats to his family. Several times, he told Vale, "It's the most natural thing in the world at this time that he chooses his loved ones over us." He would then go on to say that if Bass were truly needed here, "he'd be through that door quicker than Billy be jiggered." Vale took the Sheriff at his word but still remained anxious to talk with Marshal Bass.

This morning, on his arrival, he took over the coffee-making duties for Sherrif Mariany, allowing the older man to recline in his chair, which had been moved closer to the stove.

"Damn weather, Greg. 'Seems to be getting cold earlier and earlier each year. We'll be getting the rain soon, likely the monsoons too. 'No place for old gunhands, I'll say. I keep readin about this Florida place and how it's like a tropical paradise and all. Damned if I wouldn't like to see for myself. S'pose they need lawmen there just as everywhere else?" The senior lawman paused to consider where he was and the likelihood that his usefulness had waned. Perhaps not completely, though. He said, "I'll make my rounds later once the sun's had a chance."

"The cold ain't only a suffer to you, ya know. There was ice in the bucket this morning. Ma had me fetch water from the spring. 'Grounds near frozen, too. Pa says it's freakish early this year."

Mariany had his coffee cup in hand, ready for the first sign of percolation. "Hmm. I agree. This here's late December weather in October. Did you ride through the 'States' on your way in?"

(El Paso's residential neighborhood streets were named for the states.) "I did, Sheriff, and nothin' seemed out of place. Everything was quiet 'cept for the iron stoves. By the smoke, I'll bet them stoves was cracklin with fire this mornin."

Eddie Voer, the large, yellow-haired young man who served as the jailer, walked in through the back door of the building, allowing a gust of wind to break through and slam the door between the Sheriff's office and the cells. Bart Mariany was so startled he dropped his cup, and Greg Vale's right hand instinctively grabbed at his holster. "God and Jesus...For cryin out loud, Eddie. Did you turn your brain on when you got up this mornin?" Mariany began dabbing at the spilled coffee on his trousers, mumbling, and Greg Vale's shoulders sagged noticeably. Eddie looked sheepishly into the office and said, "Well, hell, I'm just as sorry as I can be. Next time I have to go out to use the privy, I'll just stay inside and let fly. Hate for you two to endure a little wind." Greg Vale said, "It ain't just the wind Eddie, the slamin noise surenuff spooked me good.

"Well, good heavens, ma'am. I can't say sorry enough, I guess." Eddie came into the office and poured himself a cup as well. He took a seat in one of the desk chairs and said, "You two hear the news this mornin?" Mariany answered, "No, all we heard was that damned jail door, Eddie."

Eddie went on, "I read before you boys got in this mornin that John Wesley was released from up to Huntsville on Monday. The article said he did his fifteen years studyin' law, and he planned to come here to open a practice." Mariany said, "Why in the name of sin would he come here? Did it say?"

"Nope, didn't say much more a' tall. Just that he planned to hang his shingle in EL Paso."

Greg Vale asked, "Who is John Wesley, and how come he was in the penitentiary?" Mariany was more subdued now and leaned over, staring at the floor as he spoke.

"John Wesley Hardin, son. He was the most dangerous gunmen that ever walked on two legs. Killed forty men, they say. Hicock accounted for eight." Mariany looked up at Greg Vale smiling and said, " And Hickocks' dead." Mariany stood up and swallowed his coffee. Vale asked, "Well, what'd he do to spend so long in the Pen?" Mariany, again, this time staring through the open window. "Even though he killed a bunch of people, son, probably only one or two that got proved in court. Enough to send him away." Mariany turned to face Deputy Vale. "Guess his sentence is up. Frank'll be interested in Hardin's return and where he settles."

9:00 a.m. October 18th, 1888
TwainHeart Ranch
Twelve Miles South of
El Paso, Texas

"Since we returned from Colorado, Frederick has spent more time in that horse barn than he has at his desk. And, you know what? I'm all for it." Sally was the only person who called Bass by his given first name. She liked it better than Frank. This morning, she was drinking her morning coffee in the kitchen at the TwainHeart house with their neighbor, Marianna Treece. Bass and Sally had known the young woman since she first met Theo Treece at her father's Cantina in Tularosa, New Mexico Territory, eighteen months ago. Theo had asked for Bass's help in proving his father's innocence in a train robbery, and in the course of their investigation, Theo Treece became enamored of the girl. Following the conclusion of the case, Theo and Marianna married and purchased a small ranch to the south of TwainHeart on the Rio. Now Marianna was pregnant and sought Sally's advice at every opportunity.

"As much as he's been through this year, I'd be just as glad should he quit the Marshal Service and focus his efforts on TwainHeart and his family. And not necessarily in that order."

"I understand, Mrs. Sally. I have my Theo at home every night, but his head... sometimes it stays in El Paso at the business. Even with the, ah, how you say ah Contador."

"The bookkeeper, yes, and I'm so glad Theo found one. Perhaps with time, he'll get used to having the bookkeeper. Then maybe you'll have more time with Theo at home."

"I hope so, Mrs. Sally. Even a little time would be good."

Bass and Theo had pooled their resources to purchase a feedlot in El Paso that quickly became the favorite among area stockmen. So much so that the business expanded to a second lot offering specialty grains and feed shipped by train from around the country. Theo was the general manager, with Frank Bass being a silent partner. Marianna was watching the yard through the kitchen window.

"What does Mr. Frank do in the barn for so many hours?"

"Oh, I believe it has to do with the Shire horses and the barn extension he and Silas Pratt have been working on. Frederick doesn't give Silas enough credit. He's quite a clever architect and engineer.

Our lavatory downstairs and the laundry chutes from the second floor were all his notions."

"I believe I will ask Theo to hire him to work on our house. When we moved in, there was much to be done, and we have finished many things. But with the baby, I want the house to be warmer and also to have a... ah, the baby room?"

"Nursery."

Si...yes. A nursery like you have for baby Lillian." There was a pause as Marianna poured herself another cup, "Mrs. Sally, I don't know how I ask it. But I am afraid for the baby and for me, too. I was too young to see mi Madre... my mother bring my brother to the world. I don't know what will happen?" Sally smiled. She felt more and more like a big sister to Marianna as the days went by. Chinesta and Paulo Alvarez were Bass's oldest friends and shared range land for their combined cattle herd. They lived in a house they renovated when Bass bought the place. When the previous owners decided to sell, one of the things they left behind was a Shire horse once intended for use as a draft animal. Bass took a particular liking to the giant beast, and though the registered name of the horse was Sir William, Bass thought a more fitting name would be Willy, and he decided to look for a broodmare for Shire stock.

As it happened last winter, Bass recovered two kidnapped girls and returned them to their parents. Their father worked for the XIT Ranch, the largest cattle ranch ever established in the country, and as a thank you, they sent Bass, the perfect mate for Willy. A young white Shire mare named Angel-Heart. Bass was excited to develop the breed and believed coupling the black-colored Willy with the pure white of the younger mare might produce, at some point, a coveted blue color animal. In any event, Shire horses were still unique animals on the frontier, and Bass was determined to breed them successfully.

To that end, Bass had enlisted the services of his carpenter and trusted friend, Silas Pratt. Silas had made several improvements to the ranch house in anticipation of the arrival of baby Lillian. He'd also built a working lavatory, or crapper as Bass liked to call it, in the space under the staircase on the first floor. The flushing toilet, basin, and tub all drained to buried, perforated pipes that spread out beneath the grounds between the house and the Rio. It was the first such facility in El Paso. Even the Presidio at Fort Bliss didn't have one.

Today, Bass and Silas Pratt were outside the horse barn discussing the plans for the Shire horse shelter. Bass explained,

"I'd at least like to have the foundation laid out before winter, Silas. I know it has to be large, and if you need extra help to complete the work before the frost, go ahead and hire someone. Let me know what materials you'll need, and I'll procure them through the feedlot if I can."

"Frank, these plans you've drawn require a certain amount of plumbing, and zinc pipes don't grow on trees. It has to be ordered and shipped. And the specific lengths will cost extra. It ain't like the drains I did for the house. Those pipes were random and were excess inventory. I got 'em on the cheap. Running water in both barns will mean increasing the size of the tank back on the hill, too. Or building a second one. And the lumber for such a tall structure will cost a penny, too. It'll be double to dig the holes and pour the concrete for the footings as well." Bass was unfazed. For the first time this year, he was rested, healed from injury, and excited about a project outside law enforcement.

"Silas, my friend. I have complete faith in your ability to overcome whatever odds may stand in your way. I got money salted away for this project, and while I can't just say 'money is no object, I can promise that whatever you need according to my drawings here will be paid for." Bass walked back into the horse barn and to the expanded stall that housed Willy and Angel. "Look at 'em, Silas. Have you ever seen anything so grand?"

"No, Frank, well, not up close like this, but I once saw the circus parade in Fort Worth, and by damn them, elyphants was pretty grand to look at, too. Which reminds me. There were flyers posted in Fort Worth sellin Circus manure for fertilizer. Sold by the wagon load at a nickel a yard. 'Seems to me with hay burners this size, you'd be wise to make an accommodation for their leavins.'"

You also got seven other animals in that barn, Frank, and all of them are gonna create droppings, too. Now you ain't no farmer, Frank. What use would you have of all that...that...fertilizer."

Bass considered and said, "Silas? You're a, by God, genius. We'll sell it at the feedlot, yes sir, haul it all up to town and sell it like you said for a nickel a yard." Silas shook his head at the compliment. It did his heart good to see Frank Bass in such fine spirits after the last eight or nine months he'd had. "Frank, I'll start tomorrow and work till the ground freezes. I believe we can get the eight-by-eight corner posts set in concrete by the end of the first week of December. After that, siding and the roof will depend on the weather."

"That sounds fine, Silas. You know where to find them heavy posts?"

"I do. Fort Bliss sells 'em. Keeps 'em on hand for telegraph repair and whatnot."

"Then I'll leave it to you, Silas. Thank you. Silas picked up his tape measure and level and folded his plans. By the time Bass got to the kitchen, Silas had his buggy on the drive down to the River Road.

"Marianna, it's good to see you. You're looking real pretty, all rosy cheeked and smilin. Sally says you're in a family way. How are you feelin? I know Sally had the mornin sickness all day long for a while.

"Yes, I have that matutinas feeling, si. And you know? Theo has it sometimes, too. I meant to ask Miss Salida...uh Sally, what that means when the husband is sick as well."

"Sally put her hand on Marianna's arm. "It's alright, dear. It's called sympathetic morning sickness. Some men get it, especially first-time fathers. I know Theo may not act like it, but he's just as anxious, ansioso, as you."

"What a nice way to show your love and caring. I will be sure to tell Theo. May I go to see Lilliana before I leave? I will let myself out."

"Of course, you go right ahead, Marianna." The younger woman walked out of the kitchen to Lillian's cradle in the parlor. Bass and Sally stayed in the kitchen, where Sally asked, "Did you and Silas figure everything out?"

"Yeah, well, for the most part, we agreed to get underway and set the perimeter poles in concrete. 'Want to get the concrete cured before the first frost. Once the poles are set, it's just a matter of puttin' up the plank siding and anchoring the roof in place."

"Can't you just nail it down?"

"Well, sure, but we do get the now and then tornado here, and they can pull the roof off a barn quick as a jack rabbit covers ground."

"I see. Wash up if you plan to eat. I'll get some ham and eggs on the stove here." Bass stepped to the sink and pumped the short handle of the kitchen water pump twice. Then, he waited for the clear, cold water to wash over his soapy hands. He dried them on a kitchen towel and sat at the kitchen table. He poured what would be his third coffee of the morning and dropped a tablespoon of sugar in it. Sally saw him use the sugar and said,

"Frederick, I swear your sweet tooth will break us. 'Like you think sugar grows on trees."

"Not at all, Sal. Sugar grows on canes in South Texas, along the Brazos. Though I don't 'zactly know how they get sugar outta the cane. You know they grow it in Louisiana and around the Gulf, too.

I sure can't figure why the price of sugar is so high. I mean, there's so much of it nearby. Must be in the way they process it." Bass took a swallow of his cup and was quiet for a moment. Then he said, "Seems like it ought to be a good crop to have land in. 'Believe I'll look into what processing the cane requires. Don't spoil on a store shelf, either. 'Folks pay a dollar fifty for a five-pound bag."

"Frederick, I believe you have enough on your plate as it is. You shouldn't be stretching yourself any more than you already have." There was a sudden noise from the front room, followed by the sound of baby Lillian crying. Sally dropped her spatula and dashed through the door to the front parlor, where she found Lillian standing on the floor, grasping at the rungs of her cradle. Sally was startled at first but quickly ran to the child and scooped her up in her arms. Bass was right behind and asked, "What'd she do? What'd she do, Sal? Is she hurt?" Sally turned to him smiling and said, "No, ninny. Your daughter is standing on her own. I think she may have tumbled from the cradle. She's fine, just scared."

"Standing? Why she ain't, but what? Ten months old? And standing?"

"Yes, dear, girls do these things more quickly than little boys.

"Standing. Ten months old and standing. She's a genius, Sal. Let me hold her." The baby was quiet now as Bass took her from Sally. He walked, holding her, to the large front window that looked down over a fenced meadow to the Rio. "Lil? You see out there? You're gonna be runnin all over out there soon, sweetheart." Sally watched and listened. It always warmed her whenever Bass spoke to Lil that way. After a moment, she said, "Alright, now you two, Frederick, take her back to the kitchen, will you dear? It's time she was fed. And didn't I hear you say that you were going into town today?"

"Hmm? Yes...oh yes. Say, you know what we need? Keep this from happening again. Is there some kind of a baby pen we can set up on the floor? We can put her bunny and Mr. Pony in there, and she can stand up all she wants without getting hurt. What da ya think?"

"I think it's a splendid idea. I can put the mattress from her crib in it, too. She can nap downstairs in it, and we won't have to worry she'll fall from her cradle."

"I'll ask Silas about 'for I go. And I had better hop to it, too. I need to stop at the jail and check what's happening. I've been away too much, as it is. Bart may a hired another deputy for all I know."

"Is that Greg fellow you mentioned not working out? I thought you all liked him?"

"What? Oh yeah, sure, we like him. Like him fine, 'got a good head for sheriffin'. I was just joking, thinkin that Bart maybe wanted more help, is all. I'll go get my stuff and saddle Emma."

Emma was Bass's ten-year-old mare, the horse he rode most often and knew best of all the animals at TwainHeart. She was tall, nearly eighteen hands, and was a light brown color bay that might've been mistaken for buckskin. Her mane, tail, and feathering were black, and the contrast was not only striking but identifiable. Her coloring was not common. She'd belonged to Bass since his Ranger days. He bought her as a filly and paid a tame Comanche in Fort Smith to train her.

Bass walked into the barn carrying his rifle and gun belt. He also had a black canvas duster with him in case of rain or high winds. It was a forty-five-minute ride into El Paso, and the weather in fall was changeable. He walked to Emma's stall and held her muzzle, breathing into her flared nostrils. As was his habit, he felt down all four legs to the fetlock, checking for tendon or ligament damage. Finding a hotspot would require a vet's visit. Finally, satisfied she was sound, he wiped her down and brushed her back carefully, making sure there was no foreign object beneath the saddle to cause discomfort and injury. Once his saddle was on and cinched up snug, the rifle in its scabbard and the duster tied off behind the cantle, Bass tapped his heels to her sides, and they walked slowly from the barn.

Two

10:45 a.m. October 18th, 1888
Sheriff's Office and
City Jail
St. Louis Street
El Paso, Texas

Bass reined in Emma, took her into the sheltered corral behind the jail building, and walked through the backdoor of the jail enclosure to find Eddie Voer sitting with his back to him, reading a newspaper.

"Is there coffee still, Eddie?" Voer, a strapping youth perfectly suited to the duties of a jailer, jumped from his seat, tearing the page of newsprint he was reading.

"Frank! Thank God it's only you."

"Only me, Eddie? Who was you fearin it might be walking through the backdoor of the jail?"

"Huh. I thought it might be Bart. He don't like to see me readin. 'Says it's an idler's task. I'm just tryin to keep up with things in town, is all." Bass picked up the torn sheet.

"Oh? Then why are you lookin' at the help needed ads instead of the front page? You lookin for a better job, Eddie? 'Thought you liked it here?"

"Oh, I do, Frank, I do. Only now, with Greg Vale on as deputy, Bart says he can't pay me no more than he does, and ...well, truth is me and Roxanne Purdy been keepin company..." Eddie took a deep breath, "and I was lookin for a second job so's to.... Well...so's to buy her a ring."

"I see. Well, Eddie, I think that's wonderful. 'Don't believe I know Roxanne, but I'm sure she's a fine lady. Uh, just how long have y'all been seein' each other, Eddie?"

"For a long time now, three, maybe four weeks. Frank, I think she's just a peach, sweet as soda pop. I'm so lucky."

"I'm sure she is Eddie. How did you two meet, if you don't mind my askin?"

"Say I'm glad you asked, Frank. I was just walkin down Franklin Street one mornin on my way to work, and I saw her sittin out on the front porch with some other ladies at her rooming house. She called to me to stop, and she walked right up to the gate and talked to me, Frank. And we talked and talked after that. She invited me into their Parlor, but I explained I had to work, so I left. Frank, I been back to see her just as often as I can. She lives a real poor life. Frank and I give her, you know, a few dollars each time just so she can get by. They's awfully poor in that boardin' house, you know."

"Uh-huh. Well, that's fine for you, Eddie, and I'm real glad on you for it. 'Tell you what. I'll talk to Bart 'see if we can't find a little more for you in the budget. Okay?"

"Say, that would just fix it all right, wouldn't it? Thanks, Frank." Bass smiled at Eddie as he opened the door to the Sheriff's office, and Eddie went down to cell five with his mop.

Bart Mariany saw Bass first, "Well, as I live and breathe, if it ain't the Hero of the whole state of Texas come down to earth to slum with us mortals." Bass just stood listening to his old friend and finally answered,

"G'mornin' to you too, Bart. I can't tell from that welcome whether your mood today is fair or foul." Mariany chuckled and walked to the window for a quick look outside.

"Oh, it's fair, alright, Frank. 'You happen to bring your medal in with you? Like you done fifteen or twenty times since summer?"

"No, actually. Now that you asked, Silas made a very nice oakwood case for it. I leave it to home on the mantel to remind Sally what a catch I am."

"Oh...I think she knows that already. Come on over and sit down. One or two things I wanna run by you." Bass sat at the desk, and Mariany poured more coffee into his cup.

"First off is the Dillards. Them brothers come to town, get drunk, and leave the city a little poorer for repairs when they leave. They're ornery drunks, too. Greg nearly shot one three days ago. I figure since you knew their Pa, you might have a word. Ya think?"

"Yeah, sure, Bart. I'll ride out to their spread this afternoon and talk to them. I believe they are missin their Pap... and his iron will. Ol' Mace woulda turned a blind eye to them lettin' off steam, but he never woulda allowed them to get off without payin. What else?" Mariany hung his head a little as he spoke.

"D'you know Eddie's took up with a whore? He thinks it's love, and I ain't had the heart to tell him 'bout Miss. Ladysmith's Boarding House. Such a good, sweet kid."

"Yeah, I do know. He told me about it when I came in this morning. 'Says he's lookin for a second job so he can buy her a ring. And I don't know what to do. Hell, you're older, s'posed to be wiser. What do you think we should do?"

"Aw, hell. I'll think on it some more, I guess. You think I should give him more money?"

"Well yeah, 'he keeps seein' this Roxanne, he's gonna need every penny he can get."

"Alright. 'Guess it can't hurt none.

And there's one more thing. 'Don't think you're gonna like it. John Wesley's out, and he's settin' up as an attorney in an office over on San Francisco Street. Came by to check in 'cordin to his Pardon three days ago."

"Holy.... Anything happen yet?

"Nope. Model citizen for the last three days. Frank, I know you got a history with John Wesley, but ya gotta put it all aside now. He's done his time. He looks older now... and 'seems like he bettered himself by studyin the books at the Pen."

Bass was not pleased at all. John Wesley Hardin was the most notorious gunfighter on the frontier, next to Bill Hickok. Hardin claimed to have killed upwards of forty men starting at age fifteen. He killed Indians, Mexicans, lawmen, and innocents, and whereas Hickok could be a rogue and a gambler, he was always an agent for law and order. John Wesley Hardin was his opposite.

What Bass would never forgive, though, was an incident that occurred in Comanche, Texas. Bass was a seventeen-year-old ranch hand whom Sheriff's Deputy Chuck Webb had befriended and mentored in the use of firearms and the importance of law enforcement on the frontier. One day, Hardin came up against Webb in a saloon in Comanche and asked the Deputy if he'd come to arrest him. Webb replied, 'No, that he had a warrant for another man,' and as he produced the warrant, Hardin shot and killed Webb on the spot. Hardin claimed that Webb was pulling a gun, but witnesses said differently.

When young Frank Bass heard of the shooting, his first instinct was to track and kill Hardin for his wickedness. But Webb's widow, in her grief, persuaded Bass to forego his vengeance lest he become a killer as well. Bass swallowed his anger and, a short time later, joined the Texas Rangers under Captain Leander McNelly.

Now, Bass sat in the El Paso City Jail, aware that one of the most hated men in Texas law enforcement, and a personal nemesis as well, was only a few blocks away, walking the streets a free man.

"Damn lawyer, ya say?" Mariany was studying Bass closely.

"Ats right. Over on San Francisco Street, down from the Wildcat Saloon."

"Hmm. Believe I'll stroll over and pay my respects."

"You think that's wise, Frank? Right now, I mean. Might be better to let the idea settle a bit."

"It's as settled as it's ever gonna be. Don't see a reason to wait, Bart." Bass set his cup down, stood up, and carried his hat to the door. Once outside, he set it down on his head and adjusted the brim. It was chilly when the sun hid itself behind a cloud. He decided to walk the quarter-mile distance rather than resaddle Emma. 'No point in disturbing her morning, too.

The Wildcat Saloon had a big, gaudy façade with multi-colored signs and advertisements for the dance partners inside. He could hear the banjo playing about a block away and then the piano as he got closer. The Wildcat was always busy, but oddly enough, it was not as dangerous a drinking establishment as some of the others. He could see people coming and going through the swinging steel doors and heard laughter in crescendos through the open windows. He paused as he passed by to look in. He stood in the doorway, the light from the street creating a silhouette, and as soon as he was recognized, the low roar that was almost constant in the room ceased.

"You boys go on with what you're doin'. I ain't here for any of ya." He turned and walked back out to the boardwalk and continued another two doors, where he saw a sign that read, ***John W. Hardin, Esq. Attorney at Law.*** Bass squared himself and walked through the door.

Hardin was sitting at a desk by the stove. His hair was thinning, and his coloring was prison grey. He had deep wrinkles on his forehead and a slight tremor in his left hand. He was unarmed, but Bass caught sight of his cross-draw rig hanging on the coat rack behind the door. Without looking up, Hardin said,

"Been expecting you, Marshal. 'This a business or social call?"

"Ain't nothin' social 'bout it, Hardin. More about 'old business' than anything else."

"Ah, yes. What was his name? It was so long ago I hardly recall."

"Webb, Chuck Webb. You killed him in cold blood out in Comanche."

"That's right, friend of yours, wasn't he? You know I was absolved of any guilt in that shooting."

Bass clenched his fists in anger at the cocky attitude and disrespect Hardin was showing.

"Witnesses said different. And they'd already convicted you of two murders anyway. One more woulda been water to the well."

"Bass, you know I've served my time. My debt to the citizens of Texas is paid in full, and I ain't broke no laws. 'Set myself up in business with all the legal papers to prove it. 'Happy to show 'em to ya if you want?"

"What I want is for you to take your shingle out there and hang it in another town, in another County. I don't like havin you so close."

"Ha. I'm afraid there ain't much you can do about it, Marshal. El Paso is a growin town. I figure to make riches here. And like I said, I ain't broke no laws."

"Yet...you ain't broke any laws yet, Hardin, and I plan to keep a close eye on you."

"Yes, well, do it from outside my office, will you, Marshal? You've worn out your welcome here."

Bass held Hardin's gaze for a moment, opened the door behind him, and stepped out. As he did, he made a mental note to ask Greg Vale to put Hardin's office on his daily rounds.

Back at the jail, Greg Vale had finished his morning rounds and was sitting with Bart and Eddie Voel, making a report on what he'd noticed around town. He was talking about having spotted a man who looked very similar to a wanted flyer that had come in last week. "I ain't lyin' Bart. The guy looked just like Lucas Teague from the poster. 'Can't hardly miss that scar and the feather in his hat. Big fella, too. 'Wasn't doing nothin', so I didn't stop, but I figure I outta go back and feel him out. What do you think?"

"Hell boy, if it was Lucas, we should both go. And carry extra ammunition to boot." Bass walked in at the end of the conversation.

"Ta' boot what, boys?" Bass asked.

Bart explained, "On his rounds this mornin, Frank, Greg here said he thought he spotted Lucas Teague sittin in front of Hardesty's Hardware on Texas Street. We were thinkin 'bout pickin' him up for a talkin to."

"Lucas, huh? We get paper on him?" Bart answered, "Yeah, flyer came in a week or so back, said he was wanted for robbin' the Allendale bank, near Abilene." Bass thought for a moment and said, "Well, let me do it. I know Lucas from a couple years back. If it's him, I'll know it. Tell you what. You two boys come on along but stay back. Greg, you go ahead and walk on over to the corner of Utah Street, where you can get a good view, and Bart, you back me up across the street in the alley behind Hudson's. You boys just watch. Don't play your hand till you see me call for it. If there's a game workin, there's likely to be more of 'em than just Lucas. You remember what's across the street from Hardesty's?" Bart realized what it was and spoke out. "Damn... Lone Star Savings Bank." Greg Vale swallowed hard at the thought of going up against hardened gunmen. A shootout in the street in front of the bank had become a frightening possibility.

"Alright, Greg, grab a Winchester and go ahead on over. Remember to stay out of sight on that corner." Greg had the longest distance to travel, so he left first. After he left, Bart went to the gun rack and took down a Winchester for himself. Bass then turned to Eddie Voer. "We got nobody in the cells for you to guard Eddie. 'You feel comfortable bringing that shotgun there behind you? Tell me if you don't. No shame in it at all. You're a jailer, after all." Eddie thought for a moment and then nodded his head. His mouth had suddenly gone dry, making it difficult to speak.

The three men left the office on St. Louis Street and walked the three blocks to the corner of Texas Street and Stanton Rd. The weather was breezy but not particularly cold. They could smell Osfeldt's Bakery as they passed by. Just before rounding the corner onto Texas Street, Bass took a quick look at the man sitting in front of Hardesty's. "Yeah, that's Lucas, alright." Next, he sent Eddie Voer to the bank's side door, telling him to lay low unless he heard shooting. Then he was to burst through the side door and shoot any gunman that might be trying to make an escape from the bank out the front. "They'll be tryin to get to their horses and won't expect someone to come up behind 'em. Besides, by that time, we'll all be shootin at 'em." Eddie's eyes were wide open and wouldn't blink, no matter how hard he tried. He nodded again and jogged down the alley to the bank's side door. Bass watched as he went inside.

Bass looked at Bart and asked, "You ready for this?" Bart just shook his head and said, "Hell no. But let's get it done with." Bass didn't want to cross the middle of the street, figuring he'd be an easy target if there was someone already in the bank. He stayed on the opposite side and strolled down the boardwalk, acting like Lucas wasn't there. After he'd taken a few steps, he stopped and called out, "Lucas? Lucas Teague, is that you on that bench?" Teague, who'd been concentrating on the Bank's front door, looked to the left at the figure calling to him. "God damn. That you, Frank? We heard you was quit a' your job."

"No, not hardly. I got paper on you, Lucas. You're wanted in Abilene for robbin' a bank. Can't have that, you know." There was a pause as Lucas thought what to say.

"You think I'm just gonna walk over to your jail, Frank, pretty as you please?"

"No, I don't, Lucas. But I got deputies all around you here, and I'm given you the chance." Lucas hesitated for a split second and said,

"You go to hell, Frank." Lucas Teague pulled a pistol from behind his back and got off two shots that sailed harmlessly into a plank wall before Bass could raise his Colt. Gunfire erupted from the corners of Utah and Stanton as both Greg Vale and Bart Mariany fired their rifles in Teague's direction. Both front windows at

Hardesty's were shattered, sending glass shards into the confusion around Teague, causing him to duck and cover his face. He was still standing, however, and lifting his pistol when Bass pulled the trigger on his Colt. It was all that was needed as Teague spun around, falling over the jagged glass remains in one of Hardesty's windows. Now, there was the sound of a shotgun blast as two men dashed from the bank, pistols in hand, only to fall into the street, their backsides peppered with buckshot. Eddie Voer dashed from the front door of the bank, re-loading his shotgun as he pointed it at the outlaws lying in the street. Both had tossed their weapons aside in submission. Bass went first to Lucas Teague, feeling for a pulse in the man's neck. He found none. Next, he joined Bart and Greg as they stood with Eddie Voer, smiling from ear to ear. "Did ya see, Frank? Did ya see how I got 'em? They did just what you said, Frank and I got 'em." Bass looked down at the two hapless men sprawled in the dirt, slight trickles of blood seeping slowly from their buckshot wounds. Bass asked, "I don't know you boys, do I?" One of 'em began speaking.

"No sir, you don't. Can we please get a doctor to help us? My butt's hurtin' real bad."

"Well, I dare say it is, shot where you are. You two got names?"

"Yes, sir. My name is Steven Hadley, and this is my younger brother Hugh. Can we get a doctor now?"

"Greg, run, see if you can find Doc Spalding. Ask him to meet us at the jail."

"The Jail? How 'we supposed to get to the jail, all shot up like this?"

"Well, I guess you'll have to walk. We'll help you, though." The two young men screamed as they were lifted to their feet and marched to the jail by Eddie Voer. On the way, if Eddie said it once, he said it ten times, "This will learn you 'bout robbin' banks in El Paso."

Three

2:45 p.m. October 18th, 1888
El Paso City Jail
St. Louis Street
El Paso, Texas

Bart Mariany, Greg Vale, and Frank Bass were doing the shooting reports that Bass mandated a year or so earlier. Eddie Voer, not being a Deputy Sheriff but a hired Jailer, was exempt from such reporting. He was, after all, a volunteer in the action, and he was not quite fluent in his letters. He also had two new charges in his cells, the Hadley brothers, both of whom had been treated with tweezers and witch hazel. Now, they both lay on their cots, naked, except for the blankets provided by the jail.

Greg was having trouble with his spelling and occasionally asked for help and definitions. "Say, Bart, what's it mean, *initial assault?*"

> "Means who fired first. You best always say it was the
> outlaw, lest you get a funny look from the
> judge who reads these damn things." Bass didn't look up
> from his work when he said, "He's right, Greg. Remember
> that. Outlaw always shoots first. Which, in this instance,
> happens to be the truth. Bart, do you remember if I said
> to
> drop his weapon or not?"
> "Not exactly, 'Told him *there was armed deputies all*
> *around him, and he said he weren't gonna be arrested* er
> somethin like that. Hard for me to hear with
> my teeth chatterin' like they were."
> That's a whole lot to write out. I'll just say I did tell

him, and he refused." Bart nodded and said, "Well, that's fine, boys. Then I'll just go ahead a write down that without my noble and courageous heart, the day would've been lost...Frank? How do you spell *courageous*?

"H-o-r-s-e-s... a-s-s. Bart? 'Think we should write one for Eddie? He was legally deputized, remember?" Bart Mariany looked up from his work and said, "Hell, I don't know. I spose we should. Yeah, I'll do one for Eddie. He'll be the hero of this shootout, and folks will be readin his name for a change." Bass nodded and said, "Just remember to get them flyers on Lucas pulled in. Otherwise, folks around Texas'll be seein Lucas Teague in all manner of places."

The writing continued in silence, except for the low moans that now and then wafted in from the jail. Eddie stuck his head in the door and said, "I'm headed out to the café...get the Hadley brothers somethin to eat. Neither of them fellas has et lately, and it may stop their moanin'. Everybody said ***goodbye and be careful,*** and Eddie walked out the front door of the Sheriff's Office. He still carried the Remington Pump on his shoulder rather than return it to the gun cabinet. He carried the shells for the gun

in his overalls. Bass finished his report first and said, "I'm

gonna head upstairs; there's still a stack of mail on my desk

that needs tendin.' You boys, let me know when you're

finished, and I'll run 'em on over to Judge Hobart's office. Bass stood, grabbed his hat, and left the office. He

walked up the rickety stairs on the side of the building,

promising himself with each squeak and teeter that he was

gonna get Silas to shore them up. His office above the jail

was just as he'd left it. Even though he'd waded through

much of the mail on his desk after he returned from his

leave a week ago, the stack hardly seemed to have shrunk. He hung up his hat and lit the stove in the corner

against the chilly winds that blew through the plank walls

of his office. There was dirty grey light coming through the

two south-facing windows, so he lit a lamp on his desk to

be better able to read the fine print on some of the flyers

that accumulated daily. He was able to discard many of

them because the issue dates were over two months ago. He

was still receiving congratulations for the Texas State

Medal of Honor presented in the summer for his work on

the Austin Annihilator case. The Medal sat in its display

box on the mantle at TwainHeart, and every time he looked

at it, he thought of his friend Grooms Lee, his struggle with

liquor that eventually led to his death. He was proud, of

course, any man would be, to receive such a special award,

and his work on the case and the time spent away from

home assured him of his worthiness. Still, there was a

shadow hanging over the award, one he'd always

remember.

There was a letter from his sister in Colorado saying that even in a place so far away, they saw reports of the award ceremony. "Everyone is bustin' their britches with pride that you stayed with us on our little ranch. She also reported that Lucky Fowler, the saloon keeper who was

badly beaten by the villain Tom Horn, had died of

pneumonia as a result of his beating. The family was well,

and their herd was healthy and growing in numbers. Francis, her eldest boy, wanted to follow in his

uncle's footsteps and become a "crime fighter" just like his

uncle Frank. This pleased Bass. Francis was a bright

youngster with a good heart and determined will. He had

the makin's of a fine, active law officer, and Bass said as

much in his goodbye to the boy.

Bass read the letter's closing and thought it was a

bit odd. She reported that after six weeks in a Denver

hospital lockdown, Tom Horn had escaped. "Most people

seem to think he's headed west, but I just thought I'd let

you know, for what it's worth." Bass contemplated the paid

assassin for a bit and finally pushed him out of his mind. The mail in front of him was more urgent than Tom

Horn. He decided to take the letter home for Sally to read,

so he folded it into a square and slid it into his shirt pocket.

There was a note from Theo regarding two large

expenditures he wanted to make for the feedlot, and as per

their agreement, he sent notice to Frank for his okay. The

note made Bass think of selling manure from his barns as

fertilizer to the area farmers, and he made another note

to speak with Theo about it. He decided to walk over to the

B&T Feed Lot on Franklin, just across the tracks from the

EP&SW Terminal. He hadn't been by in at least a month,

and though he saw Theo Treece regularly as a neighbor,

they rarely discussed business at those meetings. Those
were the times Theo generally picked Bass's brain

on ranching issues. Theo was in the process of building a

herd of Angus and Hereford cattle. He'd purchased

a Hereford bull he called Caesar and hoped to use Bass's

Angus Bull, Cochise. Feedlot business rarely interfered,

though the money it generated provided the flexibility for

them to indulge themselves as Gentlemen Ranchers. In fact,

the only member of their little group who relied solely on

ranching to feed his family was Paulo Armendez. Paulo
and his wife and twin girls lived on the ranch adjacent to

Bass, one that Bass had purchased when his neighbors, the

Pullholz's, quit trying to farm the gravelly soil just east of

Bass's place. Bass and Paulo had been friends for years and

had agreed to split whatever profit might be made from

selling cattle. Paulo knew as much about cattle as Bass did

about outlaws, and the partnership recorded its first profit

last spring when a small herd of Angus and Hereford
steers

were sold to a meat packer in Fort Worth.

Another bonus that Bass received from the purchase
of the Pullholz farm was the Shire Horse, Willy. Abe Pullholz
had brought Willy with him from West Virginia. "No better draft
animal ever made," he told Bass. Willy hadn't pulled a plow or reaper
since Bass had acquired him two years previously. And now, with
Angel, Bass could foresee the breed becoming popular for farm work
all over the state.

The B&T Feedlot was a five-block walk from the Sheriff's office,
but the weather had turned partly sunny, and the earth was
beginning to warm up around town. Bass walked into the large main
barn where lumber, tools, and fencing were sold and climbed the
nearby staircase to the office overlooking the floor. Theo saw Bass
and jumped to greet him.

"Frank, just the man I was thinking of. What brings you out here this afternoon?"

"Well, ya left me this note saying you wanted to discuss something that might cost some money, Theo. Thought I'd walk over and see what ya had in mind." Bass and Theo walked into an enclosed office with glass windows that looked out over the floor of the warehouse. Bass sat in his usual chair in front of the desk and held up the dram glass that was always perched nearby. Theo, without looking, went directly to the desk drawer that held the Overholts Rye and poured a healthy amount into the glass. "Was that gunfire I heard earlier, Frank?"

"Oh, yeah, 'twas. Lucas Teague and two young brothers tried to rob the Lone Star Savings Bank. Our new deputy, Greg Vale, spotted Lucas during his morning rounds. Did a real good job."

"Oh? Do I know him? This new deputy?"

"Don't believe so, but you might recognize him. The feedlot's on his morning beat.

So, what's the reason you want to spend money, and how much?"

"Well, I want to make our warehouse here a real Hardware Store. You know? Not just hand tools and nails but housewares, pots and pans, uhh, irons and small appliances like andirons and kettle cranes."

"Uh huh, how much to get it started?"

"Maybe two thousand. Buying inventory isn't as bad as I thought it might be at first, though we do have some rearranging of things to do downstairs."

"Yeah, okay. Sounds like a good plan. And considering Hardesty's just got its windows shot up, they might be our first customers. What's the other idea?"

"Say, now this is a bit more costly, and it might not start paying off till next spring. I think it might be a good idea to buy the land directly south, along the ES&SW tracks. We could use it as a cattle pen. It's a big enough piece of land, Frank, and we could start it as a crowding or sorting pen for shipping and then expand it into a feed pen. You know, fatten 'em up on corn before shipping. Why, we'd get a few cents, maybe a dollar, on each beef that ships out. Plus, feeding our provender. What d'ya think?"

"Well, Theo, it's a great idea, but how much 'you figure it'll cost?"

"Like I said, not cheap 'cause we gotta buy the land. Probably about five thousand."

"Ouch. That's a big hit, Theo. Do we have it?"

"Not quite. We're still fifteen hundred short. But I'll put up half of what's left, if you will. Whatda ya say?" Bass was looking about the room as he thought about the proposition.

"Theo, it's a good idea...'Great idea! But let's consider this. Why don't we buy the land now while the price is right and just sit on it? Then, when the timing is better, and we can afford it, we can put together a couple of feed stops inside the pen." Theo was obviously disappointed. He knew Bass was right. He was almost always right, and he generally sided with the conservative course. Usually, this was fine, but Theo sensed that this time, the proper course would be forging ahead and completing the project.

"Frank, I disagree. I believe we should strike while the iron is hot. The land, as you say, is certainly priced right, and I think the additional crew and building materials for barns and corals will come at bargain prices as well. We'll be up and running in no time, turning a profit right away."

"Theo, I know you. You're the smartest man I've ever known, probably the smartest man I ever will know, but lemme ask you this. How many cattle herds get shipped out during the winter months?" Theo saw where Frank was going, and his shoulders sagged noticeably. "Not many, I know."

"How many 'you seen in the last month?"

"None"

"That's right. And we won't be seein' anyone selling cows from El Paso probably till after branding, make that late April. That's the reason the land's cheap. Also, why material and labor costs are low. Nobody builds anything in the winter. And there ain't gonna be no need for Crowding Lots till next Spring. The land will always be there and probably at a higher price if we wait on that 'til Spring. But if we extend ourselves for lumber and builders now, we'll have no cushion against a harsh winter when our customers will need us the most. See what I'm sayin?"

Theo realized he hadn't thought it through. Not being a cattleman, he hadn't learned the tough lessons of winter on the Texas prairie. "You're right, Frank. I hadn't considered the winter months in my equation. Let me see what kind of deal I can get on the twenty-acre parcel for now."

"Sounds good. I believe Riddle Sanders owns that land, and he's not likely to be in a position to put it to any use other than makin' dust. I believe his Missus just had another baby, too, so he might be apt to sell at the first cash bid. How much cash do we have on hand?"

"About eighty-five hundred, but I haven't ordered for December and January yet. And we got payroll in about ten days."

"Okay, why don't you go see Riddle and find out how much cash he'd like to get for that land."

Theo nodded his head, and Bass stood to leave. As he was about to head down the stairs, Bass turned back and said. "Theo? Don't try to steal it from him. He's a good neighbor, and one day, he might be a customer. Deal fair with him. Always pays in the end." Bass walked down the stairs and out the door to the street. Theo Treece watched him go and sat back in his chair. He reflected on Frank's words as he sat and then thought, *I'm a bona fide genius, graduated from Purdue University at sixteen, earned a Ph.D. at twenty. I have a beautiful wife and baby on the way, a sweet little spread on the Rio, and more money with better prospects than I ever hoped to see in my lifetime. And I still*

*don't have the common sense of that man there. No wonder they gave
him the damn medal."*

Four

7:30 p.m. October 18th, 1888
Front Room
TwainHeart Ranch House
El Paso, Texas.

"Chinesta make them enchiladas? I'll say they were tasty."

"No, dear, I made them myself in our kitchen with my own two hands. Though Chinesta taught me, of course, her secret is slow-cooking the beef and then pulling it apart into shreds rather than just leaving the lumps as most Norteamericanos do."

"Norteamericanos, hell. You're startin' to sound like one a them Mexican Politicians I hear all the time in the Chamizal. What are you runnin' for down in Old Mexico?"

"Well, better wages for cooks to start with. And don't forget housekeeping and babysitting, either."

Bass lit one of his small cigars and said, "Well, sweetheart, once they raise the wages for cattle herdin', horse wrangling, and keepin' the peace on the frontier, I'll be happy to see to it you get a raise. 'Bout twenty-five cents a day, do it?" Sally threw a dish towel at him from the kitchen and then ran to him and sat on his lap, her arms around his neck. She took the cigar from his mouth, puffed on it a few times, and then asked, "How was your day in town, dear? Anything exciting going on?"

"Le'see, well, Greg Vale's workin' out real well. Bart ain't killed him yet, and Greg ain't drove Bart to drink neither. Uh, there was a small shootout next to Hardesty's, and Theo wants to buy land next to the tracks for a cattle sortin' and crowdin' pen. The land belongs to Riddle Sanders. You remember him from the town..." Sally leaned back and said, "Hold on just a minute there, Marshal. What about a small shootout at Hardesty's? Were you involved in it?"

"Oh yeah, I was there—some youngsters tryin' a bank robbery. But you know who got the fellas robbin' the bank? Eddie Voer, that's who. Filled those two boys behinds with buckshot. Took Doc Spalding near two hours to pick out all that small shot."

"I see, and did you shoot at all in this little fray of Eddie's?"

"Well, a course, Hon, I'm the Marshal. After all, it's kinda expected of me."

"Uh-huh, who'd you shoot Frederick?"

"A real bad outlaw named Lucas Teague."

"And did Lucas Teague shoot at you, too?"

"Uh,... Bart was standin' right next to me. Mighta been shootin' at him." Sally stood up and walked to the divan.

"Frederick, we talked about this on the train...you were gonna try to avoid these armed conflicts, you said."

"Yes, I know I said that, Sal, and if I didn't already know how ruthless Lucas Teague was, I wouldn't a gone over there. 'Fact is, as senior man for the District, I believed the situation called for fast action, and I thought I ought t'be there." Sally was listening, her arms crossed over her chest. Finally, she said, "I'm gonna go up and check on Lil. Be back shortly."

"Bass decided he'd need a quick shot of Overholt Rye while he waited for Sally's return. Shortly, she reappeared at the top of the stairs and walked down slowly, holding onto the railing.

"The fact is, Frederick, there's another reason why you should be avoiding these armed skirmishes."

"Oh? What's that?"

"Frankly dear, I believe your son's on the way." Bass went back to the Overfelt.

He turned back to Sally, eyes wide and a sideways grin on his face. "A little boy, sure nuf? How do you know?"

"Doctor Spalding came out the other day while you were out with Willy. He asked me all the same questions as with Lil and did the arithmetic. I told him I thought it might have been while we were on the train coming home from Colorado. Do you remember that night?"

"I surely do. I recall we shared a bottle of wine at dinner that night, too."

"Yes. 'Pretty sure he won't be the first baby that got his start at the pull of a cork. Anyway, the doctor said, 'probably late April. We talked about my cycle, and that's the time he came up with."

"April, huh? Calving and branding season. Seems like good timin'. When you was first carryin' Lil, you had the morin' sickness, as I recall. 'Had it bad, too, and for a while. You ain't been sick at all this time, what'd Doc say 'bout that?"

"Frederick, dear, I was getting sick almost every morning last month. You just haven't been around to share in it with me, dear." Bass reflected on the time frame and realized it was while he was still on leave. "Yeah. That's right. Well, how are you now, Sal?"

"I'm fine, normal. I'm not getting sick anymore, if that's what you mean. That's one of the ways Doc Spalding figured my due time."

'Well, that's good. I remember how bad you had it with Lil. Lord, that was hard to watch."

"I'm sure it was, dear. Anyway, I wanted to wait to tell you, but after hearing about your day, I thought I'd better tell you right away. Maybe now you'll be less likely to involve yourself in potentially dangerous situations."

"Yeah...I get it now. I'll start turnin' more of that kinda work over to Bart and Greg." Bass swallowed the end of his whiskey and asked, "Say, how do you know it's a little boy?"

"I don't know. 'Just feels like it, I guess. Different than Lil." Bass smiled at her, shaking his head.

"We're gonna have us quite a little family here in a few months, ain't we?"

"Damn, betcha, Pard."

9:30 a.m. October 19th, 1888

Dillard Ranch
Southeast of
El Paso, Texas

Because of the Lucas Teague incident and the subsequent paperwork requirement, Bass wasn't able to pay a call on the Dillard Brothers yesterday afternoon as he'd planned. Instead, he decided to ride up their way from TwainHeart the next morning. The River D Ranch was on the southeast side of El Paso and about ten miles distant from the city limits. Even though the Ranch owned the River D brand, the house itself was at least thirty miles distant from the Rio it was named for. There were several small feeder creeks on the property that filled tanks during the rainy season against the hot summer when the creeks were dry. In truth, water was not a problem on the River D. Wind was another matter. Whatever topsoil had favored the area had long since blown away, and now any seed planted deep enough not to be carried off in the wind was too distant from the surface for the moisture it needed to germinate.

Mace Dillard was not a cattleman. He didn't have the range for it. He looked instead to pigs and goats, both animals being suited to the climate and locale. Goats would feed on the scant goose grass and sprangletop weeds that grew wild on the prairie, and pigs could eat almost anything left over from a butchered goat or a family meal. The Dillards prospered year-round, selling their pork and goat meat to merchants on both sides of the Rio and their goat milk to cheesemakers as well.

Mace Dillard and Bass had become friends when Bass first arrived in El Paso. Mace was, in fact, the first to volunteer for posse work during Bass's early days and even offered to guard the jail whenever Bass needed to leave town on a manhunt. This was all before Bart Mariany was elected County Sheriff in 1881. Just after, Marshal Dallas Stoudenmire got himself shot in a running gun battle in the streets of El Paso.

Mace had suffered a stroke and died two years ago in December, and now the ownership of the River D fell to his two sons, Abel and Nathan. The boys had earned a reputation as hell-raisers whenever they came into town. They weren't really mean-spirited boys, but they were usually destructive when at the bottle and left without compensating the merchants for the damage they caused. Most saloons accepted such behavior from the Dillards and transient cowboys as a cost of doing business. Some others would turn a blind eye to the Dillard's mischief out of courtesy for their father, who was generally well-liked. Evidently, however, from Mariany's report, things were getting out of hand, and Bass was the only authority figure the Dillard brothers respected.

The morning was clear and cool with bright sunshine as Bass turned up the drive to the River D and opened the gate. The house was a hundred yards or so from the road, and because there was little or no vegetation, visitors were easily spotted from the house. Bass reined Emma in front of the small plank and adobe hut and looked over the place, remembering how well it appeared the last time he was there. Now it was run down, the small house barely standing. The only barn on the place was missing several siding planks, and the roof gaped with holes and missing shingles. The few chickens that pecked at the hardscrabble around the yard were scrawny-looking and sickly. Eggs were out of the question. The pigs Mace once took such pride in wandered the property covered in filth. Their eyes festered, and their feet lame. Water troughs were dry, and on top of everything, there was a foul odor about the place that spoke of unsanitary human conditions.

Bass called out, "Nathan! Nathan or Able Dillard! It's Frank Bass. Come out and talk with me, boys." There was no answer, so Bass climbed down and opened the door. As soon as he did, he was met with an odor he'd encountered all too often. He lit a lamp and opened the shutters over the windows on the front wall of the house. Able and Nathan Dillard were lying face up on the dirt floor, long dead from gunshot wounds to the chest and lower body. Bass determined the boys had been dead for some time, judging by the decomposition of the bodies, which were still intact. Bass assumed since the boys had fallen inside the cabin, the pigs and other critters hadn't been able to get to the bodies. Flies had found them, however, and the grisly scene was accompanied by the constant buzzing of the insects.

Bass took a quick look around the place, noticing that certain items of value were still in place...had not been taken. Things like the Winchester rifle over the hearth and the weapons still in the boy's belts led Bass to believe that this wasn't a robbery or renegade Indian raid. He began to wonder if the boys, in some kind of drunken frenzy, had shot each other but discounted that notion because the multiple wounds on the bodies had to have been made by a shotgun, and no such weapon was anywhere to be found inside the cabin. He stepped outside to clear the stench from his nose and walked around the property, making mental notes as to what he saw.

He found their Hampshire Boar had been shot in the head, again by a shotgun at close range, and was lying alongside the barn. He was partially eaten and covered with flies, but he was still in the place where he fell. There were no marks in the ground that might indicate the carcass had been dragged to that spot by a more aggressive predator. He also saw several sows with their pigs and shoats rooting about the property, and Bass assumed it was probably the sows that had eaten into the boar. Under extreme conditions, it wasn't uncommon for pigs to cannibalize their dead. Bass knew it would be difficult for a thief to wrangle a three-hundred-pound sow, but her offspring could easily be picked up and moved. Still, the young'uns dutifully chased after their moms around the yard, evidently unaffected by whatever calamity had struck down the Dillard boys. This was another indicator that robbery was not a motive. Bass then looked inside the barn and saw saddles and harness all sitting undisturbed. He walked around to the side of the barn and found four horses huddled in a corner of the corral near another dried trough. The animals were sluggish and seemed unaware of what was happening around them.

Bass had seen enough and decided to begin pumping water from the tanks into the troughs. He had seen there was hay up in the loft, so he climbed the ladder and pitched a generous amount of fodder into the open corral for the horses, who, by this time, were all sucking at the water that was just pumped.

He stood in the loft looking over the small yard, trying to determine what may have happened here sometime during the last ten days. There were no hoof prints that might indicate a raiding party. There were plenty of footprints in the yard, but who's to say which may have been made by the shotgun-wielding shooter? He had nearly decided to ask Doc Spalding, in his capacity as County Medical Examiner, to send some people out to have a more scientific look at the bodies when he realized there were none of Mace Dillard's goats anywhere to be seen. He also had a vague recollection of a dog that Mace claimed was 'the best goatherd in the state.'

Now, he climbed back down and started walking the perimeter of the whole yard encompassing the barn, the small cabin, and a pen of some sort that Bass figured might be for the goats. When he found the wagon tracks leading to the northeast, he stopped and whistled for Emma.

The sun was high, and shadows were barely visible as he rode alongside the wagon ruts. He tried to recall who it was that Bart said was squatting on the worthless section of land that lay in this direction. He remembered that it butted up against the EP & SW right of way. Bart told him it was an immigrant family...something like that. Russian or Prussian or Slavik, maybe? He wasn't sure.

The terrain had become hilly after a couple of miles, and soon, he noticed larger patches of chickweed and henbit growing in the unstable, gravelly soil. In the distance, he could make out a column of smoke, and as he continued, he began to glimpse a small shack no bigger than a railroad line shack or equipment shed in a cluster of large rocks. As he got closer, he could see goats, hundreds of them scattered over a quarter-mile swath. Soon, he heard a dog barking and watched as a middle-sized black and white pup came running up to him, barking and nipping at Emma's hooves. Emma didn't spook easily, but she didn't like this, and she began kicking and crow-hopping so severely that Bass had to jump off. He was trying to grab hold of Emma's reins to calm her when he heard a loud bang from the direction of the shed. The dog turned and quickly ran off toward the shed. Bass, having no choice, pulled his Colts Pistol, turned Emma's reins free, and crouched behind a large tarbrush plant.

"I'm U.S. Deputy Marshal Frank Bass on official business. Put down your weapon. I wish to talk." He heard a deep voice respond, thick with dialect and conviction.

"Not to talk for. My land. Here is my land. You go! You go now!"

"Uh huh, no, no, I can't do that. I have business with you. What is your name?"

"Is what?"

"Your name, sir. I want to know your name."

"Anatoly...Anatoly Yevonovich. This is my land. You go."

Bass immediately liked this big man, blustering over his land, poor and windblown, something he'd probably never had before. And proud that it was his.

"Can't do that, Mr. Yevonovich. Two men were killed. 'About four miles away. I followed your wagon here." Anatoly Yevonovich was quiet for a moment, and Bass decided he understood more than he let on.

"They steal from me. From me, what's mine."

"Anatoly...Did you shoot them two boys?" Again, Yevonovich was silent. Bass ventured a peek around the shrub, and he could see a large balding man with a thick gray beard, wearing bibb coveralls and muck boots, sitting on a rock near the shack. He was holding a hat of some kind, and a shotgun lay across his lap. The dog was sitting at his side.

"Anatoly? I just wanna talk. I'm comin' out now. Please don't shoot. I don't want to fight with you." Yevonovich said nothing, and Bass approached the man slowly. Bass pointed toward the dog. "I've seen him a couple times with Mace Dillard, herding his goats."

"Not Mace dog...not Mace goats. Mine."

"How's that? I don't understand."

"Mace is friend, good friend. He teaches me English talk, ah..and I give him some of my goats and to use Sergei." He nodded to the dog. "Mace now dead, and I want my dog, my goats."

"Is that why you shot Abel and Nathan?" The man gestured with his long arms.

"I ask them many times. Many times. They laugh and shoot at feet on ground, so I must jump. They shoot my foot, and I have to cut off my, my...what is word?" He kicked off the muck boot on his right foot, exposing a bullet wound on the top of his foot that looked to be septic and painful. "And they laugh more. They do not hear. Say goats are theirs. Goats are mine, Sergei is mine. I make, what is it... deal with Mace." Bass was listening and nodding his head as the larger man spoke. He wanted Anatoly Yevonovich to know that someone would listen.

"Anatoly. I think I see what happened here. I believe the goats and Sergei belong to you. But you can't shoot people over disagreements. You must settle with them using the law." Again, Anatoly Yevonovich was silent for a long minute and finally looked up at Bass. He said,

"So...what happen now. You have badge, you arrest me? What happen to goats and to Sergei?"

"I'll see to it that the goats and Sergei are cared for, but I must take you into town with me."

Anatoly put his boot back on and stood up. Bass could tell the movement hurt, but the man's pride wouldn't let him show it. He put on his hat and went to his corral to bring one of his draft horses around to where Bass waited. He pulled himself up, bareback, on the large horse and gave Sergei a command in his language. The dog seemed to pay attention because he looked at Yevonovich and then scampered away. Both men watched for a moment as Sergei circled the goat herd, moving them toward the corral, and then Bass led Anatoly Yevonovich along the railroad tracks and into El Paso. Sergei eventually caught up with them. The shadows had returned and stretched out behind them as they rode.

Five

6:15 p.m. October 19, 1888
City Jail
St. Louis Street
EL Paso, Texas

By the time Bass and Anatoly Yevonovich reached the jail, Bart had left for the day, and Greg Vale was making rounds. But Eddie Voer was still at work sweeping out the office and fetching firewood for the next morning.

"Eddie? This is Anatoly Yevonovich, and that yonder is his dog, Sergei. We're holding Anatoly for killin the Dillard brothers, found both boys shotgunned in their cabin this mornin." Eddie had a quizzical look on his face, so Bass said, "Long story, Eddie. Let's fetch 'em both some supper and make sure you put a bowl of fresh water in the cell for Sergei. They'll both be with us until I can get in to see Judge Hobart. Oh yes, ask Doc Spalding to have a look at

Mr. Yevonovich's right foot, too. I believe it's a bullet wound that's festered."

"Alright, Marshal, if you say so. This way over here, Mr. Ka ...whatsis. You two can share this cell at the end. It's the biggest one we got." Bass saw that man and dog were settled, and then he said to Eddie, "He don't speak much English, Eddie, so try to make do if he says anything. Might be best if you wrote down whatever he says so I can make the judge understand the situation better."

"Will do, Frank. You comin' in tomorrow?" They walked out to the sheriff's office and closed the door to the jail behind them.

"As to that, Eddie, I hadn't planned to, but I guess now I oughta. I wanna send the Doc out to the River D for the bodies, and then I wanna talk to the judge about what to do with the land. There's still livestock out there, horses and pigs at the River D, and a whole flock of goats beyond where Anatoly was squatted. Yeah, I'll be in tomorrow mornin, alright." Bass turned to go back out front, where the horses were tied off. As he left, he told Eddie, "he did confess to shootin them, boys, Eddie, so he might be thinkin to run if gets the chance. Oh...walk his plug out back to the corral and see he gets a good feed, will ya, Eddie?"

"Sure thing, Frank. See ya tomorrow."

9:30 p.m. October 19th, 1888
TwainHeart Ranch House
El Paso, Texas.

Bass and Sally had eaten quietly. Sally wasn't feeling particularly well, and after feeding Lil and putting her down for the night, she just wanted to go to bed. Bass had a long day and was ready for sleep as well. He had told Sally about his meeting with Anatoly Yevonovich and how he felt for the older man. He was having difficulty getting the image of the Dillard brothers lying dead on the dirt floor of their cabin out of his mind. He'd seen things, of course, that were so much worse, but the sight of two young men that he'd known for years lying dead for days without notice saddened him more than he expected. He also knew what was ahead for Anatoly Yevonovich, and that saddened him further. He thought Anatoly was probably just a hard-working immigrant trying to make a life on the frontier when circumstance and misunderstanding took hold of him and resulted in tragedy.

Still, Bass knew that every culture he'd ever heard of forbade taking human life...assigned murder its most final punishment. Anatoly Yevonovich surely knew right from wrong when he pulled the triggers on his shotgun. His description of the taunting he received and the terror of being shot couldn't justify his final action. And yet, if he fired that shotgun in direct and immediate response to the Dillards shooting...An argument for self-defense could be raised. It was a long shot and probably impossible, but Bass planned to discuss it with the judge first thing Monday morning.

10:30 a.m. October 21st, 1888
El Paso County Court House
Office of District Judge
Clarence Hobart
600 Santa Fe Street
El Paso, Texas.

"Mornin Frank, what can I do for ya? Sorry, I'm a bit rushed, but 'always seems to get like this on Mondays."

Well, Judge, let me ask, do you remember Mace Dillard?"

"Yes, I do. 'Heard he died some time ago, stroke, I think. What's this all about?"

"Uh, Mace wanted to start up a goat herding operation, good market around here, he once told me, and he got some help from a neighbor, squatter...immigrant named Anatoly Yevonovich. 'Seems Yevonovich traded Mace some of his goats and the use of his dog for Mace teachin' him English."

"Uh-huh. I suppose this story is heading someplace interesting. What say we get there quickly, Frank?"

"Yes, sir. Well, when Mace passed, Anatoly Yevonovich wanted his goats and dog back, so he went to the River D and asked Nate and Abel to return them. Them boys, bein' who they are, probably drunk, put Anatoly Yevonovich through a dance lesson and shot his right foot. 'Probably an accident, but they shot him just the same. Yevonovich gets his shotgun and goes back, wounded, mind you, and confronts the Dillards, killing them both. I found the boys last Friday. Been dead a while and followed Yevonovich's wagon tracks to his place and arrested him."

"I see, I see. So, what is it exactly you're proposing then, Frank? The Dillard boys are dead, and your squatter's shot in the foot."

"Yes sir, yes sir, that's all true, but I'm wonderin' if the law might see a bit of self-defense on Yevonovich's part. I guess I'm sayin there's mitigatin' circumstance here, Judge, and maybe you could consider that in your sentencing of the man."

"I take it then that he's confessed to you?"

"Yes, he has. He's over in the jail getting medical care for his foot...him and his dog."

"The dog, too, huh?"

"Yes, sir, smart little pup." Judge Hobart thought for a moment and said.

"Frank, I understand his situation, and I'll do what I can, but the man killed the two Dillards boys. There's gonna be a price to pay."

"I know that Judge, and so does he. 'Just askin you to consider everything is all."

"Alright, Frank, I'll give it some consideration. Let's get his foot taken care of, and I'll stop over and talk with him after a while."

"Thank you, sir. 'Preciate your time." Bass stood up and walked to the door, about to leave, when Hobart called to him, "Frank? Take care of the dog, too." Bass grinned as he put his hat on.

"Yes, sir. 'Will do."

Bass started thinking as he left the judge's office. It seemed at least somewhat likely that Hobart would take into account the possibility of self-defense and might, therefore, sentence Yevonovich to serve time in the penitentiary rather than be gallows hung, the usual sentence for capital murder. Bass knew that Yevonovich might earn parole if he kept his nose clean in prison, and if that was the case, he might want his goats and dog back at some point in the distant future.

"Bet Emil and Sarah Sigmundson might like to take on another hundred or so goats...might could use a smart dog too."

Bass decided he'd check with Emil on Wednesday... Emil always came to town on Wednesdays to deliver goat cheese and milk to the markets in EL Paso and Juarez. Bass made a note to look for him at the Chamizal early on Wednesday morning.

7:30 p.m. October 23rd, 1888
TwainHeart Ranch House
El Paso, Texas.

The previous day, Bass had spent in the company of Silas Pratt discussing plans for the new barn and the relative benefits of concrete footings and floors. Bass liked the notion that concrete was easy to clean and didn't absorb odors and stains as a simple dirt and straw floor would, but he was hesitant due to the cost of it. Additionally, the concrete needed to set or cure, as Pratt called it, once it was smoothed over, and during the rainy season, this was a serious concern. He finally decided to build the barn over dirt so there'd be shelter for the animals during the winter, and in summer, they would look to lay out a concrete floor.

Bass and Sally had finished their supper and were cleaning up while the baby played with her potatoes and corn.

"So anyway, Sal, I figured I would ask Emil Sigmundson and his wife if they'd take Yevonovich's goats and dog. 'Don't know how long he's gonna be away, could be when he gets out, he won't want 'em back, but I told him I'd watch out for 'em, and this is the best I can come up with. What do you think?"

"I think it's a fine plan, dear. I don't know the Sigmundsons well, hardly at all, actually, but if they herd goats and treat them well, I can't think of anything better. What would happen to the animals if they weren't cared for?"

"Probably turn feral, I guess, wouldn't last long on the prairie, winter comin' and all. Coyotes and wolves would take a bunch."

"Is there a reason that Emil wouldn't want Mr. Yevonovich's goats?"

"Can't say. 'Don't know much about goats. If it was cattle, 'wouldn't be a problem. But goats are different. If they don't want 'em, I'm sure there's folks in Juarez that would take 'em. The problem there is they'd all wind up in the stew pot. I'll see Emil at the Chamizal tomorrow and ask. Meanwhile, his goats are out there along the railroad tracks wanderin' about.

The rest of the evening was spent in front of the fire. Sally had begun knitting again, and Bass was cleaning and oiling his Walker Colts. The pistols were given out to Rangers in the early 1850s, and though they had their problems, some exploded at the most inopportune times. Still, the huge side arm proved itself in the Mexican-American War. Bass had received them *in recognition for courageous service* from his first Captain in the Rangers, Leander McNelly. They were then and continued to be the most powerful handguns in the world, and Bass had found use for that particular quality in more than a few situations.

Bass had the two weapons converted to use a Colt .45 caliber cartridge. Re-loading a converted pistol required a certain disassembly of the conversion cylinder, and his only occasional use of them meant regular maintenance was required. On nights such as these, a quiet evening by the fire, Bass took the opportunity to maintain his weapons.

As much as he hated cold, early mornings, he knew that to find Sigmundson at the Chamizal, he'd have to be there when trading opened. He explained his plan to Sally, kissed the baby, and went to bed.

11:30 a.m. October 23rd, 1888
City Jail
St. Louis Street
El Paso, Texas.

Bass arrived at the Jail after spending most of the morning with Emil Sigmundson and went straight into Anatoly Yevonovich's cell.

"Anatoly, I promised you that I'd see to it your goats were cared for, and this morning, I talked with another goat herder named Emil Sigmundson about watching after your goats. He said, if you agree, he'll watch your flock and care for them like his own while you're gone. When you come back, he'll turn them back over to you, kids and all. Now, this is all supposing that you're not gone for too terrible long. For his part, Emil wants the milk produced by your 'nannies as compensation for takin' them in. He says, however, that if his dog and Sergi do not get along, he will not take your dog. He'll use his dog. What do you think?" Anatoly thought on the subject for a minute and asked, "How long Judge say I am gone?" Bass wanted to be honest with the settler, "Anatoly, he did not say. I did speak up on your behalf, but only the Judge knows how he'll rule. It could be years." At this, Yevonovich recoiled, his eyes wide with fright.

"Years, Bass?" Anatoly Yevonovich's face was twisted into a plea for understanding.

"Anatoly, you know it's a serious crime to kill men, even men that are tormentin' ya."

Yevonovich softened a little.

"You take Sergei, Bass. You care for him." Bass wasn't expecting this request, but he agreed.

"He can stay here with you as long as you want, and when you have to leave, I'll take him to my house."

"No, you take him now. Good dog, ah..he work hard. Never tired. Jail not place for good dog."

"Alright, then, Anatoly, I'll take him home with me tonight. He'll have a good home. Uh...how is he with cattle?"

12:30 p.m. October 24th, 1888
Sheriff's Office
St. Louis Street.
El Paso, Texas

Rain had begun falling in the early morning hours and continued with increasing intensity through noon. The streets of El Paso, which had not yet been cobbled with concrete and river rock, were awash. The ruts carved by wagon traffic filled with water, and the dirt streets were muddied so deep that walking across one could cost the pedestrian his shoe, lost to the suction of the muck.

Bass and Mariany sat in the Sheriff's office listening to the drunken retches of two cowboys in their cells, arrested for fighting and public drunkenness the night before. The two boys, fifteen and sixteen, had awoken in their cells and immediately fell ill from the rotgut they'd consumed the night before. Bass had a measure of sympathy for the boys, but the older Mariany would occasionally call out, "Drink with the Devil, pay his price."

"By God, Bart. Weren't you ever young and foolish in your life? Or were you born old and crotchety?"

"Oh...indeed, I was young and foolish once... and often too. But I soon learned from my mistakes and became the crotchety old Sage I am today. Those boys gotta learn, or they won't last to appreciate their dotage. Too many ways for a man to die on the frontier. Death by drink oughtn't be one of 'em. Sadly, it is. You wanna get lunch?"

"You're hungry after listenin' to that?"

"No, I'm tired of listenin' to it and thought I'd swim over to the Puesta for coffee and a biscuit. You wanna come along?"

"Yeah, might as well. Somebody ought to see to it you don't fall in the street and drown. Lemme get my duster."

The Puesta del Sol was a café across the street and half a block down from the Sheriff's Office. Bass and Mariany had been regular customers for years. When they stepped outside, the cold, wet blast of an early winter storm made each man catch his breath and close the collar of his weather gear. The icy rain blown sideways by the northeasterly wind stung their cheeks red and raw. It made walking the two-by-eight-foot of plank wood that had been laid across the street for passage that much trickier. By the time the two men reached the opposite boardwalk, their eyes stung so badly they could hardly see to walk. Once inside the Café, they were warmed by two heat stoves and a cook stove to the rear. They hung their soaked coats near the door to shed the water they'd picked up coming over. One of the owners, a short, fat Mexican woman named Guadalupe, called to them across the room. "Ustedes dos sacudanse los panchos mojados antes de colgaras." Mariany had more of the Mexican language than Bass, and when he heard what Guadalupe said, he cocked his head and yelled back, "Que dijieste vieja?" Guadalupe slammed a plate down and said, "Me escuchaste vieja pedo, no empapes mi piso." Bass had been watching the exchange, and though he picked up a couple of words, he asked. "What was that all about, Bart?"

"Oh hell, the old woman told us to hang our panties up to let them dry."

"Panties, Bart?"

"That's what she said, alright, so I asked her what she was talkin about, and then she called me an old fart, said that I heard her, and don't mess up her floor.'

"Ain't wearin' panties, Bart. Are you?" Mariany looked disgustedly at Bass and stalked off to a table near the kitchen. They both sat down and shortly after, Guadalupe's daughter stopped at the table to get their order. "Señores, what is it you'd like?"

Mariany spoke first and said he wanted "Biscuits in gravy, Dolores, and not that ranchero stuff your ma always slathers over tortillas, okay? Just good brown meat gravy."

"Si Señor, y usted Marshal?"

"Same thing, hon, and a whiskey against the damps."

"Es Bueno, de immediate." She closed her pad and left. Once she was out of earshot, Bart continued to grumble. "Panties. Who the hell 'she think we are, anyway? Been comin' in here two, three times a week, and she thinks we got panties. Fool, old woman."

"You sure that's what she said, Bart? Couldn't a been another word?"

"No, no, weren't no other word. I know the Mexican word for panties, I guess. Used it often enough when I was younger."

Bass's whiskey came quickly, and he'd taken a sip when they noticed Eddie Voer standing in the doorway, dripping rain from his hat and pancho.

"Over here, Eddie," Bass called, and Eddie walked to the table. He was holding an envelope in his hand, and even though the rain was making the ink run, it was plain to see the letter was from the Governor of Texas.

"This just came, Frank. Figured you'd like to see it right away." Mariany was watching the rainwater puddle around Eddie's boots and asked, "You ain't wearin' panties, are you, Eddie?"

"Panties? What the hell 'you drinkin' Bart?"

"Never mind, just checking." Bass had opened the letter and was reading it to himself. When he finished, he slumped back in his chair, staring at the far wall and into nothingness. He said,

"From the Governor, alright, Sully Ross himself. 'Says he wants me to go to Laredo, favor to him, to look into cattle thievery from the King Ranch. I guess from what he says in the letter that Harry Gosling bought it...tryin' to catch whoever done it."

"Harry?" Mariany paused for a moment, lost in memories. "Well, he weren't no blood n guts lawman. But he was honest as today is wet. Good man. Letter say who done it?" Bass picked up the letter again and read, "Says Dan Bogan and some others shot Harry and his deputies. One of 'em survived. 'Someplace called San Ygnacio Creek, down south." Bass knew he couldn't say no. It was the Governor, after all. "Geezes. What am I gonna tell Sal?"

Six

6:15 p.m. October 24th, 1888
Main House
TwainHeart Ranch
El Paso, Texas

The rains had stopped around 5:00 p.m. but picked up again at 6:00 p.m. when the wind shifted to the Southwest. In that brief respite, Bass was able to get home and put Emma away, dry, in her stall. Now, he sat with Sally and the baby at the kitchen table. Sergei, sitting next to the baby's chair, waiting for some morsel to be discarded.

As was his nature, he chose to get the bad news out and deal with it rather than hem and haw, delaying the inevitable and waiting for a 'better time.' Sally's reaction was expected.

"Another favor, dear? Haven't you done enough for the State of Texas? All those terrible weeks in Austin, and now this fellow expects you to drop whatever else is going on in your life and travel to Laredo? God only knows where that is, and you're to track down cow thieves when you get there? It's so unfair, Frederick, unfair to you and unfair to the people of El Paso, your own District. Lil and I will be fine. We have our friends around to watch out for us. But you'll be hundreds of miles away, alone on some trail susceptible to road agents and bandits of all kinds. I hate to throw this back at you, but you swore, after Austin, you wouldn't be taking on any more 'special requests.' You wanted to stay at home and oversee Willy and Angel." Bass had listened carefully to everything Sally said. And he agreed with all of it. It was unfair to El Paso, and he did say he wouldn't take on any more favors.

"You're right, Sal, every word. And I dreaded coming to you with this letter. But the fact is that the Governor is asking for my help. The same Governor who hung that damned medal around my neck a couple of months ago. I can't just thumb my nose and say, "Sorry, but no can do, Sully." Now Sally was standing at the counter coating chicken for the frying pan. "Well, hell. Just hell and damnation is all." She was quiet for a moment and then said, "How long do you think you'll be gone?"

"Well, see, that's the thing, it's a fairly easy assignment. They want me to track a small herd from a creek down there just to see who it was mighta paid for 'em. 'Pretty easy stuff, really. Shouldn't take moren' a week of actual trackin. I don't reckon it'll take that long, Sal. You know I'd as soon stay here 'round you and Lil, but I just can't say no." Sally was silent for a few moments again, still standing at the sink. Finally, she turned to Bass.

"Frederick, I know you have to go. The fact is, if you didn't go, you wouldn't be the man I love. But I do worry, of course. Especially after all you suffered out on the Llano last winter looking for those little girls. You just make sure to take the heavy gear with you again and send wires to us whenever you can."

"I will, hon. Try not to worry too much. I've done far more dangerous tasks in my life than this."

Sally only nodded and walked to the table to hug him. He said,

"I plan to take Emma with me... she did okay on the train to Wyoming, so the trip south should be easy for her. She's real good at this kinda thing, and since I'll likely be sleepin' outside now and then, she provides a fine lookout."

"That is some comfort. I always feel better knowing you're well-mounted. When will you leave?"

"Figure 'day after tomorrow. I'll go buy the train fare tomorrow. There's a southbound every day, but I don't know exactly when it leaves or how long it takes. Imagine there ain't nothin' direct to Laredo anyway. I'm gonna go up and get my travelin gear together now. Just call me when dinner's ready." Bass kissed Sally and left the room, headed for his closet in the spare room. He pulled out his waterproof outerwear, pancho, slicker, and heavy gloves. Then he put a second change of clothing in his duffle, along with spare long drawers and pullovers. He'd wear flannel for most of the trip, and his heavy duster would be tied off on the cantle. Even though most railroad passenger cars had heat stoves built in, sometimes it wasn't enough. He took his spare boots as well. He'd waterproofed both pairs with goose grease, and though daily he wore his Frye's, the Espinozas he bought in Arizona two years back were warmer and stayed watertight. He planned to take his *North and Judd* spurs, not so much for Emma, but in case he needed to ride a second horse. It was always possible that Emma could lame up or need rest, and Bass might have to ride an unknown animal. In that case, he'd need a convincing spur with a medium rowle to communicate with a new mount. He always carried his Colt pistol on his gun belt and the Remington Smoot New Model revolver in his boot. Since he figured to be in the saddle some, he packed his Walker Colts in oilcloth for the trip and took down his Winchester 86 for cleaning. He remembered it was the one he'd picked up in Wyoming after a shoot-out with the Poudy Brothers. He grabbed a box of 45-90 shells and decided to pick up some of the bigger .50s from the jail. He normally carried a scatter gun when on the trail but didn't think he'd need one for this trip. He'd most likely be eating in cafés and diners this time.

He rolled everything up in his duffle (in days passed, he would have taken the buffalo robe, but Lil had pretty much claimed it for herself now.) except for what he'd need in the morning and went down the stairs to the lavatory to make his shaving kit ready. As he came down, Sally called him for dinner, so he stopped at the whiskey cart, as they'd named it, and poured each of them a generous dram for supper. When he walked into the kitchen, Lil was already in her chair, and she held out her arms to her father to be picked up and hugged. Bass loved everything about his daughter, and when she asked like that for cuddles, he could never resist.

Sally was a little quiet at dinner, but Lil chatted up a storm, commenting on her bibb, her spoon, and her funnel cup with apple juice in it, how it was her favorite and all. 'Of course, it all sounded like gibberish, but her parents pretended to understand and used real words to answer her. After dinner, they all sat in the front parlor near the fire and listened to the rain as it pattered on the roof over the front porch. Sergei had curled himself at the hearth and kept a watchful eye on Lil. The weather had gentled some for the evening, and Bass hoped it stayed that way. Sally was reading her Ladies Home Journal article about women's role in society. Turns out, she said, "I'm living the perfect lifestyle." Bass busied himself cleaning and oiling the Winchester for the trip. Lillian was practicing her walking back and forth between her parents. Eventually, she tired and held up her arms, yawning, indicating it was time for bed. Sally took her upstairs, and Bass gazed out the large front window at the blackness of night, the occasional glistened drops of rain that fell in the front porch lamplight. He checked his Elgin and noticed it was near 9:30 p.m. He decided to head upstairs to get himself ready for bed.

It was still warm upstairs even though the stoves downstairs were cooling down, and the hearth in the front room had fallen to embers. Sally was warm in her nightclothes and cuddled close to him, her breathing soft and rhythmic. He could hear Lil in her crib across the hall making quiet night noises, cooing to the Raggedy Ann she clutched in her sleep. Sergei lay on a rug at the foot of the bed, quiet but alert. Bass was pleased the dog seemed to be comfortable in his new home.

In all things Bass considered, he was at peace. He had another child on the way, and the added responsibility nudged him into retrospection. He'd always known Sally to concern herself with the here and now, the future she'd deal with as it came. He hadn't known many women well and supposed that to be the natural way of things.

Like most family men, he had great awareness of the future, realizing that his actions today might influence conditions for his family down the line. He also knew his career was an uncommon one in that life and death decisions had to be made in split seconds, and the likelihood of regret, guilt, and self-doubt would be high.

He reconciled his job, which at times made him ruthless, as a righteous necessity on a lawless frontier, and the ends justified the means. He was always prideful in being a *good man*, honest and straightforward, true to his morals and ideals. Hypocrisy was unthinkable to him. He also knew some men hated him. Some families loathed his being and feared his presence. But these people were society's outcasts, and most had been intent on taking his life. His convictions and skills had simply proven to be stronger. He recalled the 'vignettes' of past violence that played on his mind for so long and thankfully had stopped when he met Sally. Still at night, awake and alone, he thanked God for the power to forgive himself.

7:15 a.m. October 25th, 1888
The Horse Barn
TwainHeart Ranch
El Paso, Texas.

The rain had stopped, but the sky was still dark and threatening. The wind had backed to the northeast, and there was a distinctive autumn chill in the air. The yard from the house to the barn was muddy even though Bass had seeded and put step stones in the previous year. He finished saddling Emma for his ride into town and led her out to the hitch rail in front of the house. Sally was holding Lil, standing on the porch out of the wind, watching as he climbed the stairs to say goodbye for the day.

"I'll try to get home early, but if something big comes up, I'll have to settle it before I leave. I'll buy my tickets today, so tonight, we can write down where I'll be stopping. 'Course, I'll send a wire whenever I can. I'm going first to Laredo, 'check in with the Sheriff there. Train'll take a couple days, I figure."

Sally's face was a contrast to the dark skies. She smiled as she always did when Bass left her for work. It was advice that her Grandmother had taught her about saying goodbye to your man in the morning. "Anything can happen in the world away from you. Don't let him leave with a sullen look on your face." It was difficult some days, but Sally always tried.

She and Lil watched him close the gate down at the River Road and went back into the house to begin their day.

Bass got to his second-floor office at about 8:30 a.m. and noted happily that Eddie Voer had started a fire in his stove and put on a pot before he got there. There was still some mail left on his desk from yesterday. He answered a couple of letters from Sheriffs in his district. Both were requesting assistance in one form or another. The frontier was expanding. People were coming from the east every day now that the Indian depredations had been quelled. The smaller towns like Las Cruces and Alamogordo were growing, and the need for additional law officers was urgent. He wrote that he would try to find money in the District Marshal's budget, and failing that, he would petition District Judge Hobart for his help.

At 11:00 a.m., he locked his office and went down to the jail to see if anyone wanted an early lunch. However, according to Eddie, both Bart, and Greg were away on a domestic issue, so he decided to head to the railroad terminal for his ticket to Laredo.

The EP&SW ticket counter was inside the terminal building on Main Street, only a couple of blocks from the sheriff's office. He waited his turn in line to speak with the clerk, and when he got to the window, he said, "Need a ticket to Laredo and passage for my horse. I know there's a southbound every day, and I'd like to leave tomorrow." The clerk recognized the Marshal; almost everyone in town did, and he said. "Yes sir, just the one ticket, Marshal?"

"Yeah, just me goin this time."

"One way or round trip fare, it's a little cheaper that way, ya know."

"This time, my trip's gonna be open-ended. 'Don't know when I'll be able to break away to come home. Soon, I hope."

"Alrighty then, One way to Laredo on the 26th is forty-nine dollars for you and fifteen for your horse. Any special requirements for your animal?"

"No, 'guess I'll bring a bag of apples and carrots. Maybe some sugar. She has a sweet tooth."

"Very good then, the *Rio Flyer* leaves at 8:15 a.m. tomorrow. 'Best be maybe half-hour early to get your horse settled. Ah...water stop at Fort Hancock and arrives in El Polvo tomorrow at about 6:00 p.m. for a supper break. 'Don't know what they got to eat there, armadillo and rattlesnake, most likely. 'Train continues to two water stops and arrives in Laredo at 5:00 a.m. on the 27th. No sleepers, but there are divans and easy chairs in the Lounge Car." The clerk stamped the ticket as paid and dated today. Bass tipped his hat and collected his paperwork. He decided to eat lunch, so he walked into the Puesta del Sol, across from the Jail, and sat at the counter, which was usual when he was alone. The young man at the counter greeted Bass with a cheerful expression and set a menu card down on the counter in front of him.

"Drink from the bar, Marshal?"

"Believe so, ah, your name's Del, ain't it?"

"Yes, sir. Be right back." As he waited, Bass noticed that John Wesley Hardin had taken a table near the wall and was having his lunch with a widow from south of town. Bass couldn't quite remember her first name, but her husband, Abe Lomas, was an older man killed when his wagon tipped over on him. He wondered what Hardin might have to do with a widow woman and, of course, what she could possibly see in him. Del appeared with his rye on ice, and Bass asked,

"Say, does that fella over there, John Hardin, come in here often? It ain't real handy to his office."

"Yeah, maybe twice a week he's in here. 'Drinks more'n he eats, but he tips real good. The girls argue over who gets to serve him."

"Oh really? Why's at?"

"Oh... cause he's John Wesley Hardin, has a reputation a bein' a dangerous man. Iris, in particular, thinks he's just the bee's knees."

"Cause he's dangerous, huh?" Del nodded, and Bass went on. "Well, he is that. I doubt the families of those he killed would agree 'bout the bee's knees, though."

"That's what I tell 'em girls, but they just pooh-pooh me. And he's old enough to be their father, to boot!" Bass shied at that remark. Hardin was only a year older than him.

"One of life's mysteries, Del. Ah... bring the blue plate, will ya? And another one of these, too." Bass held up his glass.

"Sure thing, Marshal. Right away."

Bass was looking over the tickets he'd just bought, trying to remember when the last time was that he was in Laredo. He concluded it must've been during his Ranger days because he recalled crossing the Rio with a column and camping in La Cruz just north of Laredo. For the life of him, he couldn't recall the reason they'd crossed the Rio.

"You mind if I sit here?" Bass looked over and saw the scowling visage of John Wesley Hardin standing next to him. Bass had no desire to exchange pleasantries with the outlaw, so he said, "Yeah, I do mind. I got a hot lunch comin', and I don't want it gettin' cold listenin' to your palaver."

"Well, that's a fine thing to say to someone... just tryin to clear the air between us." Bass turned in his chair.

"Hardin, it'd take a pretty strong wind to clear your stench from El Paso County. Now I'm doin my best to remember you just done time for the crimes they could pin on you. But that don't mean I gotta be your friend neither. So you just move on before I arrest you for disturbin' my lunch."

"Oh, hell. Suit yourself. I'll pay your respects to Edna Lomas anyway." Bass watched him walk back to his table, paying special notice to the peculiar outline on the back of his suit jacket. It showed the telltale sign of a cross-draw shoulder holster, the one Hardin always wore before he got sent up. Bass wondered when his time to face down Hardin would come. It was surely in the air around him, though he hadn't broken any laws yet. Bass figured it probably wouldn't happen during this lunch, anyway.

Bass walked back to the jail after lunch and found Bart Mariany and Greg Vale smiling and joking about something when he walked in.

"You boys heard a good story, did ya?" Bart looked up and said, "Naw, we was just talkin 'bout Harvey and Libby Hacke over at their market on San Francisco Street. They are a pair to draw to, I'll tell ya." Greg was still chuckling as Bart related the encounter.

"The little Whatley boy that works there came a runnin in here all in a lather sayin they was gonna kill each other. Said they were goin' at each other fierce. Now you know Harvey Hacke, big as he is, he ain't got a mean bone in his body. But Libby now she's somethin' else. That little vixen's got enough temper for three women and ain't never been one to stifle it neither. So Greg and I hustle over there, and 'turns out that Harvey delivered groceries to Inez Rodriguez over on Main? You know Irene's got them big... eyes a hers that she's so proud of, and Libby felt Harvey took too long for the visit to be all business. Anyway, when we got there, she was yellin' and throwin' tomatoes, and apples, and oranges, even raw chicken at Harvey, who was crouched behind the counter with all the peppers. He was tryin to tell Libby that there wasn't nothin' goin on, that he didn't even notice Inez's... you know...eyes, which is a bald lie 'cause everyone in town knows about Inez' big eyes the way she flashes 'em around. Anyway, I grabbed Libby, say she's a strong little gal, and Greg's over by Harvey, and we're tryin to explain that it's disturbin' the peace, not to mention makin' a mess of their store, and we don't want to arrest 'em but we will. So finally Harvey came over and reassured Libby again, and she apologized for causin' a scene cause now folks were gathering outside. And everything was all right again. They started cleanin' up their store, and they gave me and Greg a bag of apples. Want one?"

"No thanks. I just ate lunch. But it's enough to know that justice was served with a minimum loss of fruit." Everybody chuckled some more, and finally, Bass asked if anything new had come in on the District wire that he needed to deal with.

The wire was a telegraphic communication set up to alert the Marshals of the southwest of potential trouble that might be headed their way. The U.S. Cavalry used a similar Heliograph or 'Flash' System before the telegraph was established in remote southwest outposts. Originally, the wire was used to advise of Indian activity, but since the old Chiefs had either died or been moved to Florida, the wire was used to transmit business and advisories. Bart glanced at his desk and said,

"Nope, nary a peep. Unless you got something of vital import to share with us, I can safely say that all is well in El Paso County. Bass took off his hat and poured coffee for himself.

"That's good. I'm leavin tomorrow mornin for Laredo and then points east. Y'all know the Governor wrote. 'Can't hardly say no, so I'm off again. 'Don't know for how long. I'll be checking in with whatever law they got in Laredo now, so I'll let you know what's what as soon as I know anything. I guess you can reach me in Laredo at the Marshal's office should somethin come up. Y'all keep safe. Oh, and keep a watchful eye on John Wesley, will you?" Bass went up to his office to make sure he hadn't forgotten any important business before he left. Then he went down to the small barn and corral behind the jail, saddled Emma, and headed out toward the Chamizal and TwainHeart on the Rio.

Seven

7:15 a.m. October 26th, 1888
EP&SW Terminal
El Paso, Texas.

Emma generally did well on the train, provided she was positioned in the freight car, so she faced forward more or less. She climbed the wooden ramp easily and followed Bass as he led her to a narrow stall at the front of the car. At each stop of more than fifteen minutes, he would lead her back down the ramp and around the right of way to keep her balance and acclimation. In addition, Doc Spalding recommended a mild dose of paraldehyde as a calming agent coupled with chamomile flower in her feed. Chamomile tea had always been a popular sedative, and paraldehyde was a relatively new drug being used both as a sedative and to control seizures. Paraldehyde was neither an opiate nor a barbiturate. In smaller doses, it could be used to control anxiety. Bass was hesitant to give the drug to Emma unless she became quite agitated in her stall or aggressive when Bass took her to walk outside at water and coal stops.

Once Emma was settled, Bass took a seat in the second coach. He sat next to a window on one of the wooden slat benches and tipped his hat at an older woman who sat next to him and introduced herself.

"I don't mean to intrude, sir, but I think I recognize you. You're Marshal Frank Bass, aren't you? The one who just received a medal from our Governor Sullivan?"

"Yes, ma'am, I am he."

"My name is Margaret Hadley. You shot my grandsons ten days ago as they were attempting to steal money from a bank."

"Yes, ma'am, though actually, it was my deputy who shot them. Peppered their behinds with birdshot, he did, as they were tryin to escape."

"Yes, that may be the case. I wouldn't know. Their mother, my daughter-in-law, related the story as she heard it. I want you to know that, first of all, I believe in law and order. Without it, we dissolve into savagery. However, I also want you to know that those boys have always been good, dutiful sons to their mother and me. Never ever in trouble with the law. It was losing their father that brought on their turn to lawlessness. Our family is destitute, Marshal. We have no prospects for income enough to feed and shelter us. It was that no-account Lucas Teague that turned them. He came to town looking for my son, their father, Cable Hadley. My son was shot in a bar fight almost a year ago in Odessa. Since then, the boys have tried to find work, but with no book schoolin', all they can find is stable help which won't keep them or their Ma in their house. They're young, Marshal, and they fell for Teague's promises of riches and adventure. I'm tellin' you all this because I hope you'll put in a kind word for them at their trial." Bass listened and thought for a moment.

"Mrs. Hadley, I will do that. I'll explain what you've told me to Judge Hobart, who is a fair-minded person. I've seen some hard men in my time, and Lucas Teague is an example. I could also tell by the boys' behavior in the jail,... the 'yes sirs and no sirs'... that somewhere along the line, they learned manners. But they also have to learn that outlawin' can't be tolerated no matter the excuse. Fortunately, no one but your grandsons and Mr. Teague were hurt in the ruckus. They were lucky in that. Was there an innocent victim of violence, they'd surely have to pay for it.

What I'll do is write a wire to District Judge Hobart, recommendin' leniency. Likely, first offense and all, they'll get probation. 'Can't make promises, you understand. The judge is a human man and might wake up cranky on the day he hears their defense." Bass paused and watched the older lady's reaction. Then he went on. "And when I get back to El Paso after my trip, I'll see if I can find decent work for 'em and some nighttime schoolin' as well."

"Oh, thank you, Marshal, for your kindness. I'm going to live with my sister in Abilene, and as soon as I arrive, I'll write to Leona, the boy's mother, of your good deeds.

"Not at all, ma'am, not at all." Bass pulled his hat down over his eyes and tried to sleep as the train left the yard.

It was 12:45 p.m. when Bass was awakened by the steam whistle announcing its arrival at Fort Hancock for a coal and water stop. He knew they'd be there at least forty minutes, so he walked to the exit and jumped down to the track bed to fetch Emma for a quick walk to regain her equilibrium. One of the roust-a-bouts helped him with the ramp, and Emma strolled into the open air like the seasoned traveler she was. A few turns around the coal pit, and she was ready to return to her stall. Bass had slept most of the way and couldn't accurately recall if there were many curves or inclines in the trip so far that might have disturbed her in the stall. She seemed fine on her walk, so Bass decided to hold off on more paraldehyde and gave her an apple when he put her back in the narrow stall.

He decided he'd sit in the Club Car for the next leg of their trip and grabbed a comfortable-looking chair near a window at the back exit of the car. There was a newspaper on the chair left by the previous occupant, Bass surmised, and he picked it up to scan the headlines.

The paper was an Austin Statesman dated the previous week. Bass was very familiar with the banner and masthead of the publication. He'd been the subject of several articles over the spring and early summer months of the year during his investigation of the Annihilator serial murders. He noticed in the lower part of the paper, below the fold, a small corner article dedicated to cattle rustling, a burgeoning occupation in the south of Texas that seemed particularly having to do with the King Ranch. The report was quite specific and mentioned *"several experiments in breeding and cross-breeding the Texas Longhorn variety."*

Bass knew the Longhorn was an ancient breed brought to the new world by Spanish Conquistadores, where it adapted and thrived on the southwestern vegetation in Mexico and the new Texas Republic. He owned several proven bulls himself, though they took little interest in the Angus cows he and Paulo also ran on their ranch.

The article explained, *"The King Ranch, one of the largest cattle operations in the world, had begun to test the cross-breeding effects of the Longhorn with the more docile Angus and Hereford breeds. The goal being the creation of a new breed of beef cattle with the leaner, less expensive feed requirements of the Longhorn with the quicker maturing and more easily managed domesticated breeds. Additionally, the Longhorn breeds at a faster rate. Calves mature more quickly than other beef animals. Coupling that bull with a Hereford cow who traditionally calves easily and with a higher success rate would improve the profitability and quality of the beef animal."*

The article went on to say that thieves had *"learned of these efforts and had begun the systematic theft of some of the King Ranch experimental herds. The rustlers work their deviltry at night and are gone with the morning mist. Rewards have proven ineffective, the article said, and in fact, several law officers had died during their investigations. Governor Ross has promised swift action in the matter."* Bass assumed he was to be the Governor's swift action.

He set the paper aside; most was devoted to the politics of the State Capitol anyway, and he ordered a rye from the barman. While he waited, he lit a small cigar, a new brand from Pennsylvania called M.C. Killion Little Rebels. He returned to his seat and watched the fragrant bluish smoke draft to the cracks in the window framing as the scenery of South West Texas slid by. The sky was grey, and the overcast hung low so that even the tops of some of the western hills couldn't be seen. He was thinking of the wording he'd use in his message to Judge Hobart about the Hadley boys when a man sat down in the seat next to him, spun his chair around to face the window, and propped his boots up on the sill.

"Fine day for a train ride, hey?" Bass looked the man over and decided quickly that he'd rather not have much to do with him—still, no cause to be impolite.

"Oh? I suppose so. Not very pretty outside today."

"'Tisn't. You bound for Laredo?"

"I am."

"What's your line, then?" Bass took a moment to answer, hoping the fellow might take the hint.

"United States Deputy Marshal. I have business in Laredo." The stranger became quiet hearing that, so Bass took another look at him. He said,

"Seems I know you, Mister. Or of you, perhaps. What's your name?"

"Why, Dick Carey, from Wyoming, Marshal. Heading to Laredo to buy horses from the Mexicans. That's my trade. Horses." Bass watched him a bit longer.

"Uh-huh. Nope, that ain't it. It'll come to me directly. How I know you, that is. Or your name."

"I ain't wanted for nothin' if that's you're thinkin.'"

"Carey, huh? 'Know of a Sam Carey. 'Laughing Sam Carey' ran with Tom Ketchum's gang. They called him Black Jack Ketchum. Train robber. You ain't plannin no train robbery, are ya?"

"What? 'Course not. What a thing to say. And I'm Dick Carey, anyway."

"Good. I can rest easy now."

"And why not?" He waived at the barman and said, "Whiskey, any'll do." He turned back to Bass and said,

"What's your business in Laredo, Marshal? On a manhunt, maybe?" Bass again took a long pause before answering.

"Hmm. Lookin into cattle theft down in that neck of the woods."

"Bad men, I guess?"

"Bad enough to kill a peace officer and his posse."

"Say now that is desperate. Well, I wish ya good fortune in that."

"Why thank you, Sam."

"Think nothin' of it..." Carey realized his mistake too late and saw Bass lookin over at him, a knowing glare in his eyes.

"Well, damn. Ya tricked me...found me out. But I ain't wanted for nothin' in Texas now, like I said."

Bass leaned back and pulled his hat down over his eyes. "Relax, Carey, I got no paper on ya anyway. Just keep your nose clean." Carey grumbled a bit and said,

"Well, there ain't nothin' I know of gonna happen on this train. So I reckon I'm safe."

"Good to feel safe. Course, if anything does happen, you'll be the one I get first."

Bass finished his whiskey and pulled his hat back down over his eyes. The two men sat quietly, neither speaking until the supper stop in El Polvo, Texas.

6:30 p.m. October 26, 1888
EP & SW Terminal
El Polvo, Texas.

"El Polvo, Texas. Ninety-minute meal stop. El Rio Café across the street." The Conductor made the same announcement in each car. As he passed through to the vestibule on the final coach, he fixed the small ladder to the gravel bed of the rail yard. Then he turned around and completed the same task at each of the two coach passenger exits. The club car had no exit of its own, so Bass and Carey were obliged to make their way to one of the rearward coaches to exit the train.

"So I reckon as you won't be speakin' with me for the rest of the trip then." Carey was naturally talkative and pressed himself on others even when it might not be appreciated. He was of average height, a little plump, with a black mustache and straight dark hair, thinning in spots. He wore a gray Derby hat, that was a size small and left a red ring on his forehead. None of his clothes seemed to fit properly, and he constantly had to push up his sleeves to free his hands. After his short nap, Bass was feeling agreeable, and he answered.

"Don't know what there is to talk about, Carey. Say, I know. How is it that they call you Laughing Sam? Ain't heard you laugh at all this trip."

"Ain't none of your business is why. And I believe I'll keep my own company from now on."

Bass was piqued now. He'd touched a nerve and didn't want to let go.

"Oh now, don't be coy with me, Carey. You're supposed to be the wanted outlaw. What does it say for your manhood bein' shy about your nickname?"

"Ain't a nickname at all, it's more like an affliction... and people shouldn't poke fun at the afflicted." They began walking together toward the café.

"An affliction, you say. How is it that laughing can be an affliction?"

"'Tain't the laughin, it's the when of it." Carey decided to explain rather than keep on defending his silence. "I tend to laugh when I get afeared. And it ain't no laughin matter, so wipe that smirk off your face."

"All right, all right, don't bust a gut. I don't believe I've heard of that particular reaction before. 'Heard of chatterin' teeth and tremblin' knees. 'Don't think I can imagine laughin. Though now that I think on it, I have heard of laughin' in the face of danger. Is that what you do, Sam Carey? Laugh at danger?" Carey took the statement as complimentary and stood up straight to answer.

"That's exactly what I do, Mr. Deputy Marshal. I laugh at danger, spit in its eye." Carey's walk took on a bit of swagger as they approached the café. "I only hope there comes a reason for you to see my reaction so's you can know for yourself." The two walked into the small café, which was busy now with passengers from the train. Bass took a seat at the counter, and Carey sat next to him. The waiter, a Mexican boy in his early teens, stopped to ask for their order.

"You got whiskey back there, son? Not tequila. Don't want tequila."

"Si Señor, weeeeskee. You want?"

"Yes, I do, and a bowl of your roast pork, cerdo, por favor."

"Si Señor. De inmediato. Y usted Señor?"

"Ah... oh hell, same thing muchacho, Gracias." The boy scribbled into a pad and smiled as he left. Carey looked at Bass,

"You wanna hear 'bout some of my exploits?"

"The ones where you admit to breakin' the law while runnin with other outlaw gangs?"

"No, I ah...I guess not then."

"Look, Carey, like I said, I ain't got no paper on you, no reason to believe you broke the law in my state. But if you start admittin' to past crimes you and others have done, I'm gonna have to arrest you and turn you over to the local marshal in Laredo. Is that what you want?"

"God no... alright, point taken. I'll keep my big mouth shut."

"Now that's a good choice."

The two men ate in silence except for each ordering a second whiskey. When they returned to the train, they each took up a comfortable chair in the Club Car and settled in for a quiet evening. Bass had intended to sleep as best he could, but the constant swaying motion of the train kept sleep at bay. He glanced at Carey once or twice and noticed that he had no difficulty sleeping. Even when the train rocked enough to roll his head from side to side, he managed to stay in slumber. Bass eventually gave up and walked about the car, looking for something to read. He found a tattered dime novel written by Ned Buntline of New York in 1869. It was titled ***Buffalo Bill, King of the Border Men,*** and told the story of one William F. Cody. Of course, Bass was familiar with Buffalo Bill Cody and had even met the white-haired old gentleman on one occasion in Washington, D.C. Cody was there to advertise and promote his Wild West Show. Bass wasn't able to see the performance as he was assigned the next day and had to leave for his District in El Paso. But he read the newspaper reports of the show, which were all favorable and spoke highly of Buffalo Bill's showmanship.

Bass thumbed through the book; several pages were torn or missing, and the bulk of the stories told were well-known to him. He compared the publication to the several books written about his own adventures by Beadle and Adams and concluded that the latter product was far superior. Still, he re-read some of the original accounts of Buffalo Bill's Indian fighting days with a smile on his face.

At about midnight, the conductor came bustling back to the club car. He was obviously hurried and jarred people awake as he passed by. When he got to Bass, he reached down and jostled the Marshal's shoulder, rousing him after reading had helped him doze off.

"Marshal...Marshal Bass. That is you, is it not, sir? I saw your name on the passenger manifest." The man was perspiring and seemed jumpy.

"What? Hmm. Ah... yes. Yes, I'm Frank Bass. What seems to be the matter?" By this time, the few other men who'd been sleeping in the car were awake and able to overhear the conversation.

"It's the engineer, sir. He's slowing down as we approach the Livingston Bend. He's flashed an alarm signal to me, sir, which can only mean he sees an obstruction ahead. That generally means... well, I imagine you know what it means. I hoped you might take charge, sir." Bass was standing, strapping on his Colt, and stretching himself after being nearly deep asleep. As he walked down the aisle, his right hand on his Colt, he glared at Sam Carey, whose eyes were wide open, remembering Bass's warning. They followed Bass as he walked through the slow-moving car. Just as Bass passed by, he could hear Carey break into a high-pitched giggle of sorts, and he thought to himself, "There he goes, laughing at danger again."

Bass proceeded to the first coach, where he found a brakeman and two porters holding lanterns on each side of the exit vestibule extended as far as they could reach. The train had slowed to a dead stop, and Bass jumped down to the gravel rail bed that was shown in the lantern light. He reached back up to take a lamp and walked slowly past the mail and baggage cars to the tender and then to the engineer's cab. The engine was hissing steam in loud chugs as the fireman slowly bled off pressure, so Bass had to yell for the engineer to hear.

"What did you see?" The moon was bright, but as the train was on a curve and canted slightly up the grade, Bass could not see much beyond the 'cowcatcher.' The engineer called down from his cab window.

"Up ahead. Maybe thirty yards. An obstruction of some sort. Saw it when we started the curve backlit by the moon." Bass held the lantern high but couldn't see anything. He withdrew his pistol and advanced slowly up the grade and around a gentle curve to the right. The sky was mostly clear, and the temperature was quite chilly. Bass could see his breath swirl in frosted clouds around him. As soon as he came around the curve, he could see, in the moonlight, a large boulder perched between the rails on the track. The hillside to the right held several other sizeable rocks and boulders. Bass surmised that recent rain may have loosened this one, and it rolled inconveniently onto the rails. He took a moment to ensure there were no other threats in the area and then walked back to the Engine. The boiler's noises had quieted some, and it was easier to speak and be heard.

"Just a boulder on the tracks. Must've come loose in the rain. I'll get some help to move it."

The engineer nodded, and the fireman jumped down from the cab to offer his assistance. Bass recruited the two porters who brought additional lanterns, and with two hearty shoves in unison, the boulder was rolled off the roadbed and down the shallow hill on the other side. After the fireman examined the tracks for damage, it was all aboard, and they were on their way.

Bass returned to his chair and sat down heavily, feeling more relieved than he expected to. He was breathing heavily, and small beads of sweat had formed at his collar even though the night was cool. An uncomfortable lump had twisted in his gut as he realized that he had expected the worst as he walked from the train to the boulder in only dim lamplight. He recalled thinking he should take the precaution of dousing his lamp so as not to be too easy a target, and yet, for some reason, he did not. Was it bravado? Or foolish habit that sent him those ninety feet into the darkness. And why, for God's sake, was he only now reacting to the event? Where was his customary caution when it was called for? Where would Sally and Lil be if he had been shot dead on those tracks? Was his laxness a result of his conversations with the buffoon Sam Carey? Had he been lulled into overconfidence by the man's foolishness? There was only one answer to these questions...his mindset had to change. He must no longer expose himself as he did tonight in the dark or as he did in broad daylight to Lucas Teague. He could fulfill the oath of his office without brazenly confronting the villains he'd sworn to apprehend. Yes, it must be so; his family, his growing family, required it.

Eight

1:30 p.m. October 27th, 1888
Onboard the EP & SW Rio Flyer
Near Del Rio, Texas

Bass leaned back in his chair, his eyes closed as he considered all this. Finally, he became mindful of the present and waved at the porter for another whiskey. "On the house, Marshal," he was told, which always made the drink more satisfying. They had about five or six hours left before reaching Laredo, and Bass decided to lean back, cover his face with his hat, and try to get more shut-eye.

Before he finished his drink, Laughing Sam Carey was next to him asking questions.

"So what was it? 'Guess it wasn't bandits, huh? I didn't hear no shootin. You probly thought I'd set you up, didn't ya? S'why you gave me that look, right? Right? Ain't you gonna say nothin'?"

Bass scowled, "Go sit someplace else. Bad outlaws like you make me nervous." Carey realized he was being made sport of and "Hmmphed" his way back to a stool at the counter.

Bass finished his drink and sat gazing out the window, watching the desert along the roadbed as it passed by, illuminated by the lights from the train. He was suddenly aware of an extraordinary weariness. One that folded over him and ached for relief. The train stopped once at Eagle Pass for water, but Bass slept right through it and didn't open his eyes until the train stopped at the Laredo station about an hour later than scheduled.

10:30 a.m. October 27th, 1888
City Marshals Office
Matamoros at Salinas Ave.
Laredo, Texas

The city marshal's office was across San Fernando Street from the city government buildings and about eight blocks east of the EP &SW Terminal. Bass had saddled Emma and tied his gear and saddlebags onto her but decided to walk her the distance to let her get her legs back. He'd only been to Laredo once in his life, and that was as a very young Ranger recruit in the early '70s. As the train approached town, he noticed Fort McIntosh to the west of the tracks, situated right on the Rio Grande. As the Rio continued south, it jutted abruptly to the east, and the principal construction of Laredo Town was along that stretch of the river. Nuevo Laredo, the Mexican sister township, was to the south and west across the Rio.

The town had grown considerably since his last visit fifteen years earlier. A high-quality coal deposit had been discovered just north of the city, and Laredo prospered by selling the mineral to industrial interests around the state and to the east.

The Town Marshal was a man named Matt Cole. He was sitting at his desk when Bass opened the door.

"You the Marshal?"

"I am. Who might you be?" Cole was a heavy-set man that Bass pegged at near forty. His curly black hair fell over his shoulder, and his black mustache needed trimming. He was a welcoming sort, extending his hand as based introduced himself, unassuming in nature and apparently good-humored.

"So, Marshal. What brings you down our way?"

"Several weeks ago, a U.S. Deputy Marshal named Harold Gosling was shot down along with several deputies while trying to capture a group of cattle rustlers. I'm here to follow up on that and try to figure out what happened to them cattle."

"Oh yeah. Seems like a pretty simple case of cattle theft to me. Uh, I heard about you and them doin's over to Austin. Someone must think these cows are pretty special, 'send you all the way down here."

"Cows are owned by the King Ranch. I believe 'an experiment in breeding. Lotta' money and time been spent on that herd. Do you know the deputy that got away?"

"Nope, I don't. All I know is it was one of the poseemen, and I got no idea who rode off with Harold that mornin.'"

"Thank you. Tell me, you got any ideas who mighta stole them animals?

"Well, sure, everybody knows it was Dan Bogan and Cherry Lennox. Probably some Mexicans, too. Ain't seen Dan around, figured he cut and run right after, but Cherry's been spendin' like a sailor for the last few weeks."

"How come you ain't picked him up yet?"

"Ain't broke no laws in town. And we ain't got no county sheriff till next month's elections."

"Uh-huh. Well, I believe I'd like to have a word with him. Where does he hang out at?"

"Mostly the Nugget Saloon. He stays at the Arbuckle Hotel, just down the street. On the other side of the Plaza."

"Nice hotel, is it?"

"Well, Cherry seems to like it. Three dollars a night...includes a bath."

"Think I'll be stayin there, then. I'll be back after a bit. Is there a livery near this hotel?"

"Right behind it. Markson's Livery and Buggy Rental."

"All right then, thanks for your time, Marshal." Bass tipped his hat and walked outside. He took a moment to gaze about the township. It wasn't much different in size and nature from El Paso. They were both border towns on the Rio, across from larger Mexican cities. Both were charged with watching the border, which was easier said than done. Bass came away with a mediocre assessment of marshal Cole. He seemed accommodating enough, but maybe he was too accommodating. He knew many border peace officers lined their pockets by looking the other way when wanted men crossed the border into their towns. Inwardly, he hoped he wouldn't have to rely too heavily on Matt Cole.

Bass mounted Emma for the ride to the hotel. The sun had burned through the autumn cloud cover, warming his face, and he thought to have a quick look around. He decided to stay on Matamoros Street, which seemed like a fairly busy thoroughfare, and he noticed businesses along his route. There were several saloons, of course, and a couple of billiard halls as well. On one corner, a bit further down, he spotted a sawmill and lumber yard that seemed to be doing a good business. He turned north on San Augustine and passed a large garden-like plaza with several tidy-looking adobe buildings around it. On one side, he saw an impressive-looking church and steeple where he read St. Peter the Apostle Catholic Church. Just beyond the church and maybe a block and a half down, he saw a sign over the boardwalk for the Nugget Saloon. He made note of it as the place where Matt Cole said Cherry Lennox liked to drink and gamble. He turned again, heading east on Washington toward the Arbuckle Hotel. He saw several businesses, including a pharmacy, a woman's hat shop, and a small hardware store next to what appeared to be a saddle shop. Next, he noticed the Rock Bottom Saloon on the same street a few doors down. Bass had no qualms about drinking before noon, and it might be a good place to stop for information. He was particularly interested in the deputy that got away, and bartenders always seemed to have answers.

The Rock Bottom was definitely an up-scale drinking establishment. There was music coming from the back of the large saloon, but it wasn't the typical piano and banjo sound he expected. This music was more subdued, reminding him of parlor entertainment more than anything else. There was a singer, too, rendering a plaintive ballad to a strumming guitar and piano accompaniment. There was no raucous undertone of voices and laughter so typical of most saloons. Rather, there seemed to be conversations in a normal voice, polite applause when the singer finished, and no yelling of any kind. The card tables were busy, and cigar smoke was thick, but these were the only things that gave away the nature of the room.

Bass stood next to the bar, which ran at least twenty feet along the side of the room. It was long enough to accommodate quite a few customers, but there were only five or six men there at this hour. The bar was a dark, heavy wood of some kind, polished to a mirror shine with rows and rows of different liquors on display behind the barmen on the back wall. There were three nicely dressed female bartenders, each attractive in her own way and all smiling as orders were placed. A dark-haired woman approached Bass and asked. "Something to drink, sir?"

Bass immediately recalled that Sally had worked as a part-time bartender in Cheyenne when they first met. But that saloon couldn't hold a candle to this one. He replied, "Rye, please, with ice if you have it." The woman smiled and said, "Comin' right up." As she turned to fetch a bottle, she opened an ice box on a lower shelf and scooped a glass full of ice, set the glass in front of Bass, and poured generously from the bottle. When the glass was full, she reached under the bar, produced a half slice of lemon, and perched it on the side of the glass. "Would you like to see a menu, sir?" Bass had never seen service like this outside of a much larger metropolitan area. He was visibly impressed and said, "Thanks anyway, but I wonder if I might talk with the owner."

"Certainly, sir, let me tell him you're here." Before Bass had finished his drink, a tall man about Bass's age appeared, neatly dressed in a dark suit and vest with a white flower of some kind in his lapel. He was clean shaven with long sideburns and sandy-colored hair parted in the middle. He withdrew spectacles from his vest pocket as he approached Bass.

"I'm Anse Halliday, how can I help you?"

"Mr. Halliday, my name is Frank Bass. I'm a U.S. Deputy Marshal from El Paso. The Governor asked me to come down here and look into the murder of Harold Gosling, as well as the cattle thievery that's been rampant hereabouts." The man's color changed a bit, and he seemed to have difficulty finding words to speak.

"Well, um, that's wonderful, and ah, about time, too. Of course, I'll help in any way I can."

"Oh yes? Did you happen to know Marshal Gosling?" Halliday looked around to see who might be in earshot. When he seemed satisfied, he said in low and confidential tones, "Marshal, I was a member of that posse. I'm the one who escaped once Harold was killed. I saw it happen." Halliday looked around again, still a bit nervous. He seemed to sense that information might one day cause him pain if the wrong people found out. He turned and called out to the bartender. "Juliette? Another drink for the Marshal, please." They sat down at the green felt-covered card table, and Juliette brought a second rye with lemon and a coaster. Once she'd left, Anse Halliday said,

"Now then, Marshal. Yes, to answer your question, Harold was a friend of mine. How can I help?"

"Harold was killed tryin to make an arrest, I've heard. Can you tell me who he was plannin to arrest, their names if you can?"

"Certainly, though I only recognized three of the men. The leader was Dan Bogan; he'd been hanging around town for about a week before this happened. 'Was well known to most of the saloons. Anyway, he did all the talking, but there wasn't much talking at all, really. Then, there was Cherry Lennox. 'Can't miss that bright red bandanna of his. He's the one who shot Harold. 'Just as quick as that, too. He kept firing that rifle of his 'til everyone was dead. Except me, of course, I turned tail and ran for my life. Not too proud to say so, either."

"Don't blame you a bit. Who was the third one you said you recognized?"

"Oh. Lonny Dahl, the young one. He spends time across the river... has a girl there, I think. He's come to town only once that I know of since the shooting. And it was just for a short time, I believe."

"And you didn't know the others?"

"No. One was a white man, American, rough-looking, and the other two were Mexican. It was one of the Mexicans that Harold shot. Never seen the two of them before, but the beaners don't come in here. Plenty of Cantinas down along the Rio Bravo side."

"All right. The City Marshal says Cherry Lennox is in town, livin at a hotel nearby. He ever come in here?"

"Yeah, he has once or twice. 'Not a regular. If he gets too mouthy or starts causin trouble, I have our lookout bounce him. He's usually a quiet drunk and lookin for a whore. The women who work here don't ply that trade. Or if they do, it ain't on my time or on my floor. They're here to dance with the customers and sell whiskey, and that's all. Probably why he don't come here as often."

"Okay, that's all for now. Can I ask, where was Matt Cole when Harold needed a posse?"

"He begged off as he usually does, sayin' his jurisdiction ends at the city limits." Bass nodded and stood to leave. "Thanks, Mr. Halliday. 'Preciate your help. I'll keep all this under my hat, a course."

"Happy to Marshal. Hope you bring those that need it to justice." Bass put his hat on and walked back outside. He climbed back onto Emma and continued heading east, down to the Arbuckle Hotel that sat along Zacate Creek.

He tied off Emma and walked into the lobby and up to the check-in counter. "I'll need a room, don't know for how long, might be a week...a little less."

"Certainly, sir... if you'll sign the register for me. Will it be just yourself staying here?"

"Yeah, that's right."

"Very good, a single then. I have a room in the front, second floor. There is a common balcony for the four rooms."

"No. If possible, something off the street, quieter."

"Very well, top of the stairs at the far end of the hall, room number twelve. The window faces the stable and the creek beyond."

"That'll do. What do I owe?"

"Three dollars a night, two nights in advance, six dollars, sir." Bass paid in silver coins and asked, "I need to board my horse in your stable. Do I pay you for it or the fella in the barn?"

"It's a private business, sir, Bill Markson's Livery. You'll pay him directly."

"I see." Bass turned to leave but stopped short of the door.

"Tell me, you got a man by the name of Cherry Lennox stayin here?"

"Yes, we do. He's been with us almost three weeks now."

"Ah. How do I find him? We have business."

"He sleeps till the late afternoon and then generally takes a meal at the Nugget Saloon. They have a café there too. Over on San Enrique Street. Usually moves on to the Rock Bottom once he's et."

"Much obliged." Bass headed out to the hitch rail and led Emma around through a side alleyway to the Livery Barn. He ducked his head inside and called out, "Bill Markson? Lookin for Bill Markson." From a stall in back, a voice answered. "Keep your shirt on, bud. I'll get to ya."

Bass watched as an older man bent forward and, listing to the right, hobbled down the center aisle of the barn. In the light at the front door, Bass saw a man who looked to be seventy, leaning on a thick hickory cane. His eyes were clear and pale blue, and he was quick to notice what was around him. "You want as I should put up your tall mare, right?"

"Yes, sir, I'd like her to get oats and anything green you may have. Pay extra, of course."

"No need, I treat 'em like my own. She's a sturdy-looking animal, twelve, I'd guess? And at least eighteen hands."

"You're guess is dead on, Mister. What do I owe?"

"Four bits a day, she needs a vet; it's extra a course."

"Course." Bass handed the man a silver dollar and said, "Two days in advance. Probly won't need her again today."

"She'll be in the corral till dark. I bring 'em in for the night."

"That's fine. Say, can you tell me where I can find a telegraph? Need to wire home."

"They got a key down at the Post Office, closes at four." Bass checked his Elgin, and it was just after two. "And how far is the Post Office?"

"Six blocks... back down to Matamoros and then right to the corner of San Dario. You'll see the park right there."

"Thanks, 'preciate your help."

"It's okay, sonny, you paid me after all." Bass smiled and walked back out to Washington Street. He turned right on Matamoros and then again on San Dario. He saw the U.S. Post Office with two flags out front. One was the Stars and Stripes, and the other was the Lone Star State flag. The small park the old man mentioned was right across the street. He entered the double doors and noticed a Telegraph window right in the lobby. He had to wait for two customers, and during that time, he considered what he'd say both to Sally and Judge Hobart. He wrote to Sally first.

Sally Bass
TwainHeart Ranch
El Paso, Texas.

Sal - Arrived in Laredo. Trip was boring. 'Staying at Arbuckle Hotel. All is well. More tomorrow. Love.

Next, he wrote to District Judge Hobart as he promised Mrs. Hadley he would.

District Judge Clarence Hobart
County Courthouse
El Paso, Texas

Judge. When sentencing Hadley boys... please go easy. They have no criminal record. Were misled by Lucas Teague. Family is poor. I'll find work for them when I return. Frank Bass.

He re-read the second telegram a couple of times and figured it conveyed his meaning. He decided maybe another wire in a day or so, just as a follow-up, would be a good idea. When he got to the clerk, he handed him the two messages and asked that he read them back to make sure the clerk could read his printing. He asked for a special delivery on both and paid five dollars for the whole package. That settled, he decided to go back to the hotel, maybe get a bath, and rest up for his evening with Cherry Lennox.

Nine

7:45 p.m. October 27th, 1888
Laila's Café
Laredo, Texas

"What can I get you, señor?" The woman taking his order was older and a little heavy, with black hair and brown eyes. She appeared to have a little of the 'Antiguas,' the Aztecs, in her features.

"I'm just lookin over your menu card here, Señora, and I see down here you have Franks and Beans?" Bass had decided to get some supper at a café down the street from The Nugget Saloon. It was early enough, and Cherry Lennox could wait until he'd eaten. He was sitting at the counter and talking with the woman who he presumed owned the place.

"Si. It is Norte-Americano, yes?"

"Well, yes, but it's just surprising to find it in a Mexican Café. It's fine, a course, but where did you hear about it? The Franks and Beans."

"Ah…I was, um, gone to the baseball game in St. Louis, yes? The St. Louis Browns, hurrah! And there they have the ah, the **hot dogs, the franks,** si?"

"Yes, that's a favorite at the games."

"So. I am very happy to have the Norte-Americano food called hot dogs con… uh, with frijoles. Would you like?"

"You know, I believe I would. And cerveza, too, please."

"Bueno." The woman left smiling, and Bass wondered how many of her customers had tried her Franks and Frijoles. It didn't matter, and Bass figured it was a good idea that she was trying to please her American customers.

After a few minutes, his beer and plate arrived. There were two sausages surrounded by frijole beans in Ranchero Sauce and a couple of flour tortillas on the side. He rolled the franks in the tortillas and swabbed them through the beans, thinking this was the best version of frankfurters he'd ever tried. He finished his plate and called the lady back over to compliment her.

"Señora, this here was just about the best Franks and beans I ever ate. What do I owe you?"

"Oh …ah dollar and como se cinquento ah…fifty, a dollar fifty cents. For everything. And gracias, señor." Bass left her two dollars and thanked her as he tipped his hat and turned to leave.

Even though he was in the southern part of the state, there was still a noticeable nip in the night air. He walked down the street, following the gas lights back to the Nugget Saloon. Three blocks to let his dinner settle and cool his collar after sitting in a stove-warmed café. It also gave him time to consider how he'd handle Cherry Lennox, an outlaw he'd heard of once or twice but had never run into. He didn't know what the man looked like except for a vague description he recalled on a wanted flyer from maybe a month before. He knew he'd be wearin a red bandana to match his name, but red was a common color. He figured since Lennox was a regular, the bartender would know him. In any event, it probably wouldn't be hard to pick him out. Bass checked the loads in his Colt as a matter of routine. He hoped it wouldn't come to shooting, but best always to be ready.

He stepped inside the saloon and waited for his eyes to adjust to the brighter light, then he made his way to the bar. The place was crowded, smoke-filled, and noisy, all conditions that could work against making a clean arrest. He walked to the bar, ordered a rye, and took a long look over the saloon. The first thing he spotted was a lookout. He was an older man seated in a corner of the small stage where the piano was playing. He was armed with a scattergun. Bass could usually count on help from lookouts as long as he was clear in identifying himself. He remembered a story he'd heard about a deputy who didn't bother identifying himself or announcing his intent and the Lookout firing a barrel of birdshot into the deputy's knees, thinking he was a drunken intruder. Bass decided to include the lookout in his plans and slowly made his way to the stage. He spoke so only the Lookout could hear.

"My name's Frank Bass, U. S. Deputy Marshal. I plan to make an arrest tonight, and I'd like your help." Bass opened his coat to reveal his gold U.S. Marshal's Badge. The older man raised his eyebrows, "Yeah? Who?"

"Cherry Lennox, for the murder of Harold Gosling 'couple a weeks ago." The lookout nodded and said. "Watch yourself. He has friends." Bass looked back at the man and said, "Plan to. Which one is he?"

"Yonder at the corner table. Derby hat." Bass looked and was startled to recognize Marshal Matt Cole at the table, laughing and drinking with Lennox and two others. Lennox was seated with his back to Bass, but there was no mistaking the very fit man in his mid-thirties. Bass could see a gun in a holster on the man's left hip and a cherry-red bandana around his collar. "Got him, thanks."

The lookout said nothing more, and Bass started walking back to that corner, turning every now and then to listen to the music. So far, Cole, who was sitting next to Lennox, hadn't seen him. Bass considered that the noise and smoke in the room may have distracted him, or maybe he was drunk. With a big man, it was hard to tell. Once Bass was near enough to the table to be heard, he drew his pistol and turned.

"You...Derby hat." Lennox looked up and began to stand. "I'm a U.S. Deputy Marshal, and you're under arrest for the murder of Marshal Harold Gosling. Before Bass could finish, Cole stood up directly between the two men and howled something about jurisdiction. There was liquor on his breath, so Bass pushed him aside to keep an eye on Lennox, but Cole started to intervene again. Bass couldn't delay any longer, so he slammed his pistol into the side of Cole's head. The big man crumbled to the floor, and as he did, Lennox made a move for his pistol. Bass fired once into Lennox's left leg, causing him to drop his weapon and fall to the floor, screaming in pain. Several men at the table and around the saloon started grumbling to themselves. Normally, a gunshot in close quarters will cause men to back off, but not in this case. Several from the group around the table started closing on Bass, but before they could reach him, there came a loud explosion from the scattergun in the lookout's hands. "Clear away! Clear away all a ya! Do it now!" At that, the men began to disperse. Bass looked at the lookout, who was reloading his shotgun, and tipped his hat in appreciation. Now, all he had to do was figure out how to get a man with a bleeding leg and an unconscious former Town Marshal into the county jail. He saw a bartender backing away from the action and called to him. "You!

You there, bartender, blue shirt. Go on and fetch a doctor. Tell him to bring a wagon. Go on now...get!"

The bartender shrugged as if to say, "Why me?" but he left the room at double time, presumably to find a doctor. After he left, Bass announced. "All Right then. Now you're all gonna sit down... on the floor if you ain't got a chair, and you're all gonna be real quiet and still. Nothin' makes me jumpier than quick movements or loud noises. I'm a Federal Marshal here with a warrant. Once the Doc gets here, I'm gonna take my prisoners out that door. If anyone tries to interfere, I'll shoot him down and get a warrant after. All right now, sit down." All fifty or so men in the saloon then slowly took a chair or sat on the floor, their eyes on Marshal Frank Bass. The room was silent for fifteen minutes when a small, bookish-looking fellow appeared at the door, saying, "I'm Doctor Gately. Who's been shot?" Bass called to him.

"Over here, Doc. One's shot, and one's unconscious." The doctor looked at Lennox first, who was still grimacing in pain and bleeding all over himself. The doctor tied a rubber tourniquet around the man's upper leg and said, "Flesh wound, but the bullet may have nicked the femoral. I'll know more when I get to my office. This one, oh for Heaven's... Marshal Cole, someone finally did for you, I see." Cole was just starting to come around. He stood up slowly and teetered a bit before vomiting on the floor and falling forward, sprawled over a table. Doctor Gately said, "Yes...well, let's get the wounded man first and deal with the ..ah...Town Marshal another time. Bass smiled at the doctor and lifted Lennox under his right shoulder. The three of them left the saloon and got Cherry Lennox into the Doc's buggy. Before he left, Doc Gately said, "I'll get back to you about your prisoner in the morning. I have hand irons in the clinic, so I'll be certain he stays the night. I plan to keep him sedated for most of the evening anyway. Good night, Marshal."

Bass watched him go and then walked back into the saloon and directly to the table where the slobbering deputy Cole sat, wiping his mouth on his sleeve.

"Give me your badge and your keys right now. If that pistol belongs to the city, I want it too." Cole handed over the badge and keys... tossed them on the table but waited a brief moment before handing over the Colt. He said, "You can't fire me...' Town council hired me, only they can fire me."

"That's not true, Cole. I'm a federal Officer. My jurisdiction is wherever I say it is, and I can do pretty much whatever I damn well want. I'll see that the Town Council knows I've relieved you, and they'll be free to start a new search for a town Marshal. In the meantime, I'll appoint someone to take your place. Who was it you ran against for Town Marshal, anyway?" Cole just laughed, "You go to hell, Bass. I ain't helpin' you to replace me." Bass shrugged and picked up the badge, keys, and pistol. "Get up, Cole. You and me are gonna walk to the jail, which is where you'll be spendin' your time til I'm finished with my investigation." Bass slipped hand irons on Cole and then stood up, yanking the drunken man's right arm and shoulder. He half dragged Cole to the door and turned back to the men in the saloon. "OK, y'all can stand up now."

4:45 p.m. October 28th, 1888
Sheriff's Office
St. Louis Street
El Paso, Texas

A tall man on a tired-looking, grulla-colored gelding walked into town from the western road. He seemed to know exactly where he was going and strolled his horse past the saloons and bawdy houses that populated that part of town. He carried a Navy Colt's Dragoon pistol on his right hip and had a Sharps 1874 Overbaugh rifle with a scope in a beaded sheath hanging from the D rings of his finely detailed Charro saddle. He pulled his horse up at the corner of San

Francisco and St. Louis Streets, tied him off to a hitch post, and walked a block and a half to the County Sheriff's office.

Bart Mariany was sitting at his desk, and Eddie Voer was cleaning out cells in the back of the building when the man walked in.

"Afternoon. What can I do for ya?" Bart didn't like the looks of the fellow right off. Maybe it was his slow, methodical way of looking over the jail, his careful movements, or maybe it was because the man's hand rested on the ebony handle of his Navy Colt.

"Understand a Federal Marshal named Bass works outta this office, 'Zat so?"

"Yeah, that's right. Who are you, Mister? What is it you want?"

"Just wanna have a talk with my old friend Frank Bass." Mariany decided his tone was neither friendly nor trustworthy.

"Well, you just missed him. He went south on a cattle theft investigation."

"Oh? Whereabouts, south?"

"Can't say, don't rightly know. Could be gone for a while." Just then, Eddie Voer walked in and asked. "Hey...Who'er you?"

The man answered before Mariany could speak, "Just an old friend of Marshal Bass." Eddie, in his straightforward, unassuming way, blurted out, "Oh well, he's got a ranch about eight or nine miles south of town on the Rio Road. You might look him up." Mariany tried to stop the young man, but the damage was done. The man said, "Thanks. Believe I will." And he turned, tipping his hat, and walked out.

"Damn, Eddie, wish ya hadn't told him that. Don't like his looks."

"You think he's dangerous?"

"Yeah, hell, I think everybody's dangerous. But hard-looking men like that who wanna see Frank...I'm generally suspicious of."

"Geeze, I'm sorry, Bart. I took him at his word."

"Yeah, well, you best learn to read between the words with men like that. Go ahead, finish up in there. I'm gonna go home soon. Vale has the watch tonight."

Mariany left the office and went behind the building to fetch his gelding, Beau. As he began saddling the horse, he started to feel uneasy again about the man he'd just spoken to. And him knowing the whereabouts of Frank Bass's spread, with Sally and the baby there alone...Mariany decided to take a ride out along the Rio just to make sure Sally was alright.

6:00 p.m. October 28th, 1888
Rio Road at the Gate to TwainHeart
El Paso, Texas

Tom Horn dismounted and grabbed a field glass from his bed-roll. He was eight miles out on Rio Road and could make out a two-story house about a quarter mile up a gradual hill. There was a large, covered veranda, and he could see the top of a barn behind it. Smoke was blowing with the light breeze from one of the chimneys, but in the fading light, he couldn't make out if anyone was inside. There was a two-horse open wagon parked in front, so he figured there had to be someone around. He opened the gate and climbed back into the saddle, grimacing slightly at pain from a four-month-old wound that hadn't healed properly. As he got closer to the house, he could see a man working on a foundation next to the barn. As soon as the workman saw him riding to the front of the house, he picked up a rifle that had been propped against the barn and began walking through the yard. That's when he called out.

"You lookin for someone?"

"Yeah. An old friend, Frank Bass. I was headed to Juarez and thought I'd surprise him. Sheriff said he lived out here." Silas Pratt looked the fellow over and decided the smile on his face was sincere enough. "The Sheriff, huh? 'Surprised he didn't tell you Frank wasn't here. Gone down to Laredo to hunt down cattle rustlers for the Governor."

"Oh yeah, Laredo. Well, he mentioned it, but I thought I'd stop by anyway to say hello to his Misses."

"Sally? Oh, she ain't here. She and the baby are off to the neighbor's visitin. Neighbors is expectin, you see."

"Ah, yeah, I do. She and the baby, huh? Well, I 'spect my trip down here was for naught. You give her my regards when next you see her, will ya?"

"I'll do that, what's your name?"

"Just tell her Tom from Denver. She'll know who I am. I'll close the gate on my way out." Tom Horn tipped his hat as he climbed back on his horse and rode back down the drive. True to his word, he closed and latched the gate.

Ten

7:00 p.m. October 18th, 1888
TwainHeart Ranch House
El Paso, Texas

Bart Mariany tossed the reins to his horse's bridle in a loop over the hitch rail in front of the house and climbed the porch steps to knock on the front door. Sally answered, holding Lil on her right hip.

"Bart, good to see you. Please come in. I think I know why you're here."

"I'm sorry to bother you, Sal, and I won't be long, but a fella came to the office today looking for Frank. Eddie bein Eddie unknowingly blurted out the location of the ranch, and I thought I might just swing on by to make sure everything was okay with you, is all."

"Oh my, Bart, that's very kind in you, and yes, the man was Tom Horn. The same man Frank did for on the train between Livermore and Denver when we went to see Frank's sister. You're right. He certainly could cause trouble. I wasn't here at the time he stopped by, but Silas also didn't know better and told him Frank was in Laredo. Silas said Horn was very cordial and left right after that."

"Well, Laredo's a long way off, but I ought to try to reach Frank with a warnin, don't you think?"

"Why yes, I was going to do it myself early tomorrow. I don't like traveling at night, but if you're going back to town, would you mind sending the wire?"

"Sure, a course. Do you know where he is?"

"Yes, I heard from him just yesterday afternoon. He's staying at the Arbuckle Hotel in Laredo." Sally showed Bart the wire she'd received.

"The Arbuckle, would you mind writin' that down so I don't forget? My age, I'm liable to."

Sally went to the kitchen, still carrying the baby, and came back with a note that read,

Arbuckle Hotel, Washington Street Laredo, Texas

Bart folded the note and put it in his vest pocket.

"Right, thank you, Sal."

"You sure you wouldn't like a drink before your ride back?"

"Well, maybe just a quick one if it's no trouble."

"Of course. Sit right over there." Mariany sat on the divan, and Sally brought back a short whiskey.

"My, how Lil is grown."

"Oh, that's not the half of it, Bart. She's walking now and getting into anything she can reach. I've put the things that might be a danger up high, but still...you never know." Bart finished his whiskey.

"Yeah, I know it's a handful, 'remember when my boys were young. 'Just means they're curious. I'd take it as a sign of intelligence. Something I'm sure she got from your side, not Frank's."

Sally smiled, "Now you know there's all kinds of smart Sheriff Bart. Be a good thing to have Frank's kind, too."

"Yes, you're right. Well, thanks for the roadie, Sal. I'll be on my way. Before I go home, I'll get this wire out."

"Thanks, Bart. Be careful on the road." Bart eased himself down the porch steps, his spurs ringing as they scraped the wood. He climbed on his horse, turned the animal's head back down the drive, and headed north on Rio Road. He'd stop at the telegraph desk at the train depot before going home.

7:30 p.m. October 28th, 1888
Rio Road
10 miles south of TwainHeart
El Paso County, Texas

Tom Horn left TwainHeart feeling good about his plan. Originally, he thought to hold the wife and child of Marshal Bass hostage until he returned to his home. The threat to his family would make Bass do anything to save them. And killing the man in front of his family would be sweet revenge indeed. But now, with the knowledge that Bass was away from home and probably would be for quite a while, he'd decided to go to Laredo and hunt the man down when he least expected it. Possibly prolong the man's death in anguish over a lie about what he'd done to his family or apply some other, more physical torture if the opportunity presented itself. He was very confident in his ability to track the man in open country. He remembered an acquaintance from years ago that had a place in Laredo and figured to look him up. He'd done some work for the man some time ago, and he thought it might be a good idea to have a friend nearby that knows the area. And if he was somehow unable to locate Frank Bass, he now knew exactly where his family would be. And nothing would draw a man like Bass in like a threat to his family.

He was heading to Fort Hancock about thirty-five miles further south. He had been to Fort Hancock once before, just after it was flooded, and helped for a while as it was being rebuilt on better ground. This was two years ago, he remembered. He also knew that the EP & SW railroad stopped there for water and fuel before it headed for Laredo.

His problem now was money. He only had a few dollars to his name, which were left over from an ambush of two cowboys traveling between day jobs outside of Santa Fe. They only had fifteen dollars between them, and it seemed a shame to die for such a paltry sum, but that was their choice. Now, he needed to find a more lucrative source of funds. The train to Laredo wouldn't be cheap.

8:30 a.m. October 29th, 1888
Arbuckle Hotel Dining Room

Laredo, Texas.

"Pardon me. Are you Marshal Frank Bass?"

"Ah, it's Deputy Marshal, actually, but yes, that's me."

"This came for you overnight, sir." The boy handed Bass a telegram, and he gave the boy a nickel. He unfolded the message and read.

Suspect Tom Horn is trailing you. 'Mistakenly advised of your whereabouts. Sally and Lil are fine.

-Bart

Bass set the message down and dropped his hands into his lap. He knew what it meant. He had another reason to keep a watch over his shoulder now. He thought about Sally next, and even though Bart said she and Lil were fine, he wanted to send a message for himself and hear from her directly. He finished his coffee and a couple of bites of his ham steak and paid the cashier. Then he went around to the stable barn and saddled Emma. He planned to stop first at the Post Office to send the wire to Sally, his neighbor Paulo Armendez, and then one to Bart as a thank you. His next stop would be the Laredo City Jail to see about replacing Matt Cole. He also expected to hear from the City Council at some point today. He knew he'd stepped on their toes, but he really didn't care. It was pretty obvious that Cole was protecting a known killer of a Deputy U.S. Marshal, and as far as Bass was concerned, that was a hanging offense.

At the Post Office, he sent out three messages first to Bart.

Bart- my thanks for your advisory – and for watchin out for Sal and Lil. – Bass

And then another to Sally:

My Love – Bart says you two are safe. 'Need to hear it from you as well. I'm sorry Horn came by the house. Will ask Paulo to check in with you. Love - Frederick

Paulo – The outlaw, Tom Horn, tried to pay Sally a visit. – Please watch over my girls for me.

-Bass

Bass paid the clerk extra for special delivery to ensure the messages would arrive sometime that morning, and then he walked back outside. He knew he'd worry until he'd heard back from Sally and Paulo, but being over six hundred miles away, he'd done all he could do.

It was warmer in the southern part of the state, and the wind didn't blow quite so hard. But the sky was grey and getting darker by the minute. Bass could smell the rain coming from the west as he climbed up on Emma and headed her back to the Laredo City Jail. He expected the place to be empty except, of course, for Matt Cole, who he walked over last night and locked in cell number one. But when he got to the jail, he was surprised to see several men dressed in business suits waiting outside the locked office door. The three men watched Bass as he tied off Emma to the hitch rail and then fumbled for the keys to the door.

The tallest of them spoke first.

"I take it you're this Federal Marshal Matt told us about. By what authority do you sweep into our town and replace on a whim our duly appointed law officer? We represent the town council. Abe, here is the Mayor, by God. Well? What have you to say?"

Bass looked at each man individually and then turned back to the lock. "Do any of you boy's know how this damn lock works? I opened it fine last night. Which key is it, do you think?" The three gentlemen acted as flabbergasted as Bass hoped they would. "Here now, this is it. Got it. Won't y'all please come in?" Bass led the way and checked first on the prisoner, who seemed still to be asleep. At some point during the night, he'd released his bladder, so Bass opened the windows to relieve the stench. Then he walked back into the office and sat in the chair at the desk.

The three men were all standing for lack of chairs. The one who was pointed out as Mayor spoke first.

"Marshal, my name's Abraham Laurey. I'm the Mayor of Laredo. We pride ourselves on our independent nature, and we wish to run our community accordingly. We received several serious reports on your actions last night, and we want an explanation."

"You do, huh? Well, that's fair enough, I guess. Several weeks ago, the Federal Marshal for this District was shot down by cattle thieves. Harold Gosling was his name. The Governor asked me to come down here and help y'all investigate his murder.

Several other members of his posse were also shot and killed. I'm sure you remember them. They were all voters. Now, one member of that posse got away and identified the culprits for your duly appointed law officer, and he did nothing about it. In fact, he wouldn't even participate in the posse to start with. He claimed a 'jurisdictional conflict,' I think is what he called it. Now, the fact is the conflict don't exist, and last night, I found your law officer drinking and gambling with one of the identified suspects. As I went to arrest the suspect, your officer interfered... twice. As a result of that interference, the suspect attempted to draw and fire his weapon at me. I was forced to shoot him in the leg. He's at Doc Gately's place, now cuffed to his bed. I had to pistol whip your Town Officer to keep him at bay as I made my arrest. After the dust settled and Doc had taken the wounded prisoner, I stripped your officer of his badge, keys, and pistol. I believe it all belongs to the city. I plan to charge him with aidin' and abettin' a known felon and person of interest in a local murder. As the only Federal Officer in this territory, it was my right and, in fact, my sworn duty to do that. Do you still have any questions 'bout any a that?"

All three men were silent and seemed contrite for their rantings. The only one of the three who had held his tongue finally asked. "Marshal? What do we do now about finding a new Town Marshal?"

"All right, fair question. Let me ask you boys this. When you appointed Cole, were there any other candidates?" The tall one spoke out. "Well, yes, as a matter of fact, Desmond Arguello, a blacksmith, asked to be considered for the job. He'd been a small-town marshal before coming here."

"Uh-huh. And why did y'all pass on him?" The Mayor said,

"Well, he's a blacksmith, and we wanted a full-time officer. He didn't seem willing to give up his business."

"S'pose we could ask him again? 'Might be he could hire someone to work in his shop. You might have to pay him a little more for it. Probly be worth it to have an experienced lawman on duty." The three men looked at each other and indicated that it might be a good plan. They left, trying to decide how to present the offer to blacksmith Desmond Arguello.

Bass closed the door and went back into the cell area. "Wake up, Cole. Wake up and face the music. You got some talkin to do, and I get real impatient with scoundrels like you."

"Ugh...Wha? Oh, you. Be damned and get away. Ain't got nothin' to say to you or anybody else for that matter."

"Uh-huh. Well, you're gonna talk to me, Buster, or you're gonna wish you had. I got you on some pretty serious charges...' means a long spell in Huntsville. And just so's you know? Convicts over there don't really go much for former law officers, dirty or otherwise. So I'm gonna give you a chance to put some plusses on your ledger before you stand before the judge. Right now, there ain't naught but minuses. Think about it while I step away. "Bass left the Cell room and locked the access door before sitting back down at the desk. He hadn't had a chance to go through Cole's desk drawers last night or this morning, and it was routine when replacing a law officer accused of wrongdoing. The top two drawers contained nothing of any interest, old wanted flyers, expired warrants, receipts for supplies, and ammunition, all usual and customary.

The two bottom drawers were locked and typically might contain a petty cash box, evidence obtained at crime scenes, and personal possessions of inmates in safe storage pending release. Bass found these types of things on the left side of the locked drawer. The right side drawer piqued his interest because there was no key for it on the key ring Bass had taken from Cole the previous night. The desk was older, made of heavy oak, and the locks were not simple cabinet locks. The drawers had a steel cylinder lock, one that would not be easily pried open. Bass stood and went back into the cell room.

"You give me the key for the desk drawer now, and it'll save me havin to search you for it."

Cole was the bigger man, and though his drunkenness made him easy to deal with last night, he was sober now, if a bit hungover, and he smiled at Bass, inviting him to try. "You go ahead, Marshal, unlock that door and give searchin' me a try." Bass shook his head and grabbed the cell keys from the hook in the office. He put the key in the lock and said. "Turn around and lace your fingers on top a your head." Cole did as he was told, waiting for Bass to begin frisking him. He figured he'd have the physical advantage then. Instead, once Cole was turned, Bass drew his pistol and whacked Cole again on the back of the head. Just like last night, Cole crumbled to the floor of his cell, dazed and bleeding slightly from his wound.

Bass worked quickly, searching through the man's pockets without finding anything but a few pennies and a lucky piece. He finally decided to check Cole's boots, and when he pulled the right one off, a small silver key fell out. Bass pocketed the key and used

Cole's kerchief to dab at the blood on the man's scalp. He locked the cell door and went to try the key in the lock. When he opened the drawer, he found two envelopes. Both contained money. One had two hundred and fifty dollars, and the other contained five hundred. One of the envelopes had a rubber Stamp on it—the stylized head of a Longhorn Steer with the letters TBR between the horns.

Eleven

10:15 a.m. October 29th, 1888
First Texas State Bank
Montezuma Street at Flores Avenue
Laredo, Texas.

Bass put a small bucket of clean water in Cole's cell and left him to come around on his own. He went to the First Texas Bank to secure an evidence deposit box for the seven hundred and fifty dollars. He kept the envelope with the brand stamped on it, figuring to check on who it might belong to. After completing his business there, he went to see the blacksmith Desmond Arguello, whose shop was in the railroad district on Eagle Pass Road and Santa Isabella Avenue. It was a larger shop than Bass expected. Arguello was not just a blacksmith. He was also a wheelwright. The two Stage Lines that operated between Laredo and Brownsville had their repair work done there, and wheels of various sizes and conditions were lined up along one of the walls.

Bass tied off at the wagon hitch in front of the barn that housed the furnaces and walked inside. There appeared to be several men working, so Bass stopped one and asked to see Mr. Arguello. The man pointed to a doorway on one side of the barn. The noise of hammers falling and bellows blowing made talking difficult. Bass walked down the short hall, as the man indicated, and knocked at the door at the end. He heard a deep voice from inside say, "What?" and Bass opened the door. Desmond Arguello was powerfully built but of average height. He was almost completely bald and was dressed in a smith's work outfit. Denim coveralls, stained with sweat, and long-sleeved drawers underneath. He sat at a desk covered with paper. In fact, the entire office was littered with printed forms, magazines, brochures, and invoices, some stacked along the wall behind the desk. Arguello looked up, a cigarette in his mouth, and said, "Who the hell 'er you?"

"My name is Frank Bass, and I'm a U.S. Deputy Marshal investigating the murder of Harold Gosling. I understand you were in the running for the position of Town Marshal."

Yeah, I was. Harold's murder, huh?"

"That's right.

"Well, Mr. Dep'aty, it's common knowledge that Cherry Lennox did for poor Harold and a couple of the other men in his group. You might start by askin' our Town Marshal, Matthew Cole, about it. He's pretty tight with Lennox, I hear."

"I have Matt Cole under arrest in a jail cell right now, and Cherry Lennox is at Doc Gately's cuffed to his bed. Shot."

"That so? Who Shot him?"

"I did."

"Good for you, dep'aty. What do you want from me? Applause?" Bass smiled at that.

"No. No, I want you to take the Town Marshal job you wanted last year but didn't get."

Des was silent for a bit and finally said, "Well, you couldn't have asked at a worse time. I just signed a contract with the EP &SW railroad to do some of their machining and maintenance, and I'm tryin' to figure how to turn this place into a bona fide foundry. 'Just got a wire from a company up north with a price on a blast furnace, so I can shape larger pieces...By God, I don't know how I'd do 'er, Marshal."

"Well, I'm glad to see you so prosperous, but this town needs an honest lawman. The Mayor and several council members will probly stop by at some point today with the same offer. I just wanted to meet you myself. If the town could come up with the money for you to hire a manager for your business, just until they could find a worthwhile replacement for Matt Cole, would you consider it?"

"Jeezes, I don't know. It might work. I'd need to hire a deputy, too, though, so I can mind my business. I can't just walk away from my business altogether, and I'd need to keep my hand in it. If that can be arranged, I might think about it."

"Fair enough. I'll encourage the Mayor to do what you asked. 'Might make them move a little more smartly on findin a replacement for you. I'll let you know what he says."

"Sounds good. I got a lot invested in this town; decent lawman ought to be expected." Bass nodded and turned back to the door.

It was nearly 11:00 a.m., a little too soon to expect answers on his telegrams, but he decided to stop at the post office to check anyway. The clerk checked his tray of incoming messages and said, "Nope. 'Sorry Marshal, nothin' here for ya yet. But it's only been a few hours. I'd give it at least two more."

"Yeah, you're right. Say, maybe you know. Have you ever seen anything that looks like what's stamped on this envelope before?" Bass handed the envelope to the clerk, who raised his spectacles to be able to see.

"Why sure. That's a ranch brand, Marshal. "Brand for the Tierra Blanca Ranch, see there? TBR. I see it come through here often enough."

"Oh yeah. Sure. Can you tell me where the Tierra Blanca is?"

"Uh, ain't never been there myself, ya understand, but I believe she's about ten er twelve miles to the north along the Rio. Big spread. Can't hardly miss her."

"Well, thanks very much, 'preciate your help." Bass tucked the envelope into his coat pocket and turned for the door. Before leaving, he turned around and said. "I'm staying at the Arbuckle Hotel, headin' there right now, get somethin to eat. Anything comes in, run it over there for me, will ya?"

"Sure thing, Marshal. 'Will do." Bass walked back out and rode Emma slowly back to the Arbuckle Hotel. He led her to a trough to drink and then tied her off at a hitch alongside the hotel.

As Bass entered the hotel, he was stopped by two younger-looking men who claimed to be from newspapers. One was a Mexican language paper called '*El Mutualista*,' and the other was the *Laredo Daily News*. Each had sent reporters to stake out Marshal Bass's hotel.

"Marshal Bass...ah Marshal Bass? A word, please, for the people of Laredo, sir?"

"All right, what's your question?"

"Is it true you arrested Town Marshal Cole last night?"

"Yes." The reporter was clearly expecting a more elaborate answer.

"Ah...what ah, was he ..ah...what were the charges, the reason for the arrest. Can you be more specific?"

"No."

"Oh. Ah...okay. Then is the town of Laredo left without the protection of a peace officer, sir?"

"No. The town is safe as it ever was."

"Oh really? Then, do we have a new Marshal? Who is he?"

"Me. Now I'm busy, boys, so please excuse me."

Bass walked into the hotel dining room and took a seat near a window along Washington Street. Just as he sat down, an attractive young Mexican woman sat at the table in the chair opposite him. Bass looked at her, scowling as he set his hat on another chair. "Miss? Something I can do for you?" The woman smiled as she answered. "Si Marshal Bass. My name is Margaretta Perez, and I'm a reporter for *El Mutualista*. I, uh, overheard your answers outside and thought I'd try ambushing you at your table. Lunch is on me, or actually, my newspaper." Bass was a bit put off, but he also knew it never served his purpose to anger the local press. "In that case, Miss Perez, I'll order an expensive meal and tip generously. Would you like a drink?"

"No, thank you, Marshal. Drinking on duty is frowned on."

"As it should be...in most occupations. Waiter? A double rye with ice for me, and my friend will have ...tea?" Margareta nodded at Bass's presumption, and the waiter hurried away.

"Now then, Madam reporter, what is it you'd like to know that I haven't already answered?"

"For starters, Marshal, who else did you arrest last night? I've heard a man was shot."

"You're right, a man was shot. I shot him in the leg because he was about to draw a weapon."

"Well, who was he? It can't be a secret, can it?"

"No, 'course not. His name is Cherry Lennox. He's being held for the murder of U.S. Deputy Harold Gosling, among others."

"Oh...yes, the cattle rustling. There were other members of the gang, I'm told. Do you plan to arrest them, too?"

"Yes, when and if I find them. Cherry Lennox happened to be drinking in that bar last night, along with former Marshal Cole. The Marshal should have been more careful in picking his drinking friends."

"And that's why you arrested him?"

"No. I arrested him for interferin' with my arrest of Cherry Lennox. Marshal Cole also had some strange ideas about the nature of his jurisdiction."

"And you do not?" Margaretta was smiling at Bass as if she enjoyed the banter back and forth.

"No, ma'am. I do not. Waiter, I'll have rib steak, rare, please, with fried potatoes and green beans. Coffee and brandy after. The finest you've got." The waiter smiled, knowing his tip would be worthwhile.

"Yes sir, and for you, Miss?"

"A cup of soup, please. Any will do."

"Yes, ma'am."

"Marshal Bass, how is it that the U.S. Deputy Marshal from El Paso winds up investigating cattle theft in Laredo? I mean, it's hundreds of miles away?"

"'Tis. 'Fact is a Federal Marshal was shot down in the line of duty. We in the Marshal Service tend to take those things serious. Also, the cattle that were stolen came from the King Ranch, which I'm sure you've heard tell of. The animals were a special breed and quite valuable."

"I've also read the stories about you, Marshal Bass, most recently that case in Austin. Seems like you're kind of a special breed yourself."

"That's all newspaper fluff, ma'am." The waiter appeared with Margaretta Perez's soup and Bass's plate. He signaled for another rye and asked, "You sure you won't have something other than tea, Miss Reporter?"

"The name again is Perez. Well, yes, I believe I'll have a bourbon on ice, please...twist of lemon." The waiter left smiling still, and Bass asked,

"You don't mind, Miss Perez, how is it you come to be a reporter? Pretty girls like you generally marry well and raise children."

"What makes you think I'm not married, Marshal?"

"Been my experience that women who work don't have time for husbands and havin babies. And there ain't no ring on your finger, neither. Pretty much a give-away."

"Well, you're right, Marshal, but I'm a reporter because my Papa taught me. He's an editor for *El Diario de Monterrey,* in Mexico. You may have noticed there aren't too many female reporters working in the newspaper business. And you're right. My looks get me in the door with most editors. But I keep my job because I'm a good reporter. Now, let me ask you something."

"Fair enough. Go ahead."

"Who do you think is responsible for your Marshal's death and the stolen King Ranch cattle?"

"Uh, I just told you I believe that Cherry Lennox killed Marshal Gosling. I have a witness that makes him the shooter. As to the cattle theft? I'm workin' on it."

"Do you believe that whoever stole the cattle is the same person that hired Cherry Lennox?"

"That's a little cart before the horse, ma'am. But I'll tell you what. As soon as I make an arrest, I'll give you the story."

"Me? Why so generous?"

"Because. You remind me of my wife. When we first met."

The rest of the meal was spent talking about families and Bass's daughter. Bass liked the young woman, and though her features were dark and definitely Mexican, her intelligence and attitude did remind him of Sally when they first met in Cheyenne. It seemed so long ago, but it was really only about eighteen months.

As Bass was having his brandy and coffee, a clerk from the hotel front desk approached and leaned over to speak in private. "This just came for you, Marshal. 'Thought you'd like to read it right away." Bass took the message, thanking the clerk, and read to himself. It was from Paulo and said simply, *Will Do – P.* Bass breathed a little easier but was still anxious to hear from Sally. Margaretta picked up on Bass's relief and asked, "Good news, Marshal?" Bass folded the note and tucked it into his vest. "Some...Yes, as a matter of fact. Thanks."

The waiter brought the bill for lunch and handed it to Bass. He glanced at it and asked,

"Now then. Who's really gonna pay for this?" Margaretta smiled slightly and said, "I thought if I said the paper, you'd open up more. How much?" Bass handed her the bill.

"Thirty-eight dollars?! ¡Santo Jesus! ¡Eso es ridicula!.

"Lotta money, huh? Well, Miss Perez, I get a real nice per diem when I'm working away from El Paso, so tell you what. I'll pay this one, and you can get the next one. How's that?"

"Very fair, Marshal. Especially since all I had was soup." Bass chuckled as he signed his name and room number to the bill. He left a Gold Eagle coin for the waiter and stood up as he reached for his hat. "Till next time, Miss Perez."

"Indeed Marshal. Take care of yourself. I don't want you to miss your free lunch."

On his way out of the hotel, he checked his wallet. "Damn. I better stop at the bank. My per-diem's getting expensive."

Bass went back to the First Texas State Bank and drew a check on his personal account at his bank in El Paso. He took one hundred dollars in coins and bills, filled his wallet, and decided to pay another visit on Anson Halliday at the Rock Bottom Saloon.

"Mr. Halliday, do you recognize the stamp on this envelope?" He handed the envelope he'd taken from the locked drawer to Halliday.

"Hell, yes, everybody knows this brand. It's from the Tierra Blanca. A place north of here."

"Do you know who owns the ranch?"

"Sure, the whole town does. Landon Atwill. He's a bit of a dandy if you take my meanin. Never married."

"Is it possible that this Atwill fella is the one who put them boys up to stealin cattle from the King Ranch?"

"It's damned likely, Marshal. When we intercepted that herd on the bridge, there wasn't but three or maybe four places they coulda been headed. Tierra Blanca's one of 'em."

"Can you direct me to this bridge? The San Ygnacio Creek Bridge?"

"Yeah, ain't hard to find. San Ygnacio Creek Bridge is maybe eight or ten miles northeast of town. You can follow the creek road all the way to the bridge. Just head east on Matamoros all the way through town until you hit the Creek Road. Then ride north to the bridge."

"Much obliged." Bass left the saloon and climbed up on Emma. He pointed her nose to the north, and when he hit Matamoros Road, he turned east.

Twelve

1:30 p.m. October 29th, 1888
Webb County Creek Road
Six Miles Northeast of
Laredo, Texas.

Bass found the County Road that was labeled Creek Road easily enough, and he followed it north just as Halliday advised. The creek itself was narrow in places and wider in others, but all along its length, Bass noted the steepness of its banks. With the rains of the previous week, the creek was running swiftly. Vegetation was thick, and in places, Bass couldn't see the water at all.

He had passed a sheer granite outcropping on the opposite side and boulders among some Virginia Pine on the near side that seemed perched and ready to fall.

After about an hour of switchbacks and overgrown brambles that snagged his clothes, he spotted the bridge about two hundred feet ahead. As he approached, he could see it was a log bridge with heavy planking over the logs and a simple post and rail guard about four feet high along each side. When he got to the bridge, he could see it's necessity. The creek, which was flowing swiftly here, was at least twenty feet below, and the banks on either side were sheer drops to the water. He backtracked a mile or so on the approach to the bridge from the east and found that the trail was smooth and wide. Wagon ruts had been worn recently into the path, the ridges were still sharp, and there were the usual amount of droppings along the way. Bass had been taught the difference between horse and cow manure as a child, and he was able to tell the difference by looking. Cow manure is generally wetter and more fully digested than horse droppings. Horse manure contains bits of straw and undigested greens like weeds and grass. It's generally more compacted and spread along the animals' path. He assumed the stolen cattle would've been the most recent of their breed to follow this path. Most of the other animals, he thought, would have been horses or mules. The bridge seemed built for horse and wagon traffic but seemed sturdy enough for tightly bunched bovines. As he continued to backtrack, he found evidence of cow manure along the road.

He rode back and crossed the bridge, following the beaten path for nearly a mile on the west side of the creek until he noticed broken and trampled shrubs and low growth along an area to the north of the road. The recent rains had renewed much of the vegetation, but that which was broken had died, leaving the watchful eye with a clear track to follow. Bass urged Emma on through the thistle brush and creosote shrub for what he figured was five or six miles. It was slow going, but when he came to a low rise, Bass could see in the distance the path made by the animals leading down to a grand arched gateway with pastures and corrals beyond. He focused his field-glass at the center of the arch and saw the outline of a Longhorn steer and the initials TBR.

Bass debated riding into the Tierra Blanca Ranch yard and interrogating Landon Atwill but thought better of it. His Elgin told him the time was almost five p.m., and he noticed dark clouds gathering in the west. If he spared Emma, he had at least an hour ride back to town, where he had several other important issues to deal with. Most importantly, he wanted to get back to his hotel to check for messages from Sally. Landon Atwill and the Tierra Blanca could wait for tomorrow.

He rode south along the River, which eventually became a County Road named Eagle Pass Road and paralleled Fort McIntosh. He didn't know much about the old installation except that it guarded a strategic river crossing and was at least forty years old. In passing by, he noticed that several barracks were lighted and smoke wafted from the camp's canteen building. There was horse-born activity around the parade grounds, but he didn't get the impression that the old fort housed a full Company.

He turned east at Matamoros and then north again to the Arbuckle Hotel. He tied off Emma at the hitch and dashed into the lobby and the front desk. There, he found two messages waiting, both from Sally, delivered at different times. He opened the first and read.

'Found out Horn was here yesterday when we were not. Silas spoke briefly, and he left. Bart came by after. Sergei is a comfort and watchful, too. We are fine. Love Sal & Lil.

Bass breathed a bit easier and opened the second. He'd forgotten they were housing a sheep/cattle dog and recalled how protective of Lil the dog had been.

Paulo and Chinesta came by. Chinesta is staying here. Rifle at the door. We are fine.

Love Sal & Lil.

Bass knew that Tom Horn, in his blind revenge, would not hesitate to kidnap or kill Sally and Lil if it led to satisfying his rage. But he also knew that Paulo would guard TwainHeart and his family with his own life if need be. And Paulo was as competent and cunning with a weapon as anyone Bass had ever known. The *rifle at the door* meant that Sally had armed herself with the Remington Rider pistol Bass had given her. The one she'd used to kill Conrad Pliny in Wyoming, saving Bass's life. It also meant that everywhere she went, she also carried a Colt-Burgess small caliber lever action carbine that Bass kept as a varmint gun. And now, there was a guard dog on the premises whose barking would alert the house to an intruder. The little guy was earning his keep.

With Paulo and Bart Mariany now on the alert and Silas Pratt doing regular day work at TwainHeart, Bass felt a little more comfortable. He had no notion of Tom Horn's plan, but he breathed easier knowing his friends were there and ready for him.

Bass went outside and climbed back on Emma for the ride to the City Jail to check up on his prisoner. He also wanted an update on Cherry Lennox's condition, so he decided to stop at Doc Gately's place on the way.

Gately had an office in a storefront on Montezuma Street at Flores Road. It was 6:30 p.m. when he arrived, and Doc was lighting the lamps around his office. Bass called to him as he tied off Emma.

"How's Mr. Lennox doin Doc? Is he alert enough to answer questions?"

"Oh, it's you. No, he ain't. Your bullet opened his femoral, and he damn near bled to death before I could get him sewn up. He's been sedated all day and likely won't be much good to ya tomorrow, either. He'll be pretty weak."

"Huh. Well, thanks for doin' all you did, Doc. 'Guess I can wait for a couple days. Say, Doc, have you heard anything about a man named Landon Atwill? Owns the Tierra Blanca north of town."

"I know of him, is all. 'Never had reason to visit him. Don't believe he's married or has any family."

"Okay, just askin' around, see what sorta' reputation he has. I'll stop by again tomorrow just to check in."

"Yeah, well, suit yourself, Marshal. I'll be here."

"It's Deputy Marshal, actually."

"Eh?"

"Nothing. See ya tomorrow."

Bass headed next to the City jail. The building was dark, as Bass expected it would be, no one to light a fire or take a match to a lamp. The jail door was latched but not locked. Bass was sure he'd locked the office when he left earlier. When he walked into the office, even in the dark, he could sense that something was wrong. He lit one of the wall lamps, and as the light filled the room, he saw that the office had been ransacked. The desk drawers had been emptied onto the floor, and the ammunition in the drawer of the gun rack had been spilled all about. He called out, "Cole? Matt Cole, 'you awake back there? When there was no response, Bass took a lamp and went back into the cell area. He found Matt Cole dead, lying face up on the floor of his cell in a pool of his own blood. His throat had been slashed. The cell door had been opened, which hinted that Cole had likely told the killer where the cell keys were. It also meant that Cole knew his killer. There was no sign of a struggle, but Bass found a cigarette butt stubbed out on the floor just outside the cell. Bass held the butt to the light and read on the paper **Allen & Ginter's – Mexico.** He then set the lamp on the cot and bent to feel for rigor mortis. It had already started to stiffen his arms, which meant Cole had been dead for about four hours. Around the time, he was out following cattle droppings. Bass took his lamp and walked back around the building and immediately noticed hoof prints around the window to Cole's cell. There was nothing distinctive about any of the prints, but Bass could guess that Cole's killer had first asked Cole if he was alone.

Bass took the cigarette stub with him back into the office for safekeeping. He had searched Cole's pockets once but not for something as small as cigarettes or matches. He decided to check more thoroughly this time but still came up empty. He concluded that the killer may have had a smoke while he talked with Cole before killing him. "Gotta be pretty cold-blooded to chat up someone just before you slit their throat.." Bass stood up, holding the lamp and looking down on the corpse, "Welp. Guess you won't be needin' supper tonight, huh, Cole."

Bass locked the jail office, planning to ask Doc Gately to pick up the body in the morning. Cole was a wastrel and probably on the take, but he still wore a star, and Bass always gave lawmen the benefit of the doubt. He deserved a proper burial, at the least. Bass would pay for it if no one else stepped up.

He rode back to the hotel and put Emma away for the night. She'd covered a lot of ground today without complaint, and he decided he'd take her an apple from the dining room after he ate. After brushing her down and seeing to her feed, Bass left Emma in the barn behind the hotel and walked around to the front of the building. He planned to have an early evening, read a newspaper, and see if there was anything in tonight's edition by Margaretta Perez. He thought about their meeting and wished he'd stated more directly that she shouldn't mention him at all in print until he'd put things to rest. Still, he'd been button-lipped whenever she'd asked anything specific, so he wasn't too concerned for it. He wanted to talk again with Desmond Arguello about the Town Marshal position and make sure that the Town Council was on board with the plan. City Budget money would be required so the blacksmith could hire a manager to watch over his day-to-day business. Bass also intended to recommend an additional deputy or maybe two for the Township. More money needed there, too. He related the size and location of Laredo to his own El Paso and wondered if maybe another deputy at home would be advisable. Probably so was his decision, and he made a mental note to discuss it again with Bart Mariany when he returned.

He bought a *Laredo Daily* and an *El Mutualista* newspaper from the news and tobacco stand in front of the hotel. It began to rain as he paid for his papers, so, carrying both, he went inside to get a drink and something to eat. Afterward, he couldn't find an apple for Emma, so he 'borrowed' a few carrots from the kitchen and took them out to her, dodging raindrops as he ran.

By 9:00 p.m., Bass was sitting in his room listening to the rain and sipping a whiskey. He read in the Laredo Daily about the shooting at the Rock Bottom Saloon and the arrest of both Lennox and Cole. It was a factual account, though a bit embellished with sensational descriptions. His name was mentioned but not in any significant or scandalous way. The *El Mutualista*, on the other hand, listed his name in bold letters as the *"fearless lawman from El Paso"* and how he *"quickly subdued the desperado, Cherry Lennox, with a well-placed shot to his leg."* It also mentioned the arrest of Matt Cole, *"who'd long been suspected by this paper of taking bribes,"* and how he was *"finally being made to face justice."*

As Bass read the article, penned by Margaretta Perez, he tried to remember if he'd said anything like what she'd printed in the paper. The part about Cherry Lennox was true enough, but he didn't recall saying anything about Cole being bribed. He didn't have any evidence of that until he opened the desk drawer. It didn't seem like a stretch to believe that Cole was on the take, but he still wanted to ask Miss Perez a question or two about her sources.

Bass blew out the lamp at 9:30 p.m. and was asleep quickly. He slept soundly through the night, content that his family was safe at home.

6:30 a.m. October 30th, 1889
EP & SW Station
Laredo, Texas.

A tall, thin man in a dark coat and vest stepped down from the coach that just arrived from El Paso. He needed a shave, and his black mustache needed trimming. His skin was ashen, and his eyes were hollow, with dark rings beneath them. He had no luggage except for the rifle and scope that he carried in a beaded leather sheath. He wasted no time in walking through the alleyways around the station until he found a sound-looking Appaloosa gelding tied off on the side of a busy café. There was considerable foot traffic, as there usually was around the train station at that hour, but he wasn't worried. He slowly untied the horse and led him into the shadows between the buildings, where he mounted up and rode back down the alley in the same direction he'd come from.

Tom Horn had money for a hotel, money that came from the Rancher he'd shot down on the road to Fort Hancock. He'd also sold his horse, the one he stole in Denver, but he'd used that money for train fare. The hotel needn't be a fine one, of course, but something clean where he might get a bath and a few hours' sleep. He spotted a sign along the road he'd come out of the alley on that said *Travis Hotel, Private Rooms / Clean Sheets*. He tied the gelding off at the hitch rail and went inside. The clerk told him one dollar fifty per day, two days in advance, which he paid without thinking about it, and he signed his name in the register. The clerk asked if he was hungry; there was a light breakfast being served for guests of the hotel. He wasn't hungry. 'Hadn't been hungry for several days. He was too anxious at the nearness of his revenge to eat. He hadn't slept either. His waking hours had been spent picturing the final moments of Frank Bass's life. He did ask about a bath, and the clerk said, "For a dime, a Mexican boy would carry hot water to a tub in the shed out back." He heard the words, but they didn't mean anything to him. He was toying now with the idea of torturing Bass, perhaps stripping the skin off his arms and torso. He imagined the glory of the man's death agony, but in the end, he realized he'd probably have to settle for a quick and clean end to the man. Torture, from his experience, was a messy business and required time and a private location.

Thirteen

7:15 a.m. October 30th, 1888
Arbuckle Hotel
Laredo Texas

Bass woke and dressed quickly. He wanted to get to Doc Gately's early enough so that Doc could fetch the body of Matt Cole before there was too much activity around the jail. The fewer gawkers, the better. The rain had stopped just after midnight, and the air smelled fresh and clean. He saddled Emma after checking her stall, a habit he'd begun after a rattlesnake had crawled into her stall at home and spooked her into injuring herself.

He rode down the near side of Montezuma Street to avoid the mud and turned onto Flores, stopping outside Gately's storefront. He could see the Doc inside talking with a young woman, and as he got closer, he could see it was Margaretta Perez.

"Mornin' Doc, Miss Perez. What brings you out so early, Margaretta? You doin' a story on the Doc here?"

"No, Marshal, I'm just asking Doctor Gately a few questions about the condition of Cherry Lennox."

"Is that right? Well, tell me too, Doc, how's he doin this mornin?" Gately's brow curled as he listened to the banter, and he finally said, "He's about the same as he was last night when you stopped by, Marshal. No better, no worse. And that's all I can tell you, Miss Reporter. I don't expect he'll be able to talk much about anything until tomorrow or the next day. So, if you'll both excuse me, I have a couple of house calls to make."

Margaretta said, "Very well, Doctor. Can I call on the man tomorrow, do you suppose?"

"Miss. You can call anytime you want; don't mean he'll be conscious enough to answer newspaper questions."

"Very well. Thank you, Doctor, Marshal." Margaretta Perez opened the door, stepped out to the boardwalk, and walked purposefully down the street.

Bass waited for the door to close behind her before he said, "Doc, one more thing. Yesterday afternoon, sometime, the prisoner Matt Cole was murdered in his cell. Throat cut."

The doctor barely blinked an eye. "Huh. Boy, you're just the life of the damn party here in Laredo, ain't you, Marshal. 'Can't say I'm surprised, though. Matt Cole walked a ragged line for most of his time in office. All right, I'll stop by and pick him up. I'll need my nephew to help out, though. Cole weren't a little man.

Anything else you'd care to share with me, Marshal?"

"Yeah, 'matter of fact, there is. 'Just as soon, keep this quiet as best we can. Rather, the papers didn't get wind of it just yet. 'Least till I have a chance to look into it a bit."

"We'll use the alleyways."

"Thanks, Doc. Don't know if he has family, but if no one steps up to pay the fee, I'm good for it."

"You are, huh? Mexican paper said his hands were greasy. But you'll pay his bill?"

"He was a lawman, Doc. At some point, he musta been a good man." Doc Gately looked at Bass's eyes for a moment and said. "Good for you, Bass. I'll go fetch him, bring him back here."

Bass said, "Thank you, Doc," and went back outside to Emma. His next stop was City Hall.

10:15 a.m. October 30th, 1888
Laredo City Hall
Park Avenue at Santa Ursula
Laredo, Texas.

The Mayor's office was the easiest to find. It was located on the first floor toward the rear of the building. There was a secretary out front whose job, Bass supposed, was to guard the Mayor's door. She was middle-aged, had a somewhat grey complexion, and her hair was piled high on top of her head. She was writing something in a steno book as Bass approached her desk.

"Excuse me, ma'am. My name is Frank Bass. I'm a U.S. Deputy Marshal. I spoke briefly with the Mayor yesterday and wondered if I might please have a quick word with him this morning?"

Without looking up, she spoke in a high-pitched and slightly nasal voice, "I'm sorry the Mayor isn't seeing anyone he's in conference with members of the Town Council. Leave your name and address in that basket, and I'll send word when the Mayor is free. Possibly the end of the week."

Bass stepped closer to her desk. "The Town Council, is it? That suits me to a T. Please let him know that I'm here."

"I will not. The Mayor is quite busy and..." Before she could finish, Bass was past her desk and through the door to the Mayor's office.

She protested as she followed him in. "Your honor, I am sorry, but this ruffian barged right past me even though I told..." The Mayor rose from his desk

"It's perfectly alright, Mrs. Flade. The Marshal is welcome anytime. Please come in, Marshal, have a seat. Now, what can we do for you?" Mayor Abe Laurey was seated at his desk, and standing nearby were the two Councilmen he met yesterday.

Bass sat at a chair in front of the Mayor's desk and began.

"Gentlemen. Following up on our conversation from yesterday, I spoke with Mr. Arguello about assuming the town Marshal position. He's happy to help the city out, but he has a problem. His business is, what's it called, a going concern, and he'd need to hire someone to run it for him, you know, day to day. Consequently, he'll get a higher salary than you had been paying Marshal Cole. I've checked the books, and I've learned that Cole was paid one hundred fifty dollars per month for his service. Arguello will need two hundred.

Additionally, I'm going to insist that the city hire at least one full-time deputy at a salary of one hundred dollars per month. I believe the size of your township, in terms of both population and geographical size, warrants the extra help. This is the recommendation I plan to present to your District Judge, James Staton, this afternoon. If you choose to disagree with these terms, speak up. So, Whatda ya say?"

The tall councilman became somewhat huffy. "Sir, I'd like to remind you that we still have a duly elected law officer on the payroll. I understand Marshal Cole may have interfered with your arrest of Mr. Lennox, but which of us hasn't had a little too much to drink from time to time? I feel we owe it to our elected Marshal to forgive and forget, ah...so to speak."

"You do. Well, Mr. Councilman, I have evidence that suggests Matt Cole was on the take, though it really makes little difference now. Marshal Cole was murdered sometime yesterday afternoon. His throat was cut. By now, Dr. Gately will have his body and will prepare it for burial." The Mayor was standing now and asked, "Murdered, you say? Who would? How did this happen? He was in the city Jail. Held under lock and key."

"He was, Mayor. While I was out tracking cattle thieves yesterday afternoon, someone broke into the jail. I believe it was someone that Cole knew. The door to the cell room was open, and so was his cell door. There was no sign of a struggle. He must've told whoever it was where the keys were. The office was ransacked, and I believe his murderer was looking for evidence that linked Matt Cole to the rustlers. Evidence that I found and promptly took to the bank for safekeeping. Now. Mr. Arguello is ready to assume his duties as Town Marshal, provided you agree to the additional terms. As a Federal Officer, I can swear him in so your town continues to have the protection of a Peace Officer.

So. I'll ask again. Whatda ya say?" After a few moments of discussion and some 'what else can we do shoulder shrugs,' The four men agreed to the terms. Before Bass left, the Mayor quickly added, "Marshal Bass, to be clear, Mr. Arguello will be our interim Marshal until an election can be held. 'City Charter requirement." Bass looked back and said, "That's fine. I'm sure he'll agree." Bass left City Hall and decided to return to the hotel. He planned to visit the Tierra Blanca Ranch today and wanted to have all the firepower he could muster, just in case.

2:00 p.m. October 30th, 1888
Tiarra Blanca Ranch
12 Miles North of Town
Eagle Pass County Road
Laredo, Texas

The belt that held his two Walker Colts was wrapped around the saddle horn, with the butt end of both weapons facing back toward the rider. Normally, when he carried them, his Buffalo Robe would conceal their presence, but ever since Lil decided the robe was hers, Bass had to do without. Today, his pancho covered them. It seemed natural enough; after all, the weather had been rainy of late. This would be his first meeting with Landon Atwill, and as such, Bass expected nothing of any great substance would come of it. The meeting itself was really a chance for the suspect to get a good look at his pursuer and vice-versa. Bass didn't care a whit that Atwill might discover he was more interested in any evidence, circumstantial or otherwise, that might ultimately lead to an arrest for the murder of a U.S. Deputy Marshal. Whether the King Ranch got their cattle back was secondary to the murder of Harold Gosling and his posse.

It took about ninety minutes to get to the Tierra Blanca front gate. Bass had steered Emma along the way to avoid any muddy patch that looked to present uneven footing. When he arrived at Tirra Blanca, he found the gate unlocked as though he was expected, and it crossed his mind that someone in town might have left early and beaten him to the ranch. He walked Emma through the gate and up the long, narrow drive Until he came to the main house. It was an impressive structure all on one level, with different wings stretching from what must have been the main living area of the house. He counted eight chimneys, all active. There was a wide covered veranda, sparsely furnished, that reached around both ends of the house. Bass liked the idea and thought about asking Silas about a wrap-around porch when he got home.

As he waited, a smallish Mexican man who appeared to have Indian blood somewhere in his pedigree approached. He was courteous but not at all friendly. There was no welcoming smile or ingratiating attitude that might make Bass feel welcome. Bass waited for him to speak.

"Can I take your horse, señor?"

"That's kind in you, but I won't be long. I've just come to ask Mr. Atwill a couple of quick questions." The man backed away and said, "Very well...I will find him for you. Please wait here." The Mexican fellow went inside, and for a few minutes, Bass felt very exposed, standing and holding his horse alone in the yard of this Grand Rancho.

Atwill appeared after a suitable delay. He wore a formal riding outfit, fitted Jodhpurs flared above the knee, a red English riding jacket that was pinched at the waist, and highly polished black knee-high riding boots with nickel coronet spurs. He extended his hand as a gesture of welcome. Bass shook his hand as the man introduced himself.

"I'm Landon Atwill. I own the Tierra Blanca... what can I do for you, Marshal?"

"Well, Mr. Atwill, I rode out here this mornin so I could introduce myself. My name is Frank Bass. I'm a U.S. Federal Marshal, and I'd like to be able to search through your herd for a number of heifers that were stolen from the King Ranch. Maybe a month ago,"

"Certainly, of course, Marshal. May I see your warrant?" Bass smiled.

"Well, you know I don't have one, 'thought we could conclude all this in a neighborly way."

"Oh? Are you a neighbor now? Have you bought a place somewhere nearby?"

"Not what I meant, Mr. Atwill, if it's a warrant you want, then I'll fetch one for ya." Just at that moment, the Tierra Blanca's foreman appeared at the corner of the veranda and said, " Mr. Atwill, I was...Oh, excuse me. 'Didn't know you had a visitor." Bass recognized the man and said. "Willy? Willy Banes? Is that you? I didn't know you was out. When'd they cut you lose?"

Oh. Hey Marshal. Been a while, ain't it."

"Oh, it's been a while and a half. Willy. You workin here now, are ya?"

"That's right, Mr. Atwill is a fine employer."

"I'm sure he is, Willy. Say, you look just fine after all those years at Huntsville. I forget...what'd I get you on?"

"Cattle theft, Fraudulent Re-Branding. But I'm clean now, Marshal."

"Well, that's good to know, Willy. So, Mr. Atwill, I was out here yesterday following the tracks of a small herd that crossed a bridge a few miles from here. You seen any small herds, say about 24 animals, walkin about out here. 'Trail leads down to that road yonder...fact it leads right up to your gate." Bass looked directly into Atwill's eyes. He was no longer smiling.

Atwill scowled first at Willy Banes and then at Bass.

"No, Marshal, can't say that I have. I certainly would have noticed."

"How 'bout you, Willy? 'Seen any cows milling about down to the gate?" Banes was obviously nervous with his answer. "No, Frank. Ain't seen nothin' like that." Bass smiled now. He was enjoying himself. "Yeah, I imagine Mr. Atwill here keeps you pretty busy, huh?"

"That's right. In fact, I better get back to that pregnant mare. She's near to burstin right now." Banes disappeared, and Bass turned back to Atwill. "Guess I better get goin too.

You may'a heard that the Town Marshal, a fella named Matt Cole, got himself killed yesterday. I had him in custody for interferin' with a lawful arrest. Someone cut his throat right there in his jail cell. Real messy... 'terrible way for a man to die, getting his throat cut." Bass paused for a moment, fixed his stare at Atwill, and said, "I'll see you again, Mr. Atwill. I'll see you again, by and by." Bass mounted up, pulled straight back on the reins, and Emma backed away from the house, still facing forward, for a good forty feet. Then Bass turned her head, touched her ribs, and she carried him, at a trot, back through the gate.

The ride back to Laredo gave Bass a chance to think of a plan to confront Atwill with the fact that circumstantial evidence pointed to him as the thief of the King Ranch cattle. Knowing now that Willy Banes worked for Atwill further solidified his certainty that Atwill had the twenty-four head that were stolen and had hidden them in a remote pasture or corral. The problem was that cattle theft, like horse theft, was no longer the deadly serious crime it once was years before. It was still illegal, of course, and still carried a possible sentence at the state prison, but Bass was much more interested in pinning the cattle theft and accessory to the murder of Harold Gosling on Atwill.

Bass knew that his only piece of tangible evidence was the cigarette butt he found at Cole's murder. The fact that cattle were stolen, resulting in a fatal confrontation at a bridge near his property, was too thin to base an arrest on. The only talking witness he had was the bar owner.

Anson Halliday, who had lit out when the shooting started. There was a bright spot in the case, however. He'd arrested a suspect at the Nugget Saloon that Halliday could identify as the man who fired the shot that killed Gosling. But he was a hardened outlaw and was severely wounded. Doc Gately had said he wouldn't be able to talk for a couple of days, but Atwill didn't know that. Bass decided his best course of action would be to keep Lennox's condition a secret and hide him somewhere in town. When he was able to talk, Bass could likely negotiate a deal with him. After all, he was facing a noose or, at best, life in the penitentiary for killing Gosling. Bass needed to protect both Halliday and Lennox. Hide them away someplace.

He'd ridden about two miles from the Tierra Blanca Gate when Emma jumped, screaming in pain, kicking her right rear leg out, and twisting away from her lead. She wanted to run but couldn't and kept stumbling on her hind leg. Bass held onto the horn and twisted around to have a look at what might have happened. That's when he saw the small hole in her right rump and the blood that seeped from it and down her right leg. Bass jumped off and went to her head. He held both cheekpieces of her bridle in his hands. He was talking low and breathing in her flared nostrils, trying to keep her focus on him. She started to calm down, but Bass knew it might be shock. She was quieter now, but blood still ran from her wound. He tied her off at a low branch of a tree and fished out his medical kit from his saddle bag. Ever since he'd been stabbed in the gut last winter as he traveled on the Llano, he carried six syringes of Morphine Sulfate in 9 mg. doses in his medical kit. As he was opening one of the envelopes, he heard a rifle shot from some distance away. He heard the bullet as it buzzed past his head and ricocheted off a large rock behind them.

He had Emma calm enough that he thought he might be able to coax her into deeper cover off the trail. He knew it was blind trust that made her follow him, wincing and limping in her pain. Once he felt that they couldn't be easily seen, he gave her two injections of morphine and used several alcohol wipes to clean the wound. He could see the bullet embedded in muscle close to the surface. He thought he'd be able to remove the slug, but he had no bandage if she started to bleed once the bullet was removed. He decided the best idea was to get her back to town, but there was still a man with a rifle out there who might be waiting for him to do just that.

He removed his Winchester and began leading her parallel to the path, but in enough cover that he felt they'd be hard targets to spot. The morphine was working, and she was able to walk slowly through the low shrubs and scrub oak as he tried to keep them as sheltered as possible. Another shot from well behind them embedded itself in a Madrone tree with a dull thud. He trained his glass in the direction of the shot but saw nothing.

He checked her wound every so often and noticed that the bleeding had slowed. After about an hour of this, he gave her another shot. She was breathing normally, which told him the morphine had continued to work. She was still struggling to walk, and Bass saw there was swelling in her leg, but she wasn't balking as much as she had, and they continued. They rounded a point and could see the outskirts of Laredo ahead. Another shot was fired from behind; this time, it hit Bass, creasing his right hip and causing him to fall. He pulled himself up using his Winchester and limped to his saddlebags for his field glass. He steadied himself on a stump and scanned the area behind them, looking for movement or a reflection of some kind. He saw nothing, so he jammed his bandana into the crease of seared skin and continued leading his horse toward town. Another thirty minutes went by before they reached the relative safety of

Arguello's Wheelwright and Smith Shop. Once inside their barn, Bass could breathe a little easier.

Fourteen

5:15 p.m. October 30th, 1888
The Hills Along the Rio
Eagle Pass Road
Western Laredo, Texas

Horn was cursing at his failure to bring down the man's horse. He figured it to be about two hundred fifty yards, but he couldn't grip the fore stock firmly, and he'd only stung the beast. The animal was still standing, still able to walk. He wanted to run Bass down on foot, hogtie him, and begin his painful procedures in the hills away from prying eyes and passersby. He'd pictured in his mind's eye all the pain he'd inflict with his knife and hatchet. Once he'd finished, he planned to drop the dead and mangled body of the famous lawman at the steps of the local newspaper so his demise would be announced to the whole world.

He even devised the manner in which he could be identified as the true killer. There were sure to be low-lives and copy-cats who'd try to take credit once Bass's death appeared in the paper. He'd cut off the trigger finger of the famous Marshal and send it in a letter to the paper itself. "By God, they'll know then that Tom Horn's not a man to be trifled with. Not by a damned sight." His blood was up now, and he damned the weapon as he slid the scope-sighted Sharps Overbaugh into its beaded scabbard. He cursed again at the "worthless, black-livered buffalo hunter" he'd killed for it. Horn had made the mistake of assuming the scope had been 'sighted in' at a goodly distance by the hunter who'd owned it. Obviously, after missing four shots, he could no longer trust the scope and reluctantly decided to remove it. He only had two rounds of ammunition left for the Sharps, and he knew better than to try to find replacements for the old-style shells in town. He'd only be giving himself away. He had two rounds left. He'd have to make them count.

As he stood next to the Appaloosa he was suddenly bone weary and even had trouble lifting his arms. He needed a place to hole up, so he began thinking of men who might help. He knew a rancher who'd hired him before and now lived somewhere in the Laredo area, but it had been so long ago and in a very distant place that he had no idea how to find him.

He could see several buildings in the distance along the Rio, but the light was fading, and he had trouble focusing. *"What was that guy's name again? Oh yeah, Atwill...somethin like that."* He decided to head back to his hotel and get some sleep. *"Start again tomorrow when I'm rested."*

7:45 p.m. October 30th, 1888
Arguello's Blacksmith and Wheelwright Shop
Eagle Pass Road
Laredo, Texas

Doc Gatley arrived twenty minutes after Arguello sent for him. Bass lay on a low table covered with metal filings, and the particles created by extreme heat burned into his back. Emma was standing stock still in an open stall not six feet away.

"Well, my God, what happened here, Marshal?" Gatley was tearing apart Bass's trousers to get a better look at the wound. Bass was pale from loss of blood, but he was still able to joke with the Doctor. "Oh, I just bumped into some barbwire couple miles back, Doc Hell, what does it look like? Someone tried to shoot me."

"Yeah, well, looks like better'n tried, son. 'Looks to me like they did shoot you, and you was lucky. Lemme see here. Bring that lantern closer, will ya?" Arguello held the lantern as Doc requested, and he turned Bass gently over on his side. "Looks like a fairly large caliber sliced

your hip fore and aft. Maya nicked the bone, too. I can just barely see the denuded bone here, which means there's likely debrided fragments to be found. I'm gonna give you an opiate and then wash out the wound with astringent... 'means alcohol. You won't feel much, though. Then I gotta probe for them fragments...that won't be fun."

"Go ahead, Doc, but then have a look at my horse in that stall. She took one in the right rump. I gave her Morphine and cleaned the wound. The bullet's right near the surface. Can you please help her too?"

"Yes, I can. Where in hell did you get them morphine syringes?"

"From my Doc back home. He knows the kinda work I do sometimes requires pain medicine."

"Did he also tell you about what else opiates do? How they create a dependence...string you out so's you need more and more?"

"Yeah, I already knew that, but sometimes you can't afford to wait if you take my meanin."

"Uh-huh, I do. How much have you given yourself?"

"None. Didn't need it. Gave my horse two of 'em."

"Well, won't hurt her none. 'Probably just took the edge off the pain. Animals are real different when it comes to pain. Handle it different. I'll look at her in a moment." Doc Gately gave Bass a morphine injection and swabbed down the wound with witch hazel. Then, he walked to the stall and climbed on a stool to examine Emma. Arguello held the lantern for him again.

"She'll be all right, Marshal. I'll be able to get the slug easy enough. No arteries in the area I know of that might burst, no bones to worry for either when I probe."

"I'd take it kindly if you'd do that first, Doc. I'm all right to wait."

Doc Gately stepped off the stool and fixed another injection for Emma. Once he'd given it to her, he again climbed down and reached for a five-and-a-half-inch forceps and probe from his bag. He had one of Arguello's assistants hold her head and whisper to her as he used his probe and then his forceps. She barely moved a muscle through the procedure. When he was finished, he flushed the area with witch hazel and applied a heavy cotton bandage with tape.

"That tape ain't gonna hold for more than an hour or two, less if she's restless. 'Need to check on that bandage every hour or so. She'll be fine, Marshal, just fine. 'Sore for a while but fine. Nothin' there but muscle where she took the slug.

Now, as to you...let's see what we got."It took nearly an hour for Doc Gately to complete his search for bone shards. Even with the morphine, Bass felt the pain along the length of the wound. "I believe I got 'em all, son, but this ain't my clinic, and in the lamplight, I mighta missed something. Bass was in a cold sweat and only heard a word or two of what the doctor said. Doc Gately turned to Arguello and said,

"Let's leave him here tonight and move him to my place tomorrow morning. I'll come by with a wagon early. If his condition should change in the night, fever and whatnot, come get me." Before he left the Blacksmith's barn, he had another look at Emma. She was standing, her weight shifted away from her wounded leg, but in general, she seemed fine. She hadn't bled through her bandage yet, but Doc asked one of Arguello's men to change the bandage every hour. He showed him how and left him a supply of astringent, cotton gauze, and tape.

5:00 a.m. October 31st, 1888
Arguello's Blacksmith and Wheelwright Shop
Eagle Pass Road
Laredo, Texas

Bass woke to the sound of Emma kicking in her stall. Bass stood uneasily and walked as gingerly as he could to her stall. As soon as she saw him, she settled. He opened the stall, knowing that her pain made her movements and actions unpredictable, and again grabbed her bridle and breathed into her nose. She jerked and complained but stayed with him.

One of Arguello's workers heard the commotion and came to see what was happening. Bass looked at the man and calmly said, "Por favor, consigue el doctor." The man rushed from the barn, and twenty minutes later, Doc Gately appeared with a sodium bromide injection to calm her down. "My buggy's out front, Marshal. You're comin back to my place. You look like death warmed up. Don't worry 'bout your horse. She's in better shape than you are. I'll keep an eye on her. Bass agreed and rode back to Gately's office on Montezuma Street. He was only partially conscious but in little or no pain. "It's the morphine. 'Was meant to keep you down all night."

When he got to the clinic, Doc helped him inside. There, he noticed Cherry Lennox cuffed to his bed, wrist, and ankle. Bass lay in the first bed and closed his eyes immediately. He was vaguely aware of activity around his hip but didn't care at all what it might be. He noticed that it was becoming light outside and fell into sleep after that.

2:00 p.m. October 31st, 1888
Doc Gately's Clinic
Montezuma Street
Laredo, Texas

Bass woke up clear-headed and alert. He knew exactly where he was and how he'd gotten there. What he didn't know was the time and how long he'd been asleep. An older woman was standing at a medicine cabinet with her back to him. "Excuse me, ma'am. How long have I been here?" The woman, hearing his voice, turned to him and smiled warmly, "Since about six this morning, Mr. Bass. How are you feeling?"

"Better than I expected. Is the Doc around?"

"He's down at Arguello's seeing to your horse. Now...you lie back and let me see that bandage." Bass nodded and laid back down. Then he heard another voice, a man's voice from the end of the room. "What happened to you, Jim-Crack? Somebody shoot you in the leg? Hurts like hell, don't it?" Bass smiled as he remembered how Cherry Lennox wound up in Doc Gately's clinic.

"Damn right, it hurts. 'Don't recommend it. But I was shot in the hip. Should heal fine and I'll be on my way. Don't guess you can say the same, can you, Mr. Lennox?" The woman was swabbing the wound with alcohol and preparing another bandage. Lennox paused before answering, and then he propped himself up on his left elbow. "Well, my future has looked brighter, but I reckon I'll be all right."

Bass answered, "You'll be all right, y' say? How so? Seems like I got you under arrest for murderin a U.S. Deputy Marshal. Just how do you think your life's gonna turn round from that?"

"Well, I ain't hung yet. And the only man that can see to that is crippled up in the bed next to me. Also...I understand ol' Matt Cole is ..ah...no long Town Marshal. And that yellow dog of a witness? He ain't likely to testify to nothin.'" Bass turned his head slightly to see the man he was talking to. Cherry Lennox was a solely unattractive person. His hair was thinning in patches, his front teeth were rotting, and from straight on, he looked cross-eyed. His eyebrows were black and seemed to be growing together, giving him the appearance of a man with a black caterpillar crawling across his forehead.

"You seem to have it all figured, don't you? Still, I wouldn't make any long-term plans if I were you. 'Might be disappointed." Bass then rolled over to indicate he was done talking. The movement hurt, but he didn't let on.

About an hour later, Doc Gately walked in and went straight to Bass. "Let's have a look at that bandage." He bent over to look at Bass's hip and said, "Huh. Martha? Did you change this bandage recently?" From somewhere else in the building, the woman answered. "Yeah, I did. You're welcome." Doc smiled and said. "Old woman's been with me for years. She's a step ahead of me most of the time." He stood up then and said, "Your horse is doing fine, Marshal. While I was there, she had a good long drink... flushed the opiates out. She ain't been bleedin anymore, either. She's sore, but I turned her out to the corral anyway. She needs to figure out how to walk with that wounded rump. I've been meaning to talk with you about that slug, Marshal. 'Strange size...like a 44.40 but lighter. Custom, maybe?"

"Maybe. I believe I know who the shooter is, but I can't say as to the weapon."

"Oh? You wanna do anything 'bout him?"

"No. He won't know where I am right away, but he may figure it out. When he does, I'll be ready for him." The Doc nodded and said. "You're gonna be gimpy for the next few days, you know.

Desi Arguello's taken on the Town Marshal duty. You want me to bring him over?"

"Well, maybe tomorrow mornin. He's got his hands full as it is." Doc Gately pulled up a chair and sat down in front of Bass.

"Been thinking 'bout your wound and your horses' too. If your shooter fired from a long distance, the trajectory and speed of the slug woulda fallen off a bit. Could explain a lot."

"Yeah, like, why he shot my horse? And then hit me in the hip?"

"Yeah, yeah. Could be. Mighta been tryin to compensate."

"Say, when d'you think can I get up and outta here, Doc? Got people to see and things to do."

"Oh...another day, maybe two. 'Wanna make sure the stitches in your side hold. And, like I said, you're gonna be gimpy. It'll wear you down at first." Bass thought for a moment and asked,

"Can I ask you to get a note to Judge Staton? Real important."

"Sure thing. What do you want to say?"

"Hand me that pad and pencil, will ya, Doc?" Doc Gately did as he was asked and took the note from Bass once he was finished. "I'll run it over on my way to lunch." When Lennox heard the word lunch, he called out after the Doc, "Say. Bring me somethin other than a damned ham sandwich, will ya, Doc? I need more 'n that ta get my strength back." Doc was gone before Lennox finished.

Bass was still thinking about trying to draw Lennox out about the shooting of Harold Gosling when he remembered Anse Halliday mentioning that he thought Lonny Dahl may have been in the group. From what Lennox had just said, Bass gathered he didn't know who the escaped posse man was. He decided he'd try to get Lennox to talk about Dahl on his own. There were actually two outlaws named Lon Dahl. One was older and supposedly "retired," living someplace in Montana under an assumed name. The man in question, Lonny Dahl 'the younger,' was a handsome young man, having been named in several bank robberies in Arkansas and horse and cattle theft in the Indian Territory north of Gainesville near the Red River. He'd run with several gangs, but recently, he'd hooked up with Dan Bogan in San Antonio.

Bass thought he'd try to soften Lennox up by talking about Dahl.

"Heard some fellas in the saloon talkin about having seen Lonny Dahl, the younger one. Was he with your bunch too, Lennox.?"

"Dahl? 'Don't know, no Dahl. Nope, it was just me an' Dan and some Mexican kid out for a mornin's ride when that posse jumped us. And anyone says different is a bald-faced liar."

"Z'at so? Why, I heard Lonny was braggin how he shot the Marshal and three deputies himself. 'Course he scampered quick back over the river once he said it."

"Yeah, well, he would. Lily-livered pup. Teach me to ride with youngsters."

"Oh, so's you was with him then...when Harold was murdered?"

"Didn't say such...didn't say anything like it. Only said I shouldn't ride with untried youngsters, is all."

"Lennox, you told me enough...I guess I heard right. 'Heard what your given name is, too. I figured Cherry was somethin you made up."

"You best shut your yap right now, Marshal."

"Or what? 'You gonna have Lonny Dahl come shoot with me? Go ahead, Cherry. Or should I a said Cherubim?" Lennox was furious and rattling the chains that held him to his cot.

"You spill my name anywhere's, I'll clean your business up real good, Buster." Bass just smiled.

Fifteen

2:00 p.m. October 31st, 1888
Travis Hotel
800 North Monterey Street
Laredo, Texas

Tom Horn had made his way back to his hotel at 11:15 p.m. the previous evening and had slept for more than twelve hours. He awoke this morning at 11:30 a.m. groggy and disoriented. He had little or no recollection of the previous three days, how he came to be in this hotel or even in the bed where he lay. He knew he had followed Frank Bass from El Paso, and he had a vague memory of being in that city, but he could not recall how he got to Laredo. He closed his eyes, and slowly, things began to return to him. The men he'd killed for their horses or their weapons and money. The surprised look on one man's face when he was struck in the breast by the bullet he fired. He remembered, with the pain in his left arm, why he'd come and what he needed to do.

Slowly, the events of the previous afternoon and evening returned. The stolen horse, the ambush, the miss-aimed shots because of the weakness in his left side. He realized the scope was accurate. It was his inability to steady the rifle properly and absorb the recoil of the shot. That's why he missed. It would be different next time. He lay, still fully clothed, on his bed, drifting in and out of wakefulness for hours until, finally, he sat straight up. "The damn blacksmith. On the river near the railroad tracks. That's where he is."

5:00 p.m. October 31st, 1888
Arguello's Blacksmith and Wheelwright Shop
Eagle Pass Road
Laredo, Texas

"I'm lookin for a man that I believe came in here last night. He would've had a gunshot wound on his side, and he was leadin' that tall mare standin out yonder in the corral."

Horn was talking to a teenage Mexican laborer who had only come to work at noon and had no idea what the man with the black mustache was talking about.

"Por favor, Señor, no se quien te refieres." Horn understood what the young man was saying and grabbed him by the shirt, pulling him in close.

"The man, ese Hombre that came in with that horse, el caballo... I want to know where he is?"

'The Mexican boy was scarred now. He had no idea what the man was saying and knew nothing about the horse.

At that time, another worker, an older man, heavily built and holding a pair of long-handled iron tongs, stepped over and interrupted. He pushed Horn's hands down and stood between the two. "Listen here, bub. Angel don't have any idea what you're talking about, and neither do I ...so do yourself a favor and back on out the door 'fore I help you find it." The larger man stayed and watched as Horn backed away and climbed on the Appaloosa.

Horn turned his head around and headed back into town. The bigger man watched him go and turned back to Angel and said in Spanish, "Angel, if you see that man again, you come get me. I don't like his looks." The boy nodded and said, "Si Ramon. Gracias."

Horn was heading back into town. He knew now where Bass's horse was. He didn't get much of a look at her, but he did see a bandage taped to her right rump. She seemed to be standing comfortably, but that didn't mean she could carry a rider. He decided his next course of action would be to check with the local doctors. 'See if any of 'em had treated a man for a gunshot wound.' He figured he'd just return to his hotel and ask the desk clerk if there were any doctors in town. 'Couldn't be more than three or four, he thought. Now, he needed to come up with a plausible reason for needing a doctor. He wasn't worried. He knew he'd think of something.

5:45 p.m. October 31st, 1888

Doc Gately's Clinic
Montezuma Street
Laredo, Texas

Bass was getting dressed. He had waited until his bandage had been changed and the older woman had left the room. Cherry Lennox was asleep, so there wouldn't be any trouble from him. Bass needed to check on the note he'd given to Doc Gately that morning, and that meant he had to get to the Rock Bottom Saloon to see Anse Halliday. His hip was sore, but with the fresh bandage, he was able to buckle his belt a bit higher. Putting his boots on was the worst, but once he was standing and ready to go, he felt pretty good.

He had to walk to the saloon, but it was only a few blocks away. When he got there, he looked for Halliday but didn't see him anywhere around the bar. He walked up to the end of the bar and waited for one of the ladies to notice him. As he stood there, he tried to ignore the pain caused by his belt, which moved with each step. Finally, a woman approached and asked what he'd like.

"A rye with ice, please. Oh, and is Anse Halliday around tonight?"

The bartender had scooped some ice and put a sliver of lemon in the glass. She answered as she poured. "Ah, no, as a matter of fact. He had to leave town rather suddenly. Something about his brother being in trouble someplace."

"Hmm. Too bad. 'say where he was going?"

"I don't think so, someplace east. San Antonio, maybe. That's two bits."

"Sure, sure. Thanks." Bass swallowed the rye, turned, and left. He was smiling as he walked through the door.

Now that he knew his note had been delivered, he decided to go back to the jail. He was well aware that Horn was in the vicinity and considered the jail to be one of the first places he might look, but he had to run that risk. He needed to talk with Desmond Arguello.

The jail was a longer walk from the Rock Bottom Saloon than he remembered it being. Of course, he'd always been on horseback when he made the trip before, and that made all the difference. When he got to the jail, Arguello was just locking the door. Bass called to him to wait and hurried his pace as best he could.

"Desmond. I'm glad I caught you. I wanted to check on Halliday's activity today. Did it all go as planned?"

"Yes, it did. Judge Staton took Halliday's Affidavit and notarized the signature. He said since he was the one who took the sworn statement, he was certain it would hold up in court."

"Good, good. I've just come from his saloon and was told he had to leave earlier today. Did he leave an address with you?"

"Yes, a place in Brownsville, though I don't know that we'll need him now."

"You're right, but you never can tell. All the same, I'm glad he's outta harm's way. I believe the owner of the Tierra Blanca is responsible for all this. I followed a weathered track of a small herd across the bridge where Gosling and the others were shot. It led right up to the front gate. On top of that, an old rustler named Willy Banes is workin there. I put him away for a few years for cattle rustling and re-branding. He's an old hand at changing cattle brands, and I bet if we lean on him a bit, he'll give up his boss."

"Alright. You tell me how you think we should play it, and we'll get it done."

"I like your attitude, but I believe we'll need a few more men than just you and me. Think you can find a few able-bodied deputies to throw in with us?"

"I think so. I'll pass the word tomorrow."

Arguello paused to take a closer look at Bass in the fading light.

"Say, Marshal, you don't look too good. 'You okay?"

"Eh...just worn. Getting shot don't agree with me. I'll be okay tomorrow." Des Arguello walked around back to pick up his horse.

He told Bass he wanted to check on his shop before he went home. Bass watched him ride off and then decided rather than walk back across town to the Arbuckle, he'd stay the night at the jail, 'sleep on one of the cots. When he tried to open the door, however, he discovered it was locked. Then he remembered he'd seen Arguello locking up as he arrived. The next closest place would be back at Doc Gately's place. He hated to go back and explain why he'd left, but his hip was hurting, and he thought a good night's sleep would do wonders.

6:30 p.m. October 31, 1888
   Doc Gately's Clinic
   Montezuma Street
   Laredo, Texas

"Damnit, Bass, up and waltzin' about town like nothin' happened. Serve you right if I have to cauterize that gash closed. Go lie down in your bed and undo your britches."

Bass did as he was told, apologizing to the doctor as he did. Gately wasn't paying much attention to what was being said. He was too busy removing Bass's boots and sliding off his trousers.

   "Martha! Come here and hold the light for me." Martha
   heard the Doc's holler and answered from

the second floor.

"All right! Keep your shirt on! I'll be there in a minute." Doc was peering at the stitches in Bass's side. "Don't look too bad. The bottom ones are stretched. Bet that hurts a bit."

"Hell, yeah, it does."

"Good. Serves you right. Now, hold still." Gately then doused the entire wound with astringent.

Bass's face turned beet red before he yelled at the pain.

"YEEEEOWWWW, God damn it, Doc" Bass's eyes were watering now, and his nose started to run.

"Oh, I'm sorry, son. I guess I shoulda warned ya or maybe hit it with anesthesia first. Damn. I'll hafta remember that for next time."

Martha showed up and apologized for taking so long, "One of the ladies upstairs, Harriet Tait, was having false labor pain. Now, what do ya want?"

"Hand me that number 22 syringe and just hold the damn light, please, so I can see to redo these last five sutures." The Doc injected pain killer into the red area around the wound.

"That more morphine, Doc?" Bass was no longer feeling pain and was observing the doctor's procedure.

"No. It's called cocaine, 'comes from the cocoa plant in South America. It ain't from the poppy if that's what you're askin?"

"Cocaine. Sure works. From South America, huh?"

"Yup. They been usin it in Europe for a few years now. Martha? Bandage that for me, will ya? I'm gonna go check on Harriet." Doc Gately dipped his hands in the wash basin and sprinkled alcohol on his hands before drying them. He grabbed his bag and took another look at Bass, smiled slightly, and went upstairs.

Bass asked Martha, "Are there women here too?"

"Well, a course you ninny. Gals need tendin too, ya know." She finished with the tape and gauze and lowered the flame on the lamp. Then she went and locked the front door and put the *closed* sign in the window.

Bass leaned back into his pillow and felt his whole body relax. He was close to sleeping when Cherry Lennox said, "So. You was out and about today. What was so important you had to get finished before Doc let you go?"

"Lennox? Unless you want to talk about Landon Atwill and them cows you took to the Tierra Blanca, I don't want to hear your voice. Got that?"

"Yeah. Well, I don't know nothin' 'bout no cows, but I been thinkin about what you said earlier about Lonny Dahl. Was you serious 'bout findin him?"

"Well, a course I am. Why? You know where he is?"

"I might. But I wanna know what kinda deal you'll make for helpin you find that cold-blooded killer?"

"Well, I don't know, Cherry. I have heard he confessed to the actual shootin, but then I got a witness who says it was you pulled the trigger."

"Yeah, well, I wouldn't count too much on that witness hangin around. I believe a serious accident might befall that poor bastard."

"Really? You think so?"

"I do."

"That's funny 'cause one of the things I did today was to look up that witness, and you know what? He was gone."

"What'd I tell ya? Some folks, I guess, are just accident-prone."

"Oh, I don't think he had an accident, Cherry. See, before he left town, he swore an affidavit to Judge Staton that it was you shot poor Harold yourself."

"What? Wait a minute. What's this Affidavid thing? Where this guy go? Is the judge gonna just take his word on that? As bein true?"

" 'Fraid so Cherry. Now, unless you have some real information about who shot who and who stole what... and for who, I'm afraid your doom is sealed." Cherry Lennox was silent momentarily and then said, "My doom, what do you mean my doom, and why has it been sealed?"

"Lennox, I'm a wounded man, and I need my sleep. Now tell me what I asked ya, or shut up and let me be." Cherry Lennox was quiet for the rest of the night. Bass took it as a good sign.

7:50 p.m. October 31st. 1888
Travis Hotel
800 North Monterey Street

Laredo, Texas

Horn still wasn't hungry, but he had a thirst he couldn't slake. He kept asking for glass after glass of water, and when the waitress asked if he wanted anything to eat, he snapped back at her, "I ain't hungry, woman, leave me be." He sat reviewing the information he'd received from the desk clerk. There were three doctors in town; all had offices with clinics, and the clerk was certain all three were competent to treat bullet wounds. There was Doctor Forsythe on Garfield Street across the Zacate Creek that split the town in two. Then there was Doc Gately on Montezuma Street and finally Doc Sebring on Jefferson Street near the Park. The clerk said he thought Sebring treated animals, too. Horn sat thinking through each name and finally decided to check with this Sebring guy because Bass's horse was wounded as well. 'Made sense to him anyway.

Sixteen

9:30 a.m. November 1st, 1888
Lionel Sebring's Office
1400 Block of Jefferson
Laredo, Texas

"I wanna see the Doc 'He here?" The young woman wearing a hairnet and starched apron answered, "No, he's not. He's making his rounds about town right now. Can I help you? Are you unwell?"

"Hell no, I'm right as rain. I'm lookin for a friend of mine 'accidentally shot hisself in the hip. 'Thought he might'a come here. 'Seen anyone with a gunshot wound in the last couple 'days?"

"No, sir. No indeed. I should certainly remember that. Whom shall I say came asking?"

"What?"

"Your name, sir? I'll tell Doctor Sebring you stopped by looking for your friend."

"Oh. Never mind. I'll look elsewhere." Horn left the office just as swiftly as he walked in. He was disappointed in that he was sure a doctor that also treated animals woulda been the first one Bass would look up. He fished a slip of paper out of his pocket and read the name next doctor on his list. Doctor Andrew Forsythe on Garfield Avenue. He had checked the city map at the hotel desk and learned that Garfield Street was across Zacate Creek, and the closest bridge was eight blocks away. He was more than a little put out that he had to travel so far just to get across a bridge, but since there was no way around it, he climbed up on his Appaloosa gelding and spurred him north to the bridge. His journey took him through a seedier part of town that had saloons and cat houses every couple blocks. Gals sportin' their 'wares' stood bold as bright colors on the streets, hooting and howling at the menfolk that passed by.

He stopped at a corner to give a particularly raucous woman a piece of his own decency when he heard a man call out,

"Say, buster. What are you doin on Goody Brown's horse? He said that horse was stole from him the other day. How'd you get it?"

Horn was taken by surprise and had no idea what to say while a crowd of young cowboys had gathered waiting for an explanation. His only thought was to spur the animal forward to escape. But by that time, there were a couple of men in front of him grabbing at the horse's bridle.

The horse spooked at the commotion and reared up, falling backward and landing on top of Horn, who was desperately trying to fish out his pistol. He heard a loud crack and then felt a blinding pain in his left ankle. His spur had caught in the stirrup rigging, and as the horse struggled to stand, his ankle snapped like turkey bone. He cried out in pain, but the five or so cowboys were more intent on retrieving their friend's horse than caring for the man who stole it.

Once the horse had been led away, a couple of bystanders came over saying things like, "Let's get a rope" and "Hold him for the Marshal." One of them said, "His ankle's broke. He ain't goin nowhere." Horn grabbed one of the men by the arm and pulled himself up onto his right leg. He brandished his pistol at the others, who immediately backed away. He was sweating like a summer hog, sick to his stomach from the pain. He could do nothing but hop to the boardwalk, where he grabbed onto a broom handle standing next to a doorway. He flipped it upside down and used it as a cane so he could hobble down an alley away from the scene.

The whole time he hopped and skipped using that broom, he cursed his luck at stealing that *"damned horse with the spotted butt."*

11:00 a.m. November 1st, 1888
Doc Gately's Clinic
Montezuma Street
Laredo, Texas

Bass had woken to the sound of Cherry Lennox rattling his shackles because he needed a bedpan.

Martha heard him and brought one to him, helping him to undo his drawers while standing up.

"This ain't right, you know. A woman seein a man's ...you know...equipment when he hasta' relieve himself." Martha answered,

"Mr. Lennox, this ain't the first time I've seen a tallywhacker, and it won't be the last. So, tuck yours away and be grateful I didn't let you piss your cot."

Of course, Bass laughed under his breath, swung his legs off the cot, and slowly stood up.

"Believe I'll walk myself out to the commode, Martha. I'll be back directly."

"Yeah? Well, see that you are. The old man'll be back soon, and if he sees you gone from your bed, he'll start treatin' you with bromide." Bass was familiar with bromide as an antiseptic. A doctor had to use it on his stab wound last winter after Bass had cauterized his wound closed. The burn became infected, and bromide was all the doctor had. Now, the scar on his belly from the burn was rippled and also perpetually pink. And it itched too whenever Bass sweat.

"Ah. In that case, I'll be right back!

Doc Gately returned a few minutes after Bass had laid back down on his cot. Doc lifted the sheet and examined the bandage and then the wound. "Well, seems to have held up pretty well. Swellings down, and the surrounding tissue is starting to look a healthy pink. You're still seeping a bit, though, Marshal, so I can't in good conscience release you just yet. Maybe this evening if it continues to look good and the bandage stays dry." Bass was fine with staying a few more hours, though he wanted to send a wire to Sally lest she worry about not hearing from him. He debated whether he should mention the encounter with Horn and the fact that Emma had been wounded, too, but he decided it would be too much to get into a wire. Once it was all over, he'd explain everything, knowing she might be a little upset but also knowing that apologizing could be fun, too.

While he was there at Doc Gately's, he decided to work on Cherry Lennox some more. He wanted to let Lennox make the opening move, so he pretended to be resting his eyes, but he already knew Bass was awake. Lennox could not have failed to overhear his conversations with Martha and the Doc.

Finally, Lennox said,

"Alright, alright, Marshal Bass...what is it you wanna know?"

"So now you're ready to talk, are you?"

"Yeah, I am."

"What is it that changed your mind?"

"How's about I don't wann'a hang for killin some lawman. Sound about right to you?"

"Yeah, 'course it does. It's the same thing I been sayin to you for two days now, Cherry. What changed your mind?"

"Well, you promise not to laugh? Won't say if you're gonna laugh 'bout it."

"I won't laugh, I promise."

"Well, last night I had a dream about my ma. And well, hell, she had such high hopes and all for her children you know? So I woke up feelin real low and figured maybe talkin about it would keep her from rollin' in her grave."

"Oh now, Cherry. I certainly would never laugh at somethin like that. Sounds kinda like a noble thing to do for your deceased ma."

"Oh, she ain't deceased, but when she hears what I done, it's likely to kill her."

Bass had a little trouble keeping a straight face at that, but he managed and went on listening to Cherry Lennox.

"So, yeah, we stole them cows, like you said, from along the Santa Gertrudis. We was bringing 'em up the San Fernando Creek to Aguileras and then west across the San Ygnacio Bridge to get 'em to the Tierra Blanca. Guy, there wanted them cattle 'cause they was a new strain of Longhorns that the King Ranch came up with."

"Okay. I pretty much have all that put together myself, Cherry. I wanna hear about the shootin at the bridge. Tell me about how that went down."

"When we got to the bridge, that's when Harold Gosling showed up with his posse. They was all armed, now, and we didn't take no advantage on unarmed men."

"I see. Go on."

"Well, Harold was at the lead, and he started askin questions of Dan and ol Dan, he didn't care to answer. That's when Ronnie Fox shot him with his rifle."

"Wait a minute. You're sayin' that 'Bloody' Ron Fox was with you too?"

"Yes, I am."

"Well, that's the first I heard a that. I knew about Dan and you and Lonny, but I never heard Ron Fox's name come up."

"Well, he was there, sittin his horse right behind Dan. Hell, Lonny's still out there runnin' free; catch him and ask him yourself."

"Then I guess I'll have to. Now tell me, Cherry, and tell me true. Who did you shoot?

"Hell, I don't know that I shot anybody. We was all shootin after Harold bought it. I mighta hit a posseman. I can't say for sure. The cows was spooked, and the horses were dancin', smoke all around. It was all real confusin.'"

Bass could see that Lennox was upset at retelling the story, and the addition of Ron Fox was certainly believable. Bloody Ron Fox was known for his hair-trigger temper. That's how he got his nickname. Bass paused for a moment and then said,

"Well, you did fine, Cherry, just fine. And you're sure about taking the cows to Tierra Blanca?"

"Oh yeah. 'At's where we was paid. All in greenbacks and gold. This little Mexican fella bring it to us once the cows was in the corral."

"Uh-huh. And what about Dan Bogan? He get paid off, too?"

"I guess so. He came over and told us all to git. So we crossed the river into Mexico and laid low for a while. Then we heard that Sheriff Cole would take twenty dollars apiece to leave us be in town here, so after a while, we came back. And then you shot me."

"Yes, I did, Cherry. But you had it comin for tryin to draw your pistol on me. And besides, look at you. You're healin' up. Now, did Ron Fox come back across the river with you?"

"Oh hell yeah, but he didn't come with us to drink and gamble. He's got a sweetheart in town."

"Oh yes? You know her?"

"Me? No. Ain't never met her, but I know her name, he talks about her often enough. Loretta. She works along Saunders Street...but not when Ronnie's around."

"You know where she lives?"

"No. Ronnie don't want nobody beatin' his time, so he keeps her a secret, you know? Real close to the vest."

"Alright Cherry. Thank you for helpin me out. Now. If it comes to it, I'll want you to say all that to a judge, you know."

"Yeah, I know. Think it'll go easier on me for tellin' all this, Marshal?"

"I'm sure of it. And I think your ma would be proud to know it, too."

Lennox nodded with a satisfied look on his face and leaned back on his pillow. Bass did the same but was planning how he'd handle the arrest of Landon Atwill and Willy Banes. He also wanted to arrest Ron Fox and considered asking the new town marshal for help, just as backup. But then he figured Desi Arguello had enough on his shoulders without asking him to back a U.S. Marshal's play in arresting a known killer outside his jurisdiction, in Mexico. Hell, he'd have trouble explaining his own actions in Mexico as it was.

2:45 p.m. November 1ˢᵗ. 1888
Dr. Lionel Sebring's Office
1400 Block of Jefferson
Laredo, Texas

Horn barged into Doctor Sebring's office in a cold sweat and sick to his stomach from the pain in his ankle.

The woman at the desk was different from the young one he had seen earlier. This one was a whole lot older and cross-lookin''' from the get-go.

"See here, what's the meaning of all this then?"

"Lady, I'm hurt. Are you blind? My damn horse stepped on my foot, and musta broke it as best I can figure. 'Need to see the Doc right away."

"All right, all right, have a seat right over here, please." Horn did as she instructed and set his broom to the side. "Now then, what is your name, please?"

"Tom Burke. Thomas Burke."

"Do you live in Laredo, Mr. Burke?"

"No, I'm just passin through, headin north for work. Where's the Doc...when can I see...?"

"Formalities, Mr. Burke. We need to know whom we are treating."

"Well, geezes, hurry it up, will ya?"

"Let me have a look." The woman bent down and tried to get a look inside Horn's boot, but when she couldn't see anything, she said, "I'm going to have to remove your boot, Mr. Burke, so I can ascertain the nature of your injury."

"Damn, woman, the nature of my injury is it hurts like hell. Don't go tryin' to take off my boot without givin' me somethin for the pain."

The older woman was beginning to look concerned. She saw no blood, but the swelling of the ankle was very apparent from the bulge showing in Horn's boot.

"Wait right here, Mr. Burke. I'll fetch the doctor."

Sweat was pouring off Horn, and drool hung from his lip when Doctor Sebring appeared.

"You've injured your ankle, I hear. Let me have a look." And then he spoke to the older woman. "Get me a number 22 syringe with 10 mg. of morphine sulfate." He injected Horn just above his boot; it was as close as he could get to the wound. "Let's wait a minute or two before we try to remove that boot of yours... Mr. Burke, is it?"

"Yeah, that's right, Doc Tom Burke. Feels better already."

"Alright, let's see about that boot then." Sebring took hold of Horn's left heel and tried slowly and as gently as he could to slide the boot off his foot. As he increased the pressure, Horne began to squirm and then finally cry out from the pain. "Mr. Burke, I'm afraid I'm going to have to cut that boot off. Your foot and ankle are far too swollen to remove it easily."

"God damn. Doc, Just plain damn. Them's fine boots, too. Just had 'em re-soled. Go ahead if ya gotta.'" Sebring turned to the woman again, "Julia, get me the heavy shears from the kitchen, please." In a few moments, Julia was back with a large pair of poultry shears.

"Mr. Burke, brace yourself while I work. I'll try not to hurt you, but the shears may press on the ankle. They did, and Horn screamed in pain and collapsed from the chair, falling to the floor and landing on his side.

"The boot is off, Mr. Burke. I'm going to give you another injection so I can feel the joint itself."

By the time it was over, Horn was as pale as a ghost and only semi-conscious. His left foot was exposed, and he could see it was twice normal size and the color of a beet.

"Mr. Burke, I'm going to get you into that bed over there, and we're going to have to wait for the swelling in your ankle to go down. Julia will keep cool compresses on it tonight, and once it's reduced tomorrow morning, I'll be able to set it in plaster and cement. Your left fibula is broken, Mr. Burke and it has separated from the talus. Setting the ankle is imperative, and I'm afraid a long recovery is the prognosis. Still, the morphine should keep you pain-free for some time. Following that, we can prescribe Laudanum for your pain maintenance." The doctor left Horn's bedside and went to another room to wash up.

When he'd left, Julia stopped by with a pad and pencil, "Mr. Burke? Do you have cash to settle your bill with us? Or will you be needing financial assistance?"

Horn, who was barely conscious, looked at her with half-closed eyes. "Oh, don't you worry. I'll settle up before I leave."

Seventeen

8:30 p.m. November 1ˢᵗ, 1888
Saunders Street at Frost Avenue
Laredo, Texas.

Loretta Rodriguez stood by a gaslight pole outside the Corners Saloon with two other women. They were all dressed provocatively even though the temperature was chilly. Each had applied enough makeup to make them look older or younger, depending on the clientele they hoped to attract.

Loretta was fifteen years old, but with enough face powder and rouge, she appeared older than her real age. One of the women, an older gal the others called Madame Fifi, wore makeup so she'd appear younger than her forty-something age would suggest. She couldn't understand why the younger girls wanted to appear older and often chided them for it. "You don't understand the basic male instinct. He wants his whores to be young and inexperienced. Now, I know none a' you are inexperienced, but hell, they don't wanna know that. And once you get up into your room and their trousers are around their ankles, they won't care how you look. Hell, most of 'em keep their eyes closed anyways. But 'till you get to that point, believe me, they wanna see 'em young and unused."

Loretta and the other younger girls had heard it all before, and they continued to ignore it.

They were sure men wanted painted floozies, and none had been proved wrong yet. None of the girls had ever had any complaint about their makeup.

Bass walked up to the group and said, "Excuse me, ladies, I'm lookin for a gal by the name of Loretta. Don't know her last name, but I'm told she frequents these streets in the evening."

Fifi was first to answer,

"You lookin for some comfort? Gentleman like you don't need to be lookin out here on the street. Why ain't you in one a' the houses, warm by a fire, drinkin' on the house whiskey? 'Could have your pick a' the gals, man that looks like you, honey."

Bass turned to the older woman, who was scantily dressed in feathers and lace on a cold night. Her face paint made it hard for Bass to guess her age. "Well, 'fact is, ma'am, I'm lookin for a particular lady, like I said. Named Loretta."

Fifi subtly motioned to Loretta to keep still. She stepped in front of Loretta, smiled, and asked, "And what's your interest in this gal, then."

Bass had caught the signal from the older woman, but he didn't want to give himself away, so he said, "Oh, no particular reason, ma'am. I was told by a friend she was particularly gracious is all. Good night, ma'am. Good night, ladies." He excused himself and moved on, planning to catch the small dark-haired girl he'd noticed when she was alone later. Bass continued to the next block and ducked into Zeke's Whiskey Saloon. It was small, dark, and seemed quiet enough.

Gately had released him after dinner, and Bass had said that he wanted to go by to see his horse. Gately cautioned him against the long walk and encouraged him to return to his hotel. Bass decided instead, as he was walking, to see if he could find Loretta on Saunders street. He believed he had just found her, though because of the darkness, he really wasn't able to see her features and hoped he'd be able to recognize her again. He sat at a table near the door, leaning sideways so as not to stretch his bandaging under his shirt.

A waitress approached his table, carrying a tray of empty beer glasses, and asked. "' Get ya' anything, chum?"

Bass looked up and smiled,

"Yeah, whiskey...rye if ya' got it, on ice?" The woman winked and walked to the bar. She set the tray down and talked to the bartender, a weasley-looking little guy with slick black hair parted in the middle and a stringy-looking mustache.

The woman turned right around and came back to Bass, setting his dram glass on the table. "Two bits... Ain't got no ice yet. Maybe in another week."

"Don't matter, this'll do. He drank it down a healthy swallow, and when he finished, he noticed the woman had sat down in the chair opposite him.

"Don't make nothin outta' this, mister. Skinny Zeke wants us to be entertainin', and you look safe to me. Just smile every now and again so he'll think I'm doin my job, will ya?"

Bass looked at her more carefully. She wasn't made up heavily like the others, though it looked like she used some powder and color on her cheeks. She had curly blond hair and some eye makeup. She might have been thirty, he thought. "Yeah, sure, no problem. What's your name?"

"Eileen Dempsey."

Bass nodded and tipped his hat.

"That really is my name, you know. Most of the girls use an alias, but I figure at my age? What the hell? What do they call you?"

"Ronnie Fox."

Eileen looked at Bass carefully for a few moments and said, "The hell you are. I know Ronnie Fox, and you ain't even close to a match. Who are you really? Bet you're the law, ain't ya?"

"That's right. I am."

"Alright. What's your name, then?"

"Frank Bass. I'm a U.S. Deputy Marshal from El Paso."

"Oh my, you're a long ways from home, aren't you?"

"Yes, I am, Eileen, but you know, it don't matter. When it comes to catchin' outlaws, I'm the law wherever I happen to be." Eileen looked across the table at Bass and watched his eyes in the dim light of the saloon. Slowly, she began to smile at him.

"Yeah, and I'll bet you're real good at it too. Alright, what do ya wanna' know?"

"Fer starters, why don't you tell me what you know about Ron Fox?"

Eileen leaned back in her chair.

"I can tell you he's a killer. He's mean, prideful, and jealous. And he hates lawmen. Hates 'em all. So. What do ya think about that?"

"He sounds like most of the fellas I run up against. Do you know where he is now?"

"Maybe."

"Maybe?"

"Yeah. He has a girlfriend, streetwalker named Loretta. Might be stayin' with her."

"I just saw Loretta out on the corner. If he's stayin with her, don't figure she'd be out lookin for company to bring home." Again, Eileen smiled. "You're right about that. Any man she brought in would be riskin' his life if Ronnie was there. Well, he's got another one across the Rio, too. He might be with her. Course, then again, he might be in Ol' Monterrey, too, the way he moves around. If he's got money to spend, he's across the river. Girl named Rosamund."

"This girl have a last name?"

"Probably."

Bass grinned.

"How about an address?"

"She works at a place called Las Angeles Cantina. 'Lives in a room up above it. It's on Calle Camargo. Take the Water Street Bridge."

Bass paused and studied Eileen for a moment. Her shoulders had drooped, she stared at the table, and her voice had become softer.

Bass asked,

"Eileen? How is it you know all this about Ron Fox?" She lifted her head, meeting his gaze directly. She straightened up and said matter of factly, "He's my husband."

Bass was silent for a long moment. He lifted his glass, finished his drink, and said,

"I'm sorry for what I have to do."

Eileen smiled slightly, "I know. It was gonna happen sooner or later. 'Truth is when I heard that he shot that marshall, I should have come forward then. But I didn't."

Bass nodded and said, "I understand. He won't know it was you told me."

Eileen looked again into Bass's eyes. "Thank you, Marshal... Don't kill him."

"Well, that'll be up to him. But I promise I'll give him a chance."

Bass stood and left Eileen sitting alone at the table, staring at the darkness through the window. He walked through the doorway and into the night. It had started to rain, and that made the night air chillier. He checked his Elgin, nearly 9:00 p.m. He had about a half-hour walk back across Zacate Creek to Washington Street and the Arbuckle Hotel. He hadn't stayed there in two nights and knew he'd owe the clerk as soon as he walked in. He'd already paid Doc Gately thirty dollars in bills, which covered both his and Emma's care. He still owed Arguello's Livery for Emma's stall and feed, and all he had in his pocket was whiskey change and a ten-dollar gold piece. He needed to send telegrams tomorrow, too, so the only thing for him to do was stop at a bank in the morning before crossing the Rio for Bloody Ron Fox.

9:15 a.m. November 2nd, 1888
Texas Cattlemen's Exchange Bank
1200 Victoria Avenue
Laredo, Texas.

The clerk had just raised the shades and unlocked the front door to the Cattlemen's Exchange when Bass appeared in the doorway. The clerk scampered quickly from the lobby to his window behind the counter, and he opened the small doors that closed the teller's cage.

"Good morning, sir. What can I do for you?"

"I need to draw on my account in El Paso. I'd like a hundred dollars cash, please, in coin and paper."

"Certainly. I'll need to get the manager's approval for that sum. Please wait here."

Bass had removed his checkbook and Marshal's Service I.D. card in advance, knowing that proof of his person would be required. The manager was a well-groomed gentleman of average height and build, somewhere in his early forties, Bass gauged. He wore a tweed suit with a cellulose collar and bow tie.

"Yes sir, my name is Reginald Banks, and you are..." Banks picked up Bass's I.D. card and read it aloud, "United States Marshal Francis F. Bass. Yes?"

"Deputy Marshal, actually. And as I already explained, I need to draw on my account in El Paso a hundred bucks to continue my stay in Laredo."

"Of course, sir. Can I ask you to make your draft payable to this branch? I can have funds for you later today."

"Why later today?"

"On large amounts, I have to get authorization from the issuing branch. Company policy, Marshal."

"I was hopin' to send telegraphs to my family this mornin'. Unfortunately, I ain't got enough in my pockets to da that. 'Hopin' to get money right away so's I could."

"I understand. Perhaps we can advance twenty dollars or so? Against your withdrawal?"

"That'd be most kind. I 'preciate it, Mr. Banks. 'Bet you get kidded 'bout your name all the time, don't you?"

"I'm sorry. Why is that?"

"Well, your last name is Banks...you work in a bank."

"Yes." Banks didn't look up from counting out Bass's twenty dollars.

"Don't you see? Banks? Works in a bank? Don't see many stable owners named Livery nor whores named Hooker, do ya?"

"I really wouldn't know. How many marshals are named Marshal?"

Bass realized he was being played and started to chuckle. "You got me good there, Reginald. Very good."

Now Banks was grinning, too, and he said, "Thank you, Frank. Come back after lunch. We should have your money by then."

Bass's next stop was the post office on San Dario Street to send telegrams first to Sally and then to Bart Mariany. He was still afoot, and unlike some other towns, there was no trolley or coach service in Laredo. The walk would be about six blocks to Matamoros and then two north on San Dario. He figured it would take near to thirty minutes to get there, another fifteen to send the messages, and then another thirty minutes to get to Arguello's Livery Barn, where he'd saddle Emma and cross the bridge into Nuevo Laredo.

It was 10:30 a. m. when he reached the post Office. His message to Sally, which he composed on his walk over, was simple,

My Lady Loves

'Making progress. Some trouble, nothing serious. Sorry for delay in wiring but all is well. 'Will need several more days. Wire when you can.

Love Frederick

He sent this to the ranch as a special delivery. Next, he sent to Bart Mariany.

Bart-

Horn is here. He missed on several tries. Will deal with him. Check for friends in Laredo. Advise Frank

This one he sent as standard delivery because he knew the telegraph office was within a short walk of the sheriff's office. He paid four dollars and fifty cents for both and headed out to Arguello's Livery on Eagle Pass Road.

11:10 a.m. November 2nd, 1888
Arguello's Blacksmith and Wheelwright Shop
Eagle Pass Road
Laredo, Texas

The weather had become cloudy, and the sky to the west over the Rio was ominous and dark gray. The breeze had picked up, too, and Bass could smell the storm, calculating that, by the afternoon, Laredo would see some heavy rain. The streets had only just dried out from the previous storm, and Bass swore to himself at the poor weather. It would make arresting Ronnie Fox that much more difficult. He was tempted to put the action off until the rain passed, but he discarded that notion when he considered the likelihood that Fox's wife might tip him off. He also considered asking town marshal Des Arguello for help, but since Bass had to cross the Rio to take Fox, Arguello's jurisdiction would be lost. Bass didn't want to give Fox a legal loophole of any kind that might keep him from the gallows.

When he got to the Livery, he asked after Emma and was told she was doing well and was in the corral. He went outside and stood near the doorway. As soon as she saw him, she walked over to him and nuzzled his neck and cheek. He took her cheek straps in his hands and placed his forehead against hers. As tall as she was, he just barely reached. He talked softly to her, breathing into her nostrils, and then gave her an apple he'd taken from Doc Gateley's. He stood to her side so she could see him fully and then walked to her rump to check her wound. The bandage was off, and her stitches were in place. The wound was dry and starting to scab.

He walked her into the barn intending to saddle her when an older man, well-muscled, balding, and in coveralls, stepped over to him. "You must be that marshal, huh?"

"That's right. She looks just fine, just fine indeed. What do I owe you?"

"Well, I'd guess it to be two dollars. She weren't no trouble. Even though you could tell she was hurtin.'"

Bass dug into his pockets and handed over three dollar bills.

"The extra's for watching over her."

"No need. Was you planning on ridin' her out today?"

"Well yeah, she seems in good shape, 'wound's startin to heal."

"Yeah, that's true, but I'd leave her be for another couple days, marshal. Horses, all animals, really, don't understand pain the way we do. They don't know it means somethin's wrong, only that they're uncomfortable. Puttin up a saddle and ridin' her would likely stretch and maybe pop them stitches. She'd feel it but wouldn't get balky. Open her up to infection all over again. If you need a horse, take one of ours. They're all sound a dollar. 'Course, not nearly so tall. Leave her here, marshal. Let her heal up and hair over 'fore you take her out."

Bass looked at the older man with appreciation. "Can I ask what your name is?"

"Sure, it's Raymond Wilke."

"Well, Raymond, you ought to run for office. Your power of persuasion would make you a shoo-in."

"I thank you for the kind words. But the folks of our district are all Democrats, you see. Now, I know they can't help themselves for it; most were born into it, but I'm Republican, and ever'body knows it. 'Wouldn't stand a snowball's chance in hell. C'mon, let's get you a horse."

Eighteen

12:15 p.m. November 2ⁿᵈ, 1888
Departamento de Policia
Avenida Galeana
Nuevo Laredo, Mexico

Bass knew that before trying to make an arrest in Nuevo Laredo, which was, after all, a foreign country, the prudent thing to do, the proper thing to do, would be to advise the local authority of his intentions. He had made arrests before in Ciudad Juarez and also one or two in Ojinaga, and in each instance, he followed protocol by advising the locals of his intentions. Consequently, his authority to make the arrest in Mexico was never questioned.

The Jefe de Policiá in Nuevo Laredo was a man by the name of José Benitez de Arriaga, and according to Desi Arguello, he was a stickler for tradition and commanded his men with an iron hand. The Departamento de Policia was across from the Plaza Hidalgo on Avenida Galeana.

Bass tied off his horse in front of the building, an impressive brick and adobe construction that stood in stark contrast to the humble, pale adobes of the neighborhood. Inside, he identified himself to a desk clerk in civilian clothes and asked to see the Chief. He was ushered immediately into the office of the Chief of Police.

"Yes, señor Deputy Bass, what can I do for you?" Jose de Arriaga was a portly man an inch or two taller than Bass, and he presented quite an impressive figure in his elaborate uniform. He rose to shake Bass's hand and smiled as he bid him to sit.

"Jefe, I am here to arrest a desperado from the United States. His name is Ron Fox, and I have traced him to a cantina on Calle Camarga. I am here to respect your office and advise you of my intent."

The Chief smiled again and asked,

"And what, may I ask, is the crime of this gringo, señor Deputy?"

"Murder, Jefe. Of another U.S. Deputy Marshal."

"Then I see. You have much reason to catch this gringo. However, I cannot allow it."

Bass sat up straight and scowled at the police chief. "Cannot allow it? I don't understand?"

"You see, we have received a, how is it called, communicate from our Comando Militar not to allow our borders to be crossed by foreign officials without ah, previa ah, previous authorizes. So I am afraid I cannot help you, señor marshal."

"Chief, that's ridiculous. I have always respected your borders, sir, but this man is an American hiding here. Are you gonna enable him to thumb his nose at our justice?"

De Arriaga maintained his composure and nodded as Bass spoke. "Senor, I have advised you of my restrictions, so I must ask you to leave. However, may I also ask that, as a guest in our city, you visit one of our charming cantinas? Of course, should you find another Americano to accompany you back across the Rìo Bravo, how could we possibly object? We are good neighbors, after all." Bass relaxed his posture and grinned knowingly at the Jefe.

"Thank you, Jefe de Arriaga. I believe I'll take you up on your invitation." Bass stood and shook the Chief's hand before leaving the building and riding to Calle Camarga.

1:00 p.m. November 2nd, 1888
Las Angels Cantina
Calle Camarga
Nuevo Laredo, Mexico

Bass tied off the gelding he'd gotten from Ray Wilke in front of the cantina that Eileen had told him about. He removed his Winchester '86 rifle from the sheath and fed five Sharps .45-90 cartridges into the tube magazine. The next thing he did before going inside was to walk around the two-story adobe building to check for windows and other exits. There was a back door on the rear alley, but he was surprised to see there were only two windows, one on each side of the first floor and none on the back on either floor. This meant that the only exit for a fleeing outlaw would be on the first floor, and the most likely exit would be the back door. Since he didn't have a deputy, he carried two large garbage bins to block the back door. They were heavy enough that Fox would have difficulty opening the door, and that might slow him down enough for Bass to make an arrest. Once that was finished, he looked about at the surroundings, picked up his Winchester, and went back to the front door.

The Las Angeles Cantina was larger than most of the other saloons in Laredo. It had a long polished oak bar, with a fair-sized dining room attached on the right side of the building as you entered. To the left was a dance floor with a small bandstand, and the gambling hall was connected to the dance floor by a double door that was probably never closed. The second-floor rooms were accessed by a staircase next to the bar, and the doors to the three rooms all opened onto the balcony above the bar.

There were serving girls shuffling back and forth between the dining area, gambling hall, and the kitchen, which Bass assumed was somewhere in the rear behind the bar. The atmosphere was different from most saloons he'd patronized. The lamps were turned up bright, and the walls and furnishings were all gayly colored. The smoke and music didn't seem to be a distraction at all; in fact, the entire place felt like a party was going on.

Bass walked to the bar and set his rifle on the floor, leaning against the bar. A heavyset Mexican fellow in dark trousers and a bright green and white shirt asked, "Què serà, señor?" Bass rubbed his chin as he looked around and said, "Whiskey, por favor." The man left and returned in a moment or two with a dram glass and began slowly pouring. As he did, he asked Bass, "Di cuàndo." Bass waited until there looked to be about three fingers of color in the glass and said, "Bien, gracias. Do you speak English, señor?" The bartender smiled and said, "Sì, un poco,...ah,..a small bit."

"Good, good. I want to find a girl named Rosamund. Do you know her?"

The bartender's expression suddenly turned sour, and he said, "No...no, No, la conozco. Bebe y vete, por favor!"

Bass frowned at the man. "Leave? I just got here."

The bartender walked quickly to the opposite end of the bar and talked with another man dressed similarly. They both looked at Bass, and the new fellow sauntered down to Bass's end of the bar and said, "We want no issues here, gringo. The ah...the girl you ask for is ah.. she is taken. So now you will leave. Yes?"

Bass took a swallow of whatever they call whiskey in Mexico and set his glass down. He looked at the new man and said, "No. I will not leave, señor. I am the law, La ley, ¿comprende? And I really don't want the woman; I want the man she's with. Now, amigo, you tell me, dìga me... donde està?" Bass emphasized his point by opening his coat and revealing both his marshal's badge and his Colt.

"Please señor, no hagas problemas. Don't make trouble in my cantina. He is upstairs in the room of the girl."

"What's your name, hombre? ¿Te llamas?"

"Federico, Maria de Santa Louisa de Cuernavaca."

"Federico, that's Frederick. That's a good name. I like it. Now, here's what's gonna happen, Federico. Which a those rooms is he in?"

"Segundo."

"All right. I want you to go up there and knock on his door. Tell him there's a woman here named Loretta. Got that?"

"Loretta, sì."

"Good. Now, as soon as you say that I want you to hightail it back on downstairs, maybe wait outside. Got it?"

"Sí señor. Outside."

Bass watched as the man walked slowly to the stairway alongside the bar. As he did, Bass withdrew his Colt pistol, checked the rounds in the cylinder, and laid it on the bar in front of him. Then he picked up his Winchester, levered a shell into the chamber, and aimed at the second door on the balcony. The people nearby, who couldn't help but hear and now see the marshal taking action, started to leave the building, not panicking but in a quick step. The idea seemed to spread around the room pretty quickly because everything in the cantina became quiet.

Federico did as he was told. He knocked loudly on the door and said in as firm a voice as he could, "Hola, señor. Una mujer llamada Loretta está aquí."

Bass could hear a male voice in the room call out something, but Federico was already halfway down the stairs. Bass heard movement in the room, and then the door flew open. Bloody Ron Fox was pulling up his suspenders with his left hand and holding his pistol with his right.

"Loretta?! You here? What the...?"

He noticed the man standing at the bar thirty feet away, pointing a rifle at him. Bass answered, "Federal Marshal, Fox. Drop your weapon. You're under arrest!" Fox looked confused at what was happening and staggered in the hallway. It occurred to Bass that the outlaw may have been sleeping off a drunk.

Fox finally seemed to grasp the situation and called out, "You son of a bitch!" He raised his pistol, and Bass pulled the trigger on his Winchester. The bullet tore through Fox's right shoulder, shattering bone and sending his pistol flying. It discharged harmlessly when it hit the floor, but the additional gunshot added to the confusion.

Blue smoke hung over the bar as Bass picked up his pistol and walked up the stairs. When he got to the top and could see that Fox was incapacitated, he called to the group below to fetch a doctor. He knelt at Fox's side and said, "Take it easy, you're gonna be alright.

'Doctor'll be here in just a minute. He could smell the tequila on the man and thought it might keep him from shock. Bass pushed his bandanna into the hole in Fox's shoulder and staunched the bleeding.

Fox was mumbling incoherently most of the time they waited, but he finally asked.

"Who the hell are you to shoot me from ambush? Like a coward from ambush."

"Twern't no ambush a'tall Fox, an' you're under arrest for the murder of Deputy Marshal Harold Gosling."

"Gos...? Oh yeah, him. 'Got him good... He went down real quick, no good law.." Fox passed out before finishing his sentence, and the doctor, a black man, was just coming up the stairs.

Bass asked him. "You speak any English, Doc?"

"Yes, of course I do. What happened here?"

"My name is Frank Bass; I'm a federal marshal. 'Came to arrest Ron Fox here for murder. He raised his gun, and I shot him."

The doctor was doing a quick examination as he listened.

"Well, he's gonna have pain whenever he moves his right arm again. 'Clavicle's busted off the Acromion just above the joint, but he'll survive, alright. 'Feels like a clean break, but the muscles and tendons won't heal, 'arm'll never be right again. 'Lost some blood, too. 'Smells like it was mostly Tequila in his veins anyway. We have a hospital here in town. I'll take him there tonight. I'd guess you can have him in three or four days."

Bass nodded. "What's your name Doc?"

"Timothy Watkins. I have an office on Calle Reynosa. I can take him there, keep him sedated, and move him to the hospital tomorrow. Ah, Doc? I got a little problem with the local authorities, so I'd rather he wasn't taken to a hospital. Can I come for him tomorrow and take him to a doctor I know in Laredo?"

"Yes, I understand, Marshal. I'll wait for you. Shouldn't be a problem once I stop his bleeding." The doctor then turned his attention to Fox. He set his right arm in temporary splints and then wrapped the splints, with heavy tape, to the man's body.

As he was preparing to leave, Bass asked. "Say, Doc, mind if I ask why you don't work across the river in Laredo? You sound like you're American."

"Oh, I am, I am. And when I came to south Texas I tried to establish myself in Laredo. But the good people of the community made it clear that they didn't want to be treated by a doctor of color."

Bass didn't know exactly what to say, so he shook his head and said, "At's a damn shame. Folks always need a good doc."

"Hey, the people of Nuevo have treated me very well. I have no complaints. And I'm needed here as much as anywhere. Just for my records, who did this fella murder?"

"A Deputy U.S. Marshal named Harold Gosling. Last month."

The doctor thought for a moment and said. "Don't worry 'bout your man. I'll watch him for you."

Bass waited as Doc Watkins helped two men load the unconscious body of Ron Fox into a wagon and leave. He turned back around to the bar and ordered another whiskey from Federico.

"Wanna thank you for your help, Federico. That was a brave thing you did." Federico poured himself a drink and toasted Bass. "To the law." He said as he raised his glass.

Bass watched him and answered. "To the people."

Bass walked back outside, moving through a small crowd of people that had gathered. As he was sliding his Winchester back into its scabbard, he heard a woman's voice from behind.

Margaretta Perez was standing with her pad and pencil not five feet away.

"So Marshal Bass. It seems you've found your man. Can you tell me who he was?"

"Sure. This for your paper?"

"Yes, it is."

"Then I'll be true to my word. I found out from Cherry Lennox that the man that shot Marshal Gosling was, in fact, the man they just took away. Bloody Ron Fox is his name, and he was one of the men who stole the cattle I mentioned last time." Margaretta Perez was jotting in her pad.

"And is the man you just shot dead?"

"Dead? No, but he's gonna be real sore in the morning."

"And you're sure that you got the right man, Marshal?"

"What? Yes. Yes, of course."

"And what makes you so sure? Is it possible that this Lennox man may have led you astray, suggesting that another man committed the shooting?"

"Say, that's an interesting suggestion. I suppose it might be possible if Ron Fox hadn't confessed to me as I stopped his wound from bleeding him to death."

"So he told you he shot Marshal Gosling?"

"Yes, he did, and I'll be questioning him further as he recovers."

"That sounds like an excellent idea, Marshal. I hope once again you'll give me the story as it unfolds."

"Well, 'don't know that I can do it just for you alone, but I'll see to it that you know what happens. Now, excuse me, I'd like to return to my hotel." Margaretta Perez bowed slightly, and Bass climbed onto the bay gelding and tapped his heels in the animal's ribs.

He rode back across the Convent Street Bridge and continued up to Matamoros, where he turned right. At Victoria Street, he stopped at the Texas Cattlemen's Exchange Bank, where Mr. Banks was waiting with his cash.

He thanked the manager and stopped at the door. He turned and said, "You know, I don't know how many Marshals are named marshal. But I bet there's a lot of blacksmiths named Smith."

Banks smiled, and just before Bass walked through the door, the manager called out, "Not half as many cooks that are named Cook." Bass kept walking but waved as he got onto his horse.

4:30 p.m. November 2nd, 1888

Bass's next stop for the day was Doc Gately's. He wanted to arrange for the Doc to take on another patient, specifically Ron Fox.

"Uh-huh. So how bad off is this fella?"

"Shot through the right shoulder. The doctor over there said he'd be alright to move once he got the bleeding stopped. He was going to take him to his office. He said something about Fox's clavicle. That's all I remember."

"Tell me, what's the doctor's name? Was it a black fella named Watkins?"

"Yeah, that's right. You know him?"

"Yeah, I know him. Damn fine young man. Pretty good doctor, too. The 'good' people of Laredo didn't want a colored doctor workin' on 'em. Damn shame. Alright, I'll send someone over to fetch him. 'Make sure he's in shackles."

"That's fine, thanks, Doc.

Bass rode back to Matamoros Street and turned left when he got to Washington. When he got to the Arbuckle Hotel, he turned up the alley to the stable behind the hotel and took care putting the borrowed horse away for the rest of the day. He planned to have dinner at the hotel and retire early, perhaps read a newspaper or magazine. He went first to the front desk to pay his bill and collect the three wires that were waiting for him. Two were from Sally, and he read them first. Both started by saying everything was fine and then spoke of the advances Lil had made. He read the latest one first.

Frederick, she's a chatterbox. it's mostly gibberish but Im sure she said Da da. she also pulled herself up to standing next

*to your chair. I fear she'll be walking soon and we'll have no
rest.*

Love your girls.

The first wire mentioned Silas Pratt and concrete. Evidently, it
was... *not curing well. Weather too cold. will angel and willy be all right
for the winter?* He decided to wait until tomorrow to respond since
there didn't seem to be anything urgent. He was sorry to miss the
advances that Lil was making and decided when he got back, he'd
hire a photographer to take pictures of all of them so they'd have
a pictorial history of her growing up. The last wire was from Bart.
Bass had asked him to look into any friends that Horn might have in
Laredo. Bart's message only mentioned one.

...Landon Atwill.

Nineteen

7:30 p.m. November 2nd, 1888
Dr. Lionel Sebring's Office
1400 Block of Jefferson
Laredo, Texas

Horn's last morphine injection was nearly four hours ago, and his ankle was hurting terribly. He had a low-grade fever and a bad case of the sweats. His bedclothes were soaked, and Sebring's assistant was leaving for dinner.

"I won't be gone long, Mr. Burke, 'just want to get some dinner. The night nurse will be in from 10:00 p.m. 'till 6:00 a.m."

"Aaarghhh! For the love of God, woman! I'm hurtin real bad here. Can you give me another morphine shot 'fore you go? It's been a long time."

"No, I can't do that. Only the Doctor can administer morphine. It's one of his rules." The woman did take pity on her patient, though she could see he was in a bad way. "I can give you laudanum for your pain. It's not as effective as the morphine injection, but it has an opium base and will help with your pain. It may also help you to sleep too. I'll fetch a pint for you."

The woman handed the bottle over and instructed Horn on how much to take. He was very familiar with the drug as he'd used it extensively after his gunshot wound from Bass in Denver. He had spent an extra seven days in the hospital, leeching the drug craving from his system. Now, he had no choice. It was either suffer the agony of his splintered ankle or dive again into the bottle of laudanum head first. As soon as the woman was out the door, he pulled the cork and swallowed nearly half the bottle. In minutes, the tincture of opium mixed with alcohol had him limp and hallucinating. He no longer felt anything, let alone pain from a broken ankle. He was still perspiring, but he didn't care. After fifteen minutes, he fell into a deep sleep, his arms twitching and his breathing sporadic.

5:30 a.m. November 3rd, 1888
Dr. Lionel Sebring's Office
1400 Block of Jefferson
Laredo, Texas

"Mr. Burke! Mr. Burke, wake up! Mr. Burke, wake up, please!" The morning assistant just happened to come in early this morning and, as usual, checked in with the night watchman sitting at the desk in the front office. He had said that all was quiet and that their one in-house patient had slept through the night. Ordinarily, this would be a good report, but as soon as she saw the nearly empty pint bottle of laudanum on the floor next to his bed, she began trying to wake him. She knew he had taken too much during the ten-hour period since Dorothy, the other nurse/assistant, left for the evening. She intended to lecture the younger woman about dispensing laudanum to unsupervised patients.

As she was wiping his face with a cold cloth, Doctor Sebring arrived. He was in early as well, but since he had a patient in his office, he had decided to come in early.

"Julia, what's going on?"

"Laudanum doctor, I believe he may have taken too much."

"Good Lord, how did he get it?"

"I believe Dorothy may have given it to him before she left last night."

"I see. Well, she's young and probably hasn't had experience with the drug in the past. I'll talk to her. How is his pulse?"

"55 but regular."

"And his breathing?"

"Shallow and irregular. Do you want to start the zinc treatment?"

"No, I don't think so. If this was a chronic case, maybe, but let's see how he is when he comes around. I want you to continue to monitor him, Julia, and if his breathing doesn't stabilize or his pulse drops, let me know right away."

Doctor Sebring left for his office upstairs as Julia continued to the cold compresses. After nearly half an hour, she heard Tom Burke stir and went to his bedside.

"Do I know you?"

"I was here when you came in, Mr. Burke. My name is Julia. I work with Doctor Sebring."

Horn was still very woozy from the drug and responded slowly in a weakened voice.

"Oh...yeah. I remember. My damn ankle."

"That's right, Mr. Burke, your left ankle is broken."

"Mr. who? Burke?"

"Yes, that's your name, isn't it?" Horn closed his eyes tightly, trying to remember the particulars of yesterday. "Yes, I'm sorry. Yes, my name."

Julia looked concerned now. It had happened more than once in Laredo that men on the dodge used aliases to get medical treatment.

She said, "You just rest easy, now. I'm going to tell the Doctor that you're awake." Horn closed his eyes and tried to remain very still. It seemed the less he moved any part of his body, the less pain he experienced. He closed his eyes and cursed his luck again for having missed his chance at Bass.

Memories came flooding back to him, the shooting on the train as he lay exposed in the undercarriage, trying to avoid detection. The pain as he rolled out of his hiding place as the train slowed at a station and then running across the railroad yard in excruciating, seeking out poor old Doc Weatherby. He remembered leaving the doc's clinic to get to Bass, riding through the rain back to the train, only to be seen by Bass and then recognizing him and falling from his horse as he succumbed to the pain. He remembered seeing Bass through the rain and blurred vision and firing his pistol while lying on the ground... and that's when his memory stopped.

When he opened his eyes, he was surprised to see Doctor Sebring standing at his bed, calling his name just as that girl had done.

"Well, Mr. Burke, it is Tom Burke, isn't it?"

"Yeah, Doc, it is. What do we do about my ankle today?"

"This morning, when I came in, you were in a laudanum-induced sleep and nearly lapsed into coma. Have you had experience with laudanum before, Mr. Burke?"

"Ah, no, Doc, I haven't."

"Laudanum is an opium-based tincture mixed with alcohol that doctors relied on heavily during the war, along with morphine and heroin. These drugs are very powerful painkillers and, when taken to excess, can cause brain damage and even death. I want you to be aware of the dangers of the drug in the future. I'll likely be prescribing it initially to control pain, but once the joint begins to heal, lesser pain remedies will be used.

"Uh, okay, Doc, whatever you say. You're the boss. So what are you going to do today?"

"I'm going to attempt to set the joint in a heavy plaster and cement cast. But first, I have to manipulate the ankle to its natural position. As I told you yesterday, the ligaments of the joint will not heal correctly; you may very well lose the function of the joint and require a cane for mobility. Never the less, it's the best I can do. Now Julia has prepared the plaster, so I'm going to give you a morphine injection at the site. I must warn you that you'll still feel some pain, but it should be tolerable. Once the plaster is on, I intend to layer on a cement coating, which will allow you to walk on the ankle in the future months.

The cast will need to be in place for at least six months. During that time, the skin and muscles around the area will atrophy. Once the cast is removed, your lower leg will take some time to strengthen. This part of the recovery is normal for all fracture victims who must suffer a cast for a prolonged time. Do you have any questions, Mr. Burke?"

"No, Doc, let her rip."

"Very well."

The doctor injected the morphine and manipulated the ankle just as he said he would. Horn cried out on two occasions, and finally, the doctor gave him a little more morphine. When the process was finished, it was just after 10:00 a.m., and Horn's left foot was coated with a heavy white cast that exposed his toes. The left ankle was slightly elevated in a kind of sling above his bed, and he felt completely immobilized. As he lay on his back, still perspiring from the pain, he called to Doc Sebring.

"Yes, Mr. Burke. Are you feeling alright?"

"Oh, yeah, Doc, I feel pretty good. I was just wondering if you might know how I can reach a friend of mine. I've worked for him before, and I thought I might come down here again to see if he needs any day workers."

"Well, I'll see that he gets the message if I can; what's his name?"

"Landon Atwill. I believe he has a ranch northwest of town."

"Ah, good."

Thanks. Say, tell me, doctor, when will I be able to get outta here? I'm gonna have to take a different job now."

"Oh, I think another two days will do. The plaster hasn't even set yet. Once that's done, baring complications, you should be mobile in two days, three at the outside."

"Alright, thanks, Doc. Any chance I could get a newspaper or magazine to read?"

"I think so. I'll ask Julia to pick something up for you when she goes to lunch. For now, just try to lie still."

"Got it." The doctor left and went upstairs to his office.

From his bed, Horn could see the activity out on the street, people coming and going, wagons laden with goods or supplies. He kept hoping he'd see Bass walk past the window, not knowing the man planning his demise was only a few feet away. He enjoyed the notion of hiding in plain sight. It added a bit of a kick to the mundane days he had ahead of him.

Before she left for lunch, Julia stopped by to say she was leaving and ask what type of magazine he preferred." "Oh, crime mysteries are my favorite, but anything about Texas will be fine."

"I'll see what I can find. I do want to remind you of payment for our service, Mr. Burke. Setting and casting your ankle will cost fifty dollars, and then, of course, there's room, board, and medications. The total will be over a hundred dollars. I just want to make sure you understand in advance."

"Oh, I know the bills do add up, and it won't be easy, but I'll settle everything before I go. Thanks for all your concern."

Julia smiled at her patient and left for lunch. Horn lay back and thought about raping her before he killed her.

1:15 p.m. November 3rd, 1888
Arbuckle Hotel,
Washington Street
Laredo, Texas

Bass had paid a call to Doc Gately at nine that morning to check on his new patient. Ron Fox was faring well, considering he'd consumed a near-fatal amount of tequila before being shot through his right shoulder. He still hadn't come around when Bass was there, but Doc Gately was certain he'd be awake later today, though he wouldn't have his wits about him for at least the rest of the day.

Gately had taken the opportunity of Fox's drunkenness to clean and stitch his wound and then bandage it when he arrived last evening. Bass asked that Cherry Lennox and Ron Fox remain housed in separate rooms so they might not have the ability to conspire. Consequently, Lennox remained downstairs, and Fox was housed upstairs, shackled to his bed, on the women's floor.

Bass had come back to his hotel because it was time to pay another visit to the Tierra Blanca, and he wanted the supplies and equipment in his saddlebags to do that. Now that he knew Tom Horn was a friend of Landon Atwill's, he wanted to see if Horn was at Tierra Blanca specifically. Perhaps he was using that as his safe haven for ambushing United States Marshals. It wasn't far from there that Horn had wounded Emma and himself, so the notion made sense.

He also wanted to see Willy Banes one on one, without the intimidating presence of Landon Atwill, and he really had no idea how to do that. He didn't know where on the ranch Banes was housed and didn't, in fact, have any idea as to the layout of ranch buildings other than what he'd seen for himself days earlier. He could assume Banes slept somewhere in the bunkhouse, but probably not with the regular hands.

So he decided to find cover and observe, through his field glass, the comings and goings of the people there over the course of several hours. It might tell him something, or it might be a waste of time. Maybe he'd have to make his observations several times over the next few days. He did know that if Tierra Blanca ran at all like his own spread, then certain things would be done at certain times. It was the nature of running a cattle business. In any event, he needed his canteen, field glass, saddlebags, and he wanted his Walker Colts.

The slope and cover that he traveled down from the San Ygnacio Creek Bridge would provide plenty of protection from anyone observing him. The rain that had fallen the previous evening had given way to bright sunshine and a pleasantly cool temperature. The good weather meant there would be activity at the ranch, and the sooner he got there, the better.

His route to the bridge would be more direct this time. He'd already established the path the stolen cattle had used, so he followed the quickest route to the bridge. He road north on San Francisco Street to a point about nine miles north of town where it intersected Creek Road. From there, he crossed the San Ygnacio Creek Bridge and followed the same cattle path he had used four days earlier. He rode about three miles northwest along that path until he came to the same rise where he first saw the gate to Tierra Blanca. He tied off his horse in a stand of scrub and black oak and made his way a little further down to a rock outcropping that would give him good advantage.

He estimated his distance from the house to be about two hundred thirty or forty yards. His glass, a John Browning binocular, was powerful enough that he could almost make out the faces of the men moving about the yard. He spotted the long, low building with multiple chimneys that he identified as the bunkhouse. He could make out two entrances and thought the second might be a separate room for the foreman. His guess was confirmed when he spotted a man who looked very much like Banes leaving through that door.

He noted two barns, one obviously by its construction was a hay barn. This told him that since there were few animals visible on the ranch, hay might be transported to other graze or rangeland not nearby. The second barn was a stable. There was an adjoining corral that held perhaps ten or twelve horses, a rather small remuda for a large ranch. Other horses might be penned elsewhere. He noted two bulls in large pen\paddocks off the corral. One was obviously longhorn, but he had to look at the other twice. From a distance, he could make out all the characteristics of a Brahman Bull. He'd only seen a handful in his life and never at beef cattle ranches in the state of Texas. He began to search his memory for breeding attributes, but since no one he knew had ever bred Brahman, he didn't know what to think. He decided to let it go and ask around town about breeding or crossbreeding Brahmans.

He stayed for another three hours and followed the activities of hands around the barn, the pumphouse, the bunkhouse, and the latrines. After all that time, he never once spotted Horn or Atwill or any particular movement about the house. He was convinced that Willy Banes's room was the second door in the bunkhouse, and he planned to pay Willy a visit tomorrow evening. By 5:30 p.m., Bass was ready to call it a day. The sun was low, casting long shadows from the west when he untied the gelding and climbed aboard for the ride back to his hotel. He'd skipped lunch to spend time at Doc Gately's and then wanted to get his observation of the Tierra Blanca underway quickly. Right now, he needed a hot bath and a good meal. The ride would take forty-five minutes anyway, so he reached into his saddlebag for the pint of rye he always kept there.

Twenty

6:15 a.m. November 4th., 1888
Dr. Lionel Sebring's Office
1400 Block of Jefferson
Laredo, Texas

Horn was standing on his own when Dorothy came down from upstairs. The assistant nurse, Dorothy, had stayed the night so the night watchman could be home with his family. She also needed the extra money. Horn decided everything was in his favor, and it was time.

"Mr. Burke! You shouldn't be testing yourself yet. That cast has only just set. My lord, aren't you in pain?"

"Yeah, maybe a little. But I can't spend another day in here laid out like a cripple. I got things to do that can't wait no more. So here's what you're gonna do. You're gonna open that cabinet and give me a bunch a them morphine needles right now."

"I will not, Mr. Burke, and I plan to tell the Doctor what you've just said as soon as he comes in. Now, you lie back down in that bed this instant." She was acting as assertively as she could, trying to make the man obey her command, but she made the mistake of approaching the bed and getting too close to Horn, and it cost her life. Horn reached out and grabbed her around the throat, dragging her down to the floor behind his bed so they wouldn't be seen from the window. She tried to scream, but he'd crushed her larynx, and her kicking and flailing about with her arms stopped as her oxygen ceased. The young woman was dead within minutes.

Horn was in more pain than he expected, and wrestling the girl to the floor and crushing her windpipe took more energy than he thought it would. He couldn't stop to rest, though, because he knew the older woman would be here in an hour or so, and then the doc himself would arrive. He'd need a weapon of some kind if he had to deal with them, and he wouldn't be spry enough to deal with both at once. He could use his gun, but the sound would give him away. And he certainly couldn't outrun any lawman. He felt the odds would be against taking both of them out.

His next thought was the medicine cabinet. He knew it was locked, and he also knew the young girl didn't have the key. She could only give him the laudanum bottle from the shelf with the others. He grabbed a canvas sack that held bandaging and tape and put four bottles of the drug into it. He still wanted the morphine and decided he'd risk breaking open the cabinet to get at it. There might be some noise, but he thought it would be worth the chance. At first, he used a steel surgical tool to try to pry the cabinet door open, but the tool bent rather easily as he applied pressure. He didn't have much time, so he covered his hand with a thick towel and broke the glass case open. In the stillness of the early morning, the shattering of the glass was deafening. He found several small vials marked Morphine Sulphate and grabbed a steel and glass syringe and several of the screw-in needles with a portable kit as well. He'd seen the doctor give him the shots often enough and felt sure he could do it himself. Finally, he hobbled to the closet for the rest of his clothing and his pistol belt. He snatched a cane from beside the door and was out of the building and around the corner on Jefferson Street before the sun peeked over the eastern horizon.

7:15 a.m. November 4th., 1888
Arbuckle Hotel,
Washington Street
Laredo, Texas

Bass was up as soon as sunlight split the curtains of his hotel window. He rolled from the bed, feeling ready for a new day. Last night, when he returned, he'd eaten well, had a relaxing soak in a hot bath, and smoked a cigar as he read the latest on the arrest of Ron Fox in Nuevo Laredo. He was glad to see that Miss Perez hadn't mentioned his name but rather had credited the new Town Marshal

Desmond Arguello for the arrest. She did mention that Fox was wounded and treated by a Doctor Watkins in Nuevo Laredo.

Today, after his coffee, he'd check on both his prisoners with the doc and then head out for another day of watching the activity at the Tierra Blanca Ranch from his hillside perch. He went down to the dining room for coffee and then out back to saddle the rented gelding for his ride to Doc Gately's.

The doctor was not available, but Martha was in and was just coming downstairs from reassuring the two women staying in the clinic that they shouldn't be so touchy that a sedated man might see them doing their necessaries.

"I had to hang a sheet between the beds to satisfy their modesty. Now, Mr. Bass, what can I do for you?"

"Ma'am, I just stopped by to see how Cherry Lennox and Ron Fox was doin? 'Need to ask Cherry some more questions."

"Well, then I can tell you he's not yet awake. We gave him a sedative last night for renewed pain. Doctor is afraid there may be some infection.

"Oh, I see, ma'am. My questions can wait till later. I also wanted to ask Doc about Ron Fox, the other man upstairs. How he's doin?"

"Well, I can tell you myself. That fella's gonna need a little more time to flush that cheap Mexican whiskey outta his system. But otherwise, he's ok. Wound is closed, and I just changed the bandage. 'Seems fine. Swollen up like a hat band, but he'll be alright."

"Good. Would you please just tell the doc I was by? I'll be out most of the day, but I should be back by this evening."

"I'll tell him, Marshal. How many more outlaws you plannin' to shoot while you're here?"

" Well, I hope this is the last of 'em, ma'am, but...you never know."

"And how is your gunshot wound doin today, Marshal?"

"Oh, it's fine, ma'am. I had a nice warm bath last night, used your astringent, and put on a fresh bandage after. 'Feels just fine today."

"All right, Marshal. Take care of those stitches now." Bass tipped his hat as he left.

9:00 a.m. November 4th, 1888
Eagle Pass Road
North of Laredo, Texas

Horn had stumbled onto a buckboard tied to a post outside of a general store on Jefferson Street and quietly led the plug, pulling the wagon to the side alley before trying to climb in. The plaster and cement weighed heavily on the ankle as he tried to lift it into the footwell of the wagon. He was sweating profusely now and could only think about putting distance between himself and Doc Sebring's office. He knew as soon as Julia arrived, all hell would break loose, and his only saving grace would be they'd have no idea where he might've gone.

He eased the wagon down the alley, but as soon as he passed the loading dock of the general store, somebody behind him yelled out, "Hey! You there! That's my wagon! Stop! Thief! Stop!" The man jumped down from the loading platform and began giving chase. Horn knew he'd be caught before long in the narrow alley, so he grabbed his army Colt and fired without aiming at the man behind him, hitting him in the head and stopping him cold in his tracks. When Horn saw the man drop to his knees and fall face forward, he cursed his own bad luck for having to fire. "Damn. They'll be relentless now."

The sound of the pistol shot drew attention from the shopkeepers and clerks arriving for work, but because it was still relatively early, the streets were clear of traffic and commerce. He yanked on the right rein at the end of the alley, and the animal turned himself onto an open lane heading south. Horn whipped up the animal and turned him right again onto Garden Avenue, heading west. He planned to run for the Eagle Pass Road and turn north, hopefully making it to Landon Atwill's place without a posse following. He could see the park ahead, the one he passed when he first came into town, and he turned right again to head north on Eagle Pass Road. By the time he got to Chicago Street in the northern part of town, he could see no one behind him for blocks, so he reined in the tired old horse and let him walk for the next few miles.

He took a long swallow from one of the bottles of laudanum and tried to ease himself into a more comfortable position. The sun was out now and warming him slowly, or maybe it was the laudanum. He decided that he'd pull over in a few miles to rest the horse and maybe give himself a morphine injection.

8:30 a.m. November 4th, 1888
Dr. Lionel Sebring's Office
1400 Block of Jefferson
Laredo, Texas

Julia arrived at Doctor Sebring's office about a half hour late. She knew that Dorothy had stayed the night, so she took some extra time in the morning for her breakfast. As soon as she arrived, she knew something was wrong. The front door was cracked open rather than being locked, and as she entered, she saw that Mr. Burke wasn't in his bed.

She lit a lamp on a side table, looked again at the bed, and saw the girl's feet protruding from the other side on the floor. She looked closer and saw Dorothy's body, her death mask, eyes open, terror and confusion on her young face. She could see the terrible bruising and ruptured blood vessels in her neck, and she began to cry. Softly at first and then louder, with more panic in her screams. Neighbors heard, and one by one, they came in. Doctor Sebring was sent for, as well as Desmond Arguello.

9:15 a.m. November 4th, 1888
   A Position of Cover
   Hillside on Eagle Pass Road
   North of Laredo, Texas.

Bass had taken the same route as the day before and took his same position. He thought about moving back up the slope to gain a broader view but didn't want to sacrifice the clearer focus of being nearer. About twenty minutes after he began watching, he saw a fancy coach drawn by two black horses pull out from one of the smaller buildings next to the horse barn. The driver stopped in front of the house, and shortly after, the small Mexican-Indian-looking fellow came out and climbed onto the seat as he took the reins. Minutes later, Atwill emerged from the house, dressed as dandified gentry, and he sat down in the passenger seat behind the driver. As they pulled onto the road, they turned north, and Bass was able to see the Circle A brand on the side of the coach.

Bass watched until they were out of sight and decided the time was right to get down to that bunkhouse to talk to Willy Banes. He decided that he'd be less obvious if he left the horse behind and walked onto the ranch property farther down the road. He hoped his presence might go unnoticed, but if he was seen, he might be considered just another day worker. He left his frock coat and badge with the horse, who was happily cropping the green grass that had sprouted after the rains. It took twenty or thirty minutes to get through the cover to a point where he could cross the road without being seen. Naturally, he was moving cautiously. Once he had crossed and managed to hop the white rail fence, it only took a few minutes to come to the door at the small end of the bunkhouse.

Bass decided not to knock. He looked around to make sure no one would see him going in, then he pushed the latch and slipped inside.

Willy Banes jumped at the sight of the marshal, who had previously been sent away. He'd been eating a biscuit and drinking coffee from a pot that still hung from the fireplace crane.

"Frank...What are you...how come...?"

"Mornin' Willy. How's tricks? Bet you been up to your old ways again, ain't you?"

"C'mon, Frank. What daya' wanna say somethin' like that for? I'm just a hired man."

"Oh, now Willy, don't you try to kid a kidder. If you was just a hired man, you wouldn't have this fine suite provided for you. Say, Is that a set of runnin' irons I see on the wall behind you? Willy, you know how them things can get you into trouble."

"Aw, damn." Banes was caught, and he knew it. He knew it inside when he first saw Bass in the yard that day. "Alright, Frank, listen. You know there wasn't nobody hirin' old wranglers when I got out. I couldn't make a wage. And I tried too, marshal, I tried hard. Then, when Mr. Atwill came to see me at my sister's in Brownsville and made me the offer, I said okay. Didn't have no choice, and that's a fact."

Bass listened to Willy and knew his story was mostly true, but there were other ways for old drovers to make a living. Every cattle ranch needed herders and counters. And cow separators who knew a yearling from a two-year-old were always in demand somewhere.

"Willy, I've heard that sad song many times before. You know as well as I do that there's plenty of ranch work for seasoned men like yourself. I know you can't sit a horse all day, but that don't keep you from workin' on your feet. Now I'm gonna ask you some questions, and you, by God, better tell me the truth. Because right now, you're what's called an accessory after the fact to murder."

Banes's eyes opened wide at the mention of murder, and he eased himself back down into his chair.

"Frank, you gotta believe I didn't have nothin' to do with killin them boys at the bridge."

"Oh, I know you didn't, but the law says as soon as you knew who did it, you should'a come forward."

"Yeah, and if I did that, I'd be dead too." Bass paused and looked at the older man.

"Yeah, Willy, I believe you're right. So. I'm gonna give you the chance to come clean. I can't make no promises, but if you help me put these scoundrels away, I'll speak to the judge for you. Who knows? You might just walk away free."

Willy's eyes lit up again, but he began to sweat.

What's to keep them from getting to me at night when I'm asleep? I'll tell you that little Mexican, Mateo, is a damn master with a knife. He cut Dan Bogan's throat just as quick as kiss my hand and watched him bleed out right yonder by the porch. And Mr. Atwill tells him what to do. I heard a couple of the boys talkin' an' word is they're unnatural together if you take my meaning."

"Uh-huh. Listen, Willy, and I'll tell you what. You come with me right now, and I'll see to your protection. You can give your testimony, and then we'll round up these vermin and lock 'em away."

"Oh, Frank, you don't know these two. I heard the Mexican got into the jail and did for Matt Cole. Now I know he ain't much of a loss, but if they got to him in jail, they can get to me."

"Then I'll tell you what. I'll hide you out someplace else. Maybe a fine hotel. What do ya say?"

Willy Banes looked as forlorn as a lost sheep, but he knew that Frank could arrest him on the spot anyway.

'Wouldn't be much he could do about it. So he finally said,

"Well, okay, Frank. But you gotta protect me 'cause I ain't no hand with a gun, never have been."

"Don't worry 'bout that a bit. I'll always be around. Now, just like nothin' happened, I want you to get your horse and ride down the Eagle Pass Road to town. I just saw Atwill and his Mexican drive out headin' north."

"Yeah, they was goin to check on them cows they stole. They're on some graze up to Botines."

"Well, there you are. By God, 'couldn't be better. My horse is in cover on the other side of the road, so I'll fetch him and meet you down the road a few miles so no one will put us together."

Again, Willy Banes showed his nervousness, but he did as Bass instructed. Bass went back the way he came and found the horse and his things right where he'd left them. He figured to join up with Willy on the outskirts of town.

Twenty-One

10:45 a.m. November 4th, 1888
Eagle Pass Road at Pace Avenue
Laredo, Texas.

Bass caught up to Willy Banes just at the Pace Avenue intersection. "Willy? About a mile or so down this road is a livery. It's owned by a man named Desmond Arguello. I just made him the acting town marshal. I wanna stop there for a bit."

"A livery?! You said you'd put me up at a fine hotel in town, not no livery barn."

"Willy, relax. My horse was injured some days ago, and I just wanna check on her. You have any trouble on the road?"

"Nah. Just some fella in a buckboard with a broken down ol nag pullin' it."

"' You recognize him? Did he know you?"

"Never seen him before in my life. I just tipped my hat as I passed by."

"Good." They continued to Arguello's livery, and Bass told Willy to come in with him. "No point in you standin out here in the open to be recognized."

Willy tied off his bay mare at the corral, and Bass led the gelding in through the open doors.

Ray Wilke was cleaning the hooves of a large draft horse when he saw Bass come in.

"Well, you're back. Good timing, too, 'cause I believe she's ready."

"That's fine, Ray, just fine. I've missed her. Lemme have a look." Bass had to stand on a hay bale to see, but her wound looked much better. There was no swelling, and the singe marks had gone away. "What do you think about the scar up here, Ray?"

"Probably always be there. 'Don't believe hair'll

grow over. But you might check with the doc. He'd know best."

"Okay. Don't make a difference. She looks good to me no matter what."

"You headin into town, I s'pose?"

"Yeah. Takin' my friend here to find him a hotel. Why? What's goin' on?"

"Probly ought to check in with Des. Was a woman killed at a doc's office this mornin and a man shot dead in an alley nearby not long after. 'At's all I know, but he may need some help."

"I'll stop by soon as I get my friend situated."

Bass saddled Emma and led her out of the barn. He looked at Willy Banes as he mounted up and said, "Gotta move, Willy. We'll get you a room first, but then I need to see the new marshal."

The two rode directly to the Arbuckle Hotel and tied off out front. They both walked in, but only Bass went to the front desk. He told Willy to go to the bar and have a drink. Bass would come for him in a minute. Bass didn't want anyone to know who was going to be using the room, and he didn't want the desk clerk to be able to describe him if someone came asking.

Bass got a room toward the back of the building with only one window. If Willy needed to escape, the window would work as well as any. On his way into the bar to fetch Willy Banes, he purchased two newspapers and a cigar from the newsstand out front, and he took Willy out the side door. They went first to get Willy's horse, and Bass paid for three days feed and board at Marson's Livery and Buggy Rentals behind the hotel. He then took Willy in through the back door and up the rear stairs to his room.

"Now listen up, Willy. Tomorrow, I'm gonna find a judge so you can make your statement. It's called an affidavit. 'Means you're swearin' what it says is true. After that, I can go arrest Atwill and his little buddy, and your worries will be about over. I got you two newspapers here from a couple days ago, a fine, fat cigar, and a pint of Old Crow. If you need to go to the latrine, use the back stairs. Otherwise, do not leave the room. Got it?"

"Yeah, Frank, I got it. Just one thing: I don't know how to read. 'Meant to learn in Huntsville, but...'"

"Well, just look at the drawin's then. Maybe work on what you remember from the penitentiary.

Now, I gotta go see the town marshal about those killin's that Ray spoke of. You stay put, Willy."

"Don't worry, Frank. Ain't goin nowhere."

"Lock the door, and when I come back, I'll knock four times." Bass closed the door behind him, feeling fairly confident in Willy's safety... at least for the night.

3:00 p.m. November 4th, 1888
City Marshals Office
Matamoras at Salinas Ave.
Laredo, Texas

Bass walked into the jail office and found Marshal Arguello at his desk questioning what looked to be a grocer or clerk wearing an apron."

"Marshal Bass, I'm glad you're here. This man is a clerk at Bonie's General Store. He got a look at the man that shot down Elmore Bone this mornin.'"

"Is 'at right, sir? You saw the man?"

"I saw him as he drove off in the buckboard, and when he turned to shoot Mr. Bone, yes, I did."

"Well, good. Thanks for stepping up. Can you describe him?"

"Not very well. He was sittin in the buckboard, but he didn't have his shirt on, or at least not all the way on. And, I know it sounds funny, but he only had one leg in his trousers."

Bass said, "Sounds like he wasn't dressed and needed to make a fast get-a-way."

Arguello added, "There was a nurse strangled to death at

Dr. Lionel Sebring's office shortly before all this. Doc Sebring's office is pretty close by the general store."

Bass thought for a moment and asked.

"Did you happen to get a look at the man's face?"

"Yes, kinda. He had dark hair and no hat on. His hair was short and pushed back on his forehead, and he had a black mustache. Nothin' special about it, though."

Bass shook his head and said,

"That's real good. Last question. Did you happen to see which way he went?"

"Yes, I did. He turned the horse right on Garden Street and then right again on Eagle Pass Road. I know 'cause I followed after him on foot."

Arguello said, "That was a very brave thing to do. He'd just shot Mr. Bone for following him."

"I know. But Elmore Bone was my friend. Had I a pistol, I would'a shot that man."

Arguello stood up and walked around his desk. "Mr. Bradley, I wanna thank you for comin' forward. I'm sure we'll be able to catch your friend's killer. You go on home now and get some rest."

The man picked up his hat and looked at both Bass and Arguello. Then he stood up straight, set his hat on his head just so, and left the office. Arguello sat back at his desk.

"Marshal Bass, any ideas?"

"Yup, could be an outlaw I have some experience with. I have a prisoner who passed him on Eagle Pass Road today. 'Can't explain why he wasn't dressed. Maybe he was recognized and had to make a quick escape. He's here lookin' for me. 'You remember when I came to your livery? 'Shot in the hip and my horse hurt too? Well, he's the reason. He's the man who shot me an' my horse. 'Wants to get even with me for shootin' him and turnin him in up in Denver last summer. He came here lookin for me, shot me and my horse, and now he's killed a grocery clerk and maybe a nurse, too."

Arguello thought for a moment and said,

"Wanna know what I think? I think he was at Doc Sebring's for somethin', and when he didn't get it, he killed Doc's nurse and took off. Stole Elmore Bone's wagon and fled."

"That sounds likely. I think you're close. I'll bet you, since he wasn't dressed, he was at the Doc's cause he needed treatment for somethin. And when the nurse lady wouldn't help him, he killed her and ran. Stumbled onto the wagon and killed Mr. Bone."

"Think maybe he was a patient there, at Doc Sebring's?"

"Let's go find out, what do ya say?"

4:30 p.m. November 4th, 1888
Dr. Lionel Sebring's Office
1400 Block of Jefferson
Laredo, Texas

Doctor Sebring was still cleaning up the broken glass and mess made in his office. He'd seen to the care of his nurse, Julia, who was distraught at the death of the younger girl. The Doctor had taken her home and given her a sedative, and stayed until she was asleep. He left instructions with the owner of the boarding house to fetch him when she woke up, be it night or day. Now he was back at his office cleaning up after the 'hurry-up' wagon called for Dorothy's body. He had no idea how he would explain her death to her parents in Waco.

Bass and Arguello arrived just after 4:30 p. m. and walked quietly into the doctor's office.

Arguello spoke first. "Lionel? I'm very sorry to disturb you. I know you're sorry for your nurse, but we have some questions. This is Deputy U.S. Marshal Frank Bass, and he's investigating a case that may be connected."

"Alright. Ask away." The doctor sat resignedly in a chair and looked up at the two men.

Bass started. "Doctor, did you have a patient here, a man about six feet tall with a thin, black mustache?"

"Yes, that would be Tom Burke. He came in with a broken foot. Horse accident, I believe."

"And did you treat him?"

"Of course. The man was in terrible pain. I had to give him an opiate just to get his boot off."

Arguello asked, "Doc, how long was he here?"

"Three days, I believe. The first night, he overdosed himself on laudanum that our poor Dorothy mistakenly gave him."

Bass asked, "Doc, what did you do for him? How did you treat him?"

"I set his broken foot and ankle in plaster."

"And when was that?"

"As soon as he recovered from his overdose. That evening. Say, what's this all about, anyway. Who was he?"

"Doctor, the man's name is Tom Horn. I arrested him in Denver earlier this year, and in the process, he was shot. I believe he's here lookin for me. He tried to kill me a few days ago."

Arguello added, "And he killed Elmore Bone while he was escaping from murdering your nurse."

The doctor slumped forward. "Dear God in Heaven. Two innocent people dead. Well. Gentlemen, I hope you find this bastard quickly before he does any more damage. If you feel a reward will help find him, I'll be happy to put up the funds."

"Actually, Doc, I believe I know where he is."

Bass and Arguello stepped outside, and Arguello asked, "Well? You gonna tell me where the bastard is?"

"Not sure, but I arrested a fella named Willy Banes earlier out at the Tierra Blanca. Banes and I have a history, and I let him ride off the place on his own so his pards wouldn't suspect the law took him. I have him stashed over at the Arbuckle. Anyway, he saw the man in the buckboard on his way in. 'Said he may have been heading to Tierra Blanca. 'Almost certain it's Tom Horn.

I got a wire from the Sheriff back in El Paso that Horn knows Landon Atwill. Maybe worked for him in the past."

"Well, hell, depaty, let's go git him."

"Hold on, hold on. I want Atwill and that little Mexican, too. I believe Atwill hired out for the killing of Marshal Gosling and his men and probably Matt Cole as well. Those he hired stole the cattle from The King Ranch, too. I wanna take 'em all together. Otherwise, they'll split up, and we'll never see 'em again."

"Is it just them three we want? If 'tis should be easy to haul 'em in."

"I got two of the riders that was there when Gosling was shot, on ice back in town."

"Well, why ain't they in my jail like they're supposed to be?"

"They're both shot is why. They're chained to their beds at Doc Gately's. I'm tryin to get 'em to turn on Atwill. One already has; the other is still unconscious."

"I see. You got a plan?"

"Not yet. But I'm workin on it, I'm workin on it."

Arguello looked around the street. He was quickly getting anxious to make arrests. "Well, don't take too long. Atwill's likely to hire an army out there to watch out for him. Man's got more money than a hound has fleas."

"You'll be the first to know, marshal. I'd like you to keep an eye on my two prisoners at Doc's.

Might do to let 'em know that it ain't just me they're dealin' with."

"Alright, you say so. What are you gonna do?"

"Right now, I'm hungry. Gonna find somethin to eat. Then tomorrow I'm goin' back out to the Tierra Blanca, 'got a hidey hole out there...keep an eye on the place. See how things work out there."

6:45 p.m. November 4th, 1888
Arbuckle Hotel,
Washington Street
Laredo, Texas

Bass sat down at a corner table, one that gave him a view of both Washington and Montezuma streets. He ordered pork chops and greens and a dram glass of rye whiskey and started to consider what he ought to do first. He knew Cherry Lennox would tumble the way he figured, but he wasn't too sure about Ron Fox. He figured he needed to spend more time with Fox to convince him that speaking out about Atwill's involvement would be to his advantage. Then he started to think that maybe neither of these outlaws ever had any direct dealing with Atwill. It was certain that one of 'em, probably Fox, had pulled the trigger on Marshall Gosling. But if Dan Bogen had done all the legwork and talkin, setting up the cattle rustling, it could be that neither of these men had any direct evidence linking Atwill to the theft. In that case, the best he could hope to charge Atwill with was receiving stolen property. Banes could testify to that. And riding out to arrest Tom Horn, while he would get a world of pleasure doing it, would only put Atwill on alert.

No, he had to find a link between Atwill and Bogan that proved Atwill ordered Bogan to steal the cows. The fact that Bogan was dead, according to Willy Banes, made things more difficult. The one avenue he hadn't tried yet was Ron Fox. If he did the shooting, he might be willing to give up Atwill as the mastermind of the whole opera. On the other hand, he might just as quickly clam-up, 'hire a lawyer to do his talkin'. He decided to see Fox in the morning before riding out to observe the activities at the Tierra Blanca. He hoped, by this time, Bloody Ron Fox would be conscious enough to remember.

8:45 a.m. November 5th, 1888
Doc Gately's Clinic
Montezuma Street

Laredo, Texas

Bass arrived at Doc Gately's office, and being familiar with everyone there, he walked in unannounced. Doc was not around, and there was some confusion and activity going on in the stairwell to the second floor. Bass hoped the ladies up there were alright, and when he finally saw Martha, she hurried to him, a concerned look on her face.

"Marshal, I'm so terribly sorry for all this. It really is impossible to watch everyone all the time. And last night, we were so busy with Abigail Rull, and her baby hadn't turned. I am so sorry for you."

"Well, I'm sorry too, but what else happened? Why are you sorry for me?"

"Why, your prisoner, Mr. Fox. I thought Doc may have told you. He grabbed a syringe sometime in the night and gave himself an opiate injection. It was much too much, I'm afraid, and he's dead. We only noticed it this morning when we lit all the lamps." Bass was stunned. He was hoping to get additional information from the man, and now he'd accidentally killed himself.

"Marshal? I really am so sorry. We're just not used to having manacled prisoners, and he evidently was able to reach an opium kit."

"I understand, Martha. I'm sure there was nothing you could do. Is the doc out doing rounds?"

"No. He's upstairs with Abigail. It's going to be a hard one, poor dear. She's such a small thing, too."

Bass went into the downstairs clinic room and saw Cherry Lennox sitting on his bed.

"Hard thing, ain't it, marshal? Ol' Ronny off's hisself that way. I guess you won't be able to get your affydavid from him now, will ya?" Cherry was grinning as he spoke.

"Lennox? Now ain't the time, buster. I'll see you later."

Cherry Lennox laid back on his cot, quietly looking at the ceiling.

Bass walked out into the street, trying to think of what might be his next move. He wanted to get Willy Banes in to see Judge Staton for a deposition. After that, he planned to head back out to the Tierra Blanca for more observation.

He rode back to the Arbuckle Hotel and knocked on Willy's door four times as agreed. Willy opened the door and said, "Glad you're back, marshal. I'm getting the creeps just sittin around here."

"I understand, Willy. I'm going to take you over to Judge Staton's office now, and you can tell him your story about what you've seen and what Atwill asked you to do."

City Hall was only a few blocks away, and with the weather being sunny and mild, they decided to walk to City Hall on San Eduardo Street.

By this time, it was mid-morning, and the judge had finished with hearings for the day. He was in his office reading evidence for a trial due to begin that afternoon when Bass knocked on his door.

"Yes? Come. Ah. Deputy Bass, who do you have here?"

"Judge, this is an old acquaintance of mine, Willy Banes. Willy is employed by Landon Atwill out at the Tierra Blanca, and he has some things he'd like to report, upstanding citizen that he is."

"I see. Marshal, is Mr. Banes to give sworn testimony? And does he understand the laws of perjury?"

"Yes, and yes, your honor. I should add that Willy is a former cattle thief and brand forger who has paid his dues for those crimes. He's well aware of how the system works, sir."

"Uh-huh. And have you promised him anything for his testimony, marshal?"

"Your honor, I told him the law looks favorably on citizens who come forward with the truth."

"I see. And is he to be released after I've taken his statement?"

"Yes, your honor. Willy? You go straight back to the hotel now when the judge dismisses you, hear?"

"Oh, I will, Frank. Got no place else."

"Good. Your honor? I'll leave him in your care. Willy? You tell the Judge just what you told me.

"I will, Frank."

Bass left the office and walked back to the Arbuckle, relieved that he'd have a sworn statement from Willy Banes, taken by the District Judge no less, as part of his case against Atwill. When he got back to Emma, he talked softly and low to her, patting her neck and touching his forehead to her muzzle as he always did. The he climbed aboard and headed her west from the hotel on Washington to San Bernardo and turned North. He was still searching for another way to find a link between Bogan and Atwill, but he kept drawing a blank. He already had Haliday's affidavit, and soon he'd have Willy's. He also knew what Cherry Lennox was going to claim.

But without Ron Fox, there was no way to make any connection to Atwill or determine who the actual man was that pulled the trigger on Harold Gosling. As he rode, he considered questioning Fox's girlfriends in Laredo and Nuevo Laredo, thinking Fox may have done some bragging while with them. Of course, that would all be hearsay, but it might lead him elsewhere. He'd almost gotten to the San Ygnacio Bridge when he remembered his first talk with Anse Haliday. He'd said there'd been another with them. Lonny Dahl. Of course. Lennox didn't have a very high opinion of him, 'said Dahl had gone across the Rio, that he had a girlfriend over there. Bass had no idea if Dahl could be found or add anything to the investigation, but it was a new thread to follow.

Twenty-Two

11:15 a.m. November 5th, 1888
A Position of Cover
Hillside on Eagle Pass Road
North of Laredo, Texas.

Bass resumed his lookout position in the same area he'd spent hours in before. He held his glass to his eyes as soon as he'd tied Emma off and saw nothing to speak of happening in the ranch yard. In fact, nothing at all happened in the yard. This was not usual. There were always hands and wranglers doing any of the hundreds of tasks required to keep a spread like Tierra Blanca working.

Even if it was only carrying water to the animal troughs, there should be people milling about among the buildings. After about fifteen minutes of this, he saw the door to the bunkhouse open, and he watched Atwill and his Mexican aide stride across the yard to the house. Atwill seemed upset because he kept slapping his gloved hand with his quirt. Shortly after going inside, the Mexican came scampering out of the house and headed into the stable barn.

Bass continued to watch for movement, and eventually, men from the bunkhouse slowly began to emerge to begin whatever tasks had been laid out for them. He saw four of the men head to the corral, where they each picked a horse and began the saddling process. Once they were all mounted, they walked the animals to the front of the house, where the Mexican stood holding a handsome-looking dappled grey horse. Once Atwill came out and mounted up, the five of them, with Atwill in the lead, headed out through the gate and turned to the north.

Bass wondered if the meeting in the bunkhouse was because Willy Banes had disappeared, and now this new committee of riders was off to try to find him. Bass thought briefly about heading down to the house to look for Tom Horn and question the Mexican but thought better of it. If what Banes had said about their relationship was true, it wasn't likely Bass would get anything incriminating out of him. And if Horn was there, he'd be giving himself away arresting him. Instead, Bass decided to follow the five riders north, discreetly, of course. He bet they were heading wherever the stolen cows were being kept, and once he could tie in Atwill with the stollen cattle, he could make a stronger case than just receiving stolen property. He decided to give the riders about ten minutes head start. He'd need that time to re-saddle Emma.

He stayed in cover until he thought he was far enough away from the house that he wouldn't be seen, and then he came down to the road. Following the recent tracks of five riders was easy enough, and even more so because one of the animals had a loose shoe. It made a very distinctive footprint as they headed north.

After six miles, Bass estimated they turned to the northeast on a narrow path that was rocky and unstable. He was still far enough away from the group that his dust or Emma's scent to the other animals wouldn't give him away. He followed another six miles and stooped dead on the path. Well, in the distance, he could see several men, including Atwill, riding amongst a small herd of Longhorns, obviously the animals stolen from the King Ranch. He dismounted and had Emma lie on the ground as he watched them through his glass. He couldn't hear anything, but he could see Atwill, obvious in his white Panama hat, giving orders. He could see two of the hands riding the perimeter of the cattle, their heads looking down as they rode. Obviously, they were searching for some sign that perhaps Banes had been there. Atwill and the others were examining the animal's hip brands and ear markings. Again, he could see that Atwill was upset about something.

It occurred to him that it might be time to get off the path, so he had Emma stand, led her several hundred feet south of the path, and asked her again to lie down. He did the same and watched as the five of them left the animals to graze and rode back on the path directly over his position. They did not notice any of their prints or the soil disturbed by the recumbence of a large animal near the path. Why would they? They weren't looking for them." Bass decided he'd seen enough and decided to head back into town. He could now place Atwill at the hidden location of the stolen longhorns. It was a good start, but he still wanted to find Lonny Dahl to see if he could make a connection to Atwill ordering the theft. That would make him an accessory to the murder of Harold Gosling, and it would mean serious time in Huntsville.

He wanted to get back to town to talk to Cherry Lennox and then Marshal Des. Arguello.

4:45 p.m. November 5th, 1888
Doc Gately's Clinic
Montezuma Street
Laredo, Texas

Bass tied Emma off to the hitch rail in front of the Docs and went inside. Martha was coming down the stairs with an armful of linens, looking like she'd been chasin after bull calves in springtime.

"Evenin' Martha. Say, how did that difficult birthin' go this mornin?"

"Eventually, it worked out fine, but it took quite a while. Poor Abbey's gonna be sitin' funny for some time, I'm afraid. 'You lookin for Doc? Or that worthless Lennox man?"

"Actually, right now, I'd like to talk to the worthless one, but if Doc's around, tell him I'll buy him a drink later, would ya? I have some questions for him about Ron Fox."

"I will. He needs that drink, too. His butt's not as sore as Abbie's, but he's near as tired. He' ain't a youngster no more, ya know."

"I do. I'll only be a couple minutes with Lennox. But I wanna get over to the telegraph office to send a wire home. I'll be back after that." Bass tipped his hat before taking it off and turned left into Doc's infirmary. Lennox was sitting up on his bed, his left arm extended due to the shackles. Bass noticed as he walked in that Cherry Lennox's left arm was worn and bleeding. He also noticed that he no longer had leg shackles on.

"Say, tell me, Cherry, what happened to the leg irons I locked on you?"

"Cherry looked indignant at the question. 'Took 'em off. The lady got tired of unlockin' and re-lockin' 'em when I had to use the pan or go out to the latrine. 'Sides, they hurt my shot leg."

"Oh, what happened to your wrist there? Looks mighty painful."

"Huh? Oh, that. I toss about when I sleep, and the damned cuff chafes at me."

"Ah, well, ya ought ask Doc to give you somethin to help you sleep. Bet he would."

"Listen, the reason I'm here is the other day, you mentioned Lonny Dahl had a girlfriend. She here in town or in Mexico?"

"Don't know for a fact, but the little pecker kept talkin 'bout her like she was in Mexico."

"Don't suppose you know her name, do ya?"

"No, I don't...' Think it maya started with an E though, like Ellen or Edith or somethin."

"Well, if you think of anything else about her, you let me know, will ya?"

"Ya, ya....Say, I do remember she's a friend of that girl, Loretta. The one Ron Fox liked."

"Okay, that's somethin to go on. Thanks, Cherry. Bein helpful like this will work in your favor when I talk to the judge."

"Yeah? Well, it better... and I'm gonna hold you to it, Marshal."

6:45 p.m. November 50th, 1888
U.S. Post Office
San Dario Street
Laredo, Texas

Bass had left Doc Gately's and headed directly to the Post Office to send a wire to Sally. He hadn't sent a message for several days and knew she'd worry about him. When he arrived at the San Dario Street office, there was a sign in the window indicating that the telegrapher was out getting his supper and would return in thirty minutes. The post office was closed, but the outside window for the telegrapher's desk was open twenty-four hours a day. Since he had at least a half hour to wait, he decided to go back to Doc Gately's and see if he wanted to get a bite to eat. When he arrived, Gately was coming out of his office, his coat over his arm and his sleeves still rolled up.

"Hey Doc, Gonna catch your death out here tonight if you don't put your coat on. Crystal clear tonight means it's gonna get cold tonight."

"Yeah, well, bugs don't like the cold either, so I'm probably safe for a short while anyway. Martha said you were by and offered to buy me a drink. Is at so?"

"You bet it is. Let's go up yonder to the Black Crow Saloon. I'll treat."

Bass tied Emma off in front of Doc's again, and the two men walked a block on the boardwalk to Easterbrook's Black Crow Saloon. They took a table at a corner window not far from the hearth. As soon as they sat down and Bass set his hat on an unoccupied chair, a middle-aged woman stopped by the table.

"Well damn, it is you, Doc. At first, I thought my eyes were playin' tricks on me. 'Haven't seen you in here for what?...a couple weeks, right? Who's this?"

"Sheila Easterbrook, this is Marshal Frank Bass. Be careful what you say, dear. He's a Fed."

"A Federale, huh? Well, since you're with Doc, I won't charge you double, honey. "Sheila Easterbrook was a full-figured woman who carried the extra weight well. She wore a bit too much rouge and eye makeup, and her curly red hair tumbled over her shoulders, enhancing her ample bustline. Bass figured as a young woman, she would have been a beauty.

"Thank you, ma'am. Say, if you don't mind my askin', is this saloon yours?"

"Bet your butt it is, Mister. My husband, 'name was Early. 'Died and left it to me lock, stock, and barrels. We started it together twelve years ago after we got hitched. He was a little older but was plenty feisty when it was called for, if you take my meanin'." Bass chuckled and said,

"Well, he was a lucky man, then. Do you mind my asking what happened to him?"

"Hell no, common knowledge. One night, we were both bein' ah... feisty, and I guess I got the better of him 'cause he died right there in the marriage bed. He once told me when his time came, that's the way he wanted to go, and I'm comforted to have obliged him. Now, what can I get you, gents."

Bass was having trouble keeping a straight face, so Doc ordered, "Two rye drams, Sheila, doubles if you please." Sheila winked and walked off to the bar. Bass turned to the Doc and said,

"By God. She's a right kick in the head. Was all that true?"

"Oh yes, absolutely. I pronounced Early dead that night, directly upstairs. Just a quick word: Sheila talks a good game, but she loved ol' Early very much. She misses him more than she lets on."

'I understand. Still, she's awfully likable." Bass paused as he looked out the window. "Say Doc, while we wait, I wanted to ask you about Ron Fox. I heard from Martha, of course, that he done it himself, but I wanna get your take on it, too."

"Is that what she said? That he injected himself? ...Well, Frank, if he injected himself with enough morphine to be fatal, he'd a had to be a contortionist. The needle marks were in his left hip, and he was lying on his stomach with both hands shackled to the bed irons.

And here's something else to consider. I don't keep any morphine upstairs. It's all under lock and key in my office downstairs." Bass's face turned grey. He knew immediately what had happened. Cherry Lennox with scraped and bleeding wrist. He was silent for a moment and then asked,

"Have you checked your cabinet yet today, Doc?"

"Well, no, I haven't. Pregnant women can't have it, and that Lennox fellow only needs it twice a day. Wait...You think he did it?"

"Yup, I do. To keep Fox from sayin it was Lennox that pulled the trigger on Howard Gosling."

"Well then, I'm sorry Martha misled you, Frank, though she was tired herself and probably didn't give it much thought."

"No, no, it's alright, Doc. In fact, it might work out just fine. Only next time Cherry Lennox asks for pain killer, tell him you're out of morphine and can't understand it. Okay?"

"Sure. Only how did he get free to get the drug and then get upstairs?"

"He convinced Martha to remove the leg irons so she could walk him to the latrine. He still had the manacles and chain on, but his wrists this evening... were scraped raw and bleeding."

"Well, that explains it, I guess. Anything else you want me to do?"

"No. Just play along with him like nothing's wrong. He's confident that I'm gonna talk to the judge on his behalf anyway, so he'll be fine waiting it out until his leg is healed. Actually, you might let on to him that his wound isn't looking so good, and he should plan on at least another couple of days in your infirmary. Can you do that?"

"With pleasure. In fact, if it wasn't against my oath, I'd tell him he needs a bromide treatment. That'd serve him right, by Jove." The two men finished their rye and headed out the door in different directions.

8:45 p.m. November 5th, 1888
Arbuckle Hotel,
Washington Street
Laredo, Texas

After stopping at the telegrapher's window at the post office, Bass headed back to his hotel. He was tired and hungry, a little chilled, and though he knew a hot bath would set him up well, he was too tired to wait.

He put Emma away for the night at Markson's livery behind the hotel and went directly to the dining room to get something to eat. Fortunately, they were still serving, so he sat at a corner table, ordered a drink, and reviewed what his next plan of action should be. He still wanted more information about Landan Atwill. Still, he also didn't want Atwill to put together the idea that Willy Banes's disappearance was tied to him giving evidence to the law. He certainly wanted Tom Horn dealt with once and for all but remembered his injury probably would keep him from another ambush. And he probably wasn't going anywhere soon anyway. Then, he focused on Atwill. If he had to take Atwill on the cattle theft conspiracy alone, then that would have to suffice, but he sure wanted someone to go on record saying that Atwill ordered the whole thing, which would make him guilty as an accessory to the murder of Harold Gosling. He concluded his last chance for that was to find Lonny Dahl's girlfriend, and the best source he would have had might be the woman who had pointed him to Ron Fox.

10:30 p.m. November 5th, 1888
Zeke's Whiskey Saloon
Saunders Street at Frost Avenue
Laredo, Texas.

Bass walked the few blocks to Zeke's Saloon and sat down at the same table where he'd talked with Eileen Dempsey days before. It was very dark in the place, and being a Monday, there weren't many patrons at the bar or the few tables toward the rear. Still, the piano was playing, and the place smelled of cigars and whiskey, so Bass felt comfortable there. There were only a few lamps lit, and he couldn't really see if Eileen was working, so when another younger gal approached, he asked after her.

"Eileen? Oh hell, Mister, she quit a few days ago. Didn't say why, or goodbye, or have an apple. Just didn't bother to show up. Sometime last week. What can I get you?"

"Huh. That's a shame. Uh… I guess I'll have a tall whiskey. Ice if you got it."

"Believe we're outta ice, but I'll check. Be right back."

As Bass waited, another woman, wearin a thick coat of powder and rouge, stopped by his table. She was tall with yellow hair, though Bass thought it might be a wig. Sally would say she was 'willowy,' and with all the paint, Bass had no way to guess her age.

"Say handsome. You lookin for some fun?"

"Oh, not really, Miss.. ah, what's your name?" the girl's eyes opened wide as she said,

"Fiona. 'Pretty nifty name. Buy me a drink? I'll just keep you company."

"Alright, Fiona. Sit down. The waitress showed up with Bass's whiskey on ice, set it down without sayin a word. She walked off quickly, and Bass wondered why she was suddenly so cool.

"That's Josie…Josephine. She don't like pushin' drinks. 'More interested in the upstairs service, you know? Not me, though. I like to drink and laugh and dance…how about you, mister?"

"Yeah, I like to have fun too, but I'm just real tired tonight, you know?"

"Oh sure, honey, I get it. It's late anyway." Fiona paused and then asked, "What's your name, sugar? You ain't a regular here."

"Names Frank Bass, Fiona,… I'm from El Paso."

"Well, you're a long way from home…business?"

"You might say. I'm lookin for a man named Lonny Dahl, 'used to work with him. 'Heard he was somewhere around here, so I thought I'd look him up."

"Lonny? Oh sure, honey, he comes in now and again. He's young, right? Real good lookin boy. I haven't seen him lately. He was spendin' pretty big a while back, so he maya ran out of money."

"Zat, right? Well, I just thought I would try to find him, is all."

Fiona tilted her head and said,

"It's a shame he could have any of us white girls, but I believe he's partial towards Coloreds and Mexicans. He sees a little Colored gal 'cross town, then scoots back across the Rio. She works at a house east of here. Yeah, maybe seven or eight blocks. Place run by Frenchy Barlow near Saunders and Jarvis Street, I think it is. Don't know the girl's name though, only that she's in the trade, if you know what I mean?"

"I do. A comfort house east of here, you say?"

"Comfort house? That's a good one. That's rich. Never heard 'em called that before."

"Well, maybe I'll check around then. Thanks for the information, Fiona." Bass left a dollar on the table for his drink and gave Fiona another two dollars for her time.

"My, my. Two dollars'd get you a full hour of anybody in here tonight. You keep throwin' money around like that, and you won't have none to spend when you get there." Bass smiled at her joke, picked up his hat, and walked back out to the street.

It was too late and too cold to walk anywhere but back to his hotel. He decided to look into Frenchy Barlow's business tomorrow evening and get a good night's rest tonight.

Twenty-Three

8:45 a.m. November 6th, 1888
Arbuckle Hotel,
Washington Street
Laredo, Texas

Bass sat reading a newspaper and drinking his third cup of black coffee in the hotel dining room when a messenger walked in, calling his name. "Frank Bass. Telegram for Frank Bass." Sally knew never to send a message to him using the term Marshal. He'd explained that it might give him away. He looked around the room and saw no interested faces watching the messenger, so he raised his hand, and the kid walked over. "You, Mr. Bass?"

"Yes, I am." Bass took the half-page message and handed the boy a dime."

The message was from Sally in response to what he'd sent last night. All was still well, and Sally was feeling fine now that the morning sickness had stopped. *'Silas was working on the play enclosure for Lillian.'* Bass figured maybe snow had fallen, which shut down work on the new barn altogether, so Silas was working on a four-foot square enclosure to keep Lil from walkin into trouble. Sally said he was *'making it to be moveable.'* Bass pictured some kind of hinged arrangement, the kind of thing that Silas was so good at. Sergei was still sleeping with Lil. And he was reminded that they now had a watchdog\house pet. Bass suspected that Silas had sent the wire for Sally from town this morning. It would have been difficult for her to get into town with the baby if it had been cold enough to snow.

He always enjoyed hearing from home, even if it was something as mundane as the weather or whatever Silas was working on. It served to keep him focused on his own progress so he could get back to TwainHeart as soon as possible. Looking at the date, he realized he'd already been gone for ten days, not as long as he'd been in

Austin last Spring, but still too long to be gone on this case. Emma was nearly healed, and his wounded hip was beginning to itch. Bass decided it was time to speed things up a bit. He was going to ride out to Saunders and Jarvis Street and wake Frenchy Barlow up if he had to. He saddled Emma and rode down Washington to Saunders and turned East.

Jarvis Street was nearly at the end of the town's border. He could see open prairie beyond the intersection. It wasn't difficult to determine which place was Frenchy Barlow's. There was no street number, but it was the only two-story structure anywhere around. The front of the place looked well cared for. A long veranda spanned the front of the dwelling and ran down both sides to the rear. Three gables protruded from the roofline, and he counted at least four chimneys. Bass could see five latrines dug a good way from the house, and there looked to be a stable barn and corral directly behind. Three saddle horses were standing with a cocked rear leg tied to the front railing. He supposed the animals had been there most of the night.

He climbed the steps to the wide veranda, noticing the isinglass windows were curtained shut. He struck the heavy brass knocker three times and waited. Finally, he heard movement behind the door, and it opened. A middle-aged woman in a revealing housecoat appeared. She stood barefooted, with her arms crossed, and said, "You're a lawman, ain't ya.?" Bass removed his hat, smiling. "Is it really that obvious, ma'am?"

"Mister, wouldn't be nobody else callin' on me at this hour who wasn't drunk and half naked and desperate. What do you want?"

"My name is Frank Bass, ma'am. I'm a U.S. Deputy Marshal investigatin cattle rustling, and I'd like to talk to one a your gals."

"Eugenia. You wanted to talk to Eugenia."

"How do you know that?"

"You're lookin for Lonny, ain't you? Well, he's a regular customer a hers. Come on into the parlor, and I'll fetch her down. You wanna drink?"

"Thank you, no, ma'am. 'Bit early."

"Yeah, well, not for me, it ain't. I still got hold overs from last night. Sit down, sit down. Make yourself comfortable." Frenchy poured herself a shot of what looked like gin and swallowed it quickly. She then walked up the stairs in the front hall, presumably to Eugenia's room.

Bass looked around at his surroundings and was impressed. There was a hearth on one side of the room and an upright player piano near the door. The furniture was covered in blue velveteen, and the small bar in the room had ornate gold-colored metalwork. The walls were covered in some peach-colored wallpaper, and portraits of several older men in gold-painted frames were hung about on the walls. Through the hallway, he could see another room that looked similar, except the fireplace was not visible, and there was no piano. He'd been in cathouses before, of course, but this was the nicest one he could ever remember seeing.

After a few moments, Frenchy Barlow appeared on the stairs with a petite, almost frail-looking colored girl. They came into the room, and Frenchy said, "Now, honey, this fellas' the law, but he ain't here to harm us. He wants to talk to you about Lonny. You tell him the truth now so we can all get back to business." Frenchy poured another gin and sat in a chair with her feet curled under her.

"You wants to hear 'bout my Lonny?"

"Yes, Eugenia, I do. I want to know where he is so I can talk to him. Maybe keep him from being hurt."

"Isn't no lawman going to watch over him? You wanna 'rest him for his law breakin'? I know that."

You're right, Eugenia, but if Lonny isn't protected from the other men he was with, they will certainly do him harm. It's already happened to some. I can hide him and keep others away. Do you know where he is?" Eugenia was chewing her lip and watching Frenchy Barlow. Then she said, "Listen up. If I tell you where he is...will they pay reward money?" Bass was startled. He had just assumed that Lonny Dahl and Eugenia were sweethearts. He could have gone right to the reward first thing had he known.

"Yes, there is a reward for information leading to his capture. It's two hundred dollars, Eugenia."

Eugenia's eyes got wide for a quick moment as she thought what two hundred dollars could do for her.

"Well...All right. He's asleep upstairs in my room. Now, when do I get my money?"

"Eugenia, I have to arrest him first and hopefully get some information from him. But I'll be sure to say you're due the award right away. 'Shouldn't be too long. Now, which is your room?"

"Second one on the left. The doors don't lock." Bass tipped his hat and began slowly walking up the stairs to keep his spurs quiet.

When he reached the second floor, he saw the hallway went both left and right. So he tried first going to the right and opening the second door on the left. As he did, a half-naked woman quickly turned her back to him and said, "Unless you got the fee, you don't get the show." Bass muttered, "Excuse me," and went back down the hall. This time, as he slowly opened the door, he found a young man asleep and snoring softly in a comfortable looking bed. He drew his pistol and approached, conscious of the fact he might be playing possum, and when he got to the side of the bed, he nudged the man firmly.

"Huh? Genia...wha? Bass pulled back the hammer of his Colt to full cock and said,

"You're Lonny Dahl?" The man was still half asleep.

"Yeah, who...?"

"I'm a U.S. Deputy Marshal, and you're under arrest for murder and cattle theft. Put your pants on." Dahl looked to be no more than twenty years old, peach fuzz instead of whiskers. He shook his head and began to fumble with his trousers. Bass noticed a gun belt hanging on a wall hook. 'Looked to be a sizeable piece of iron resting in it, though he couldn't recognize it.

"Wh...where's Genia? What's happened to her? She weren't no part of it."

"I know that, son, but you were, and that's why I'm takin you in."

"Well, is she all right? Is she hurt? Where is she?"

"She's downstairs, she's fine, ain't hurt." The boy put his boots on last and buttoned his shirt up. Bass could tell it was homemade. If this boy had any money, it sure didn't show anywhere on him. Bass suspected he spent it all on Eugenia. Bass put his cuffs on the boy and asked. "You gotta horse, kid?"

"' Course I do. She's out back." Bass slung Lonny Dahl's gun belt over his shoulder and said, "Okay, let's go find her."

The boy led the way downstairs, and as they walked through the first-floor hallway, Bass noticed that both Eugenia and Frenchy Barlow were nowhere to be seen. They went out the back door to a corral, where he whistled up his mare and saddled her. Bass looked the boy's rig over closely, thinking it looked like every cowboy's rig he'd ever seen: simple latigo, no fancy scrollwork or conchos, a bedroll, and empty saddlebags. There was one exception, however. There was no saddle gun. No rifle."

The boy mounted up, and Bass led the horse around to the front where he'd left Emma. Then, together, they rode back into town and down Matamoros Ave. to the Town Marshal's office and the city jail.

10:45 a.m. November 6th, 1888
City Marshals Office
Matamoras at Salinas Ave.
Laredo, Texas

Marshal Arguello stood up as Bass came through the door with his prisoner.

"Who's this now, Frank?"

"This here's Lonny Dahl, the younger one, a most ruthless outlaw, Marshal. I believe he should be kept in your most secure cell."

"Hey, wait now, that ain't fair...nor true neither. I know I was with them fellas that stole those cows, but I never did any ruthlessness at all. It was all on them other guys, you gotta believe me. I didn't shoot nobody...ever in my life."

Bass wanted to sweat the boy a little longer before he started questioning him, and he winked at Arguello. Then he said, "Yeah, yeah. I hear that all the time. Lock him up Des." Arguello took the boy to the corner cell in back and had him reach his hands through the bars to remove the cuffs. Arguello had picked up on Bass's ploy and played along. You're one lucky kid, I'll say. You know who that is? That's Marshal Frank Bass, boy. He's known to shoot down outlaws he catches to save the costs of a trial. He comes back you best be on your best behavior." He left the cell room, shut the door, and went back out front.

"Where'd you find that pup, Frank?"

"Oh, he was out to Frenchy Barlow's whore house with a colored gal named Eugenia. She's got two hundred dollars comin in reward, I promised."

"Two hun...? Where do you think that kind a money's comin from to pay off a whore?"

"Hell, I don't know. Bill it to Atwill when we arrest him. I wanna talk to the boy after he's had a chance to fester a bit, maybe tomorrow. Depending on what I find out, I think we'll be ready to move on Atwill's place the day after. Start thinkin on guys you can trust to ride out there with us, guys that won't be trigger happy or too shy to be any good."

"Alright. Anything else I should know about what we'll be up against?"

"I followed Atwill and four riders out to a pasture maybe twelve to fifteen miles northeast of his spread. That's where he's got the cows. I think we can assume that he's got other guns hired to work for him other than just those five—figure on maybe eight to ten total. There's also that Mexican to deal with and Tom Horn, too, if he's still there. I guess we'll need at least ten men with us. Tell them they will all be deputized by me and will draw down federal deputy pay for their time. Right now, I'm gonna go see Willy Banes, 'ask if he knows how many hands Atwill might have." Bass smiled and said, "Then I'm going to torment Cherry Lennox for a while. I get such a kick outta that. I'll let you know what I find out from Willie Banes." Bass put his hat on and rode back to the Arbuckle Hotel.

Noon, November 6th, 1888
Arbuckle Hotel,
Washington Street
Laredo, Texas

Bass went straight to Banes's room and knocked on the door four times as agreed. "Willy, it's me. Open up. I wanna talk to you, 'got a few questions. Willy?! Bass suddenly noticed a slight odor, one he'd smelled too many times before, and his mind immediately imagined the worst. He tried the door, and the bolt moved freely. Bass entered the room and saw Willy Banes lying face up in the middle of the room. There was a gaping slash across his throat, and he lay in a pool of his own blood. Some of the blood had dried, and his body was becoming flexible. That meant rigor was passing, and he was starting to decompose. He'd been dead over twenty-four hours. Bass knew it had to have been the Mexican; it was his method of choice, and he must've been waiting for Willy when he returned from his meeting with the judge. Bass leaned over to close Willy's eyes and stood over the body of the older man. As he looked down at Willy Banes, he silently promised himself that he'd finish the Mexican along with Tom Horn.

Twenty-Four

2:15 p.m. November 6th, 1888
Doc Gately's Clinic
Montezuma Street
Laredo, Texas

Bass had ridden to Doc Gately's and asked that he send a wagon for Willy's body. For some reason, Willy's murder hit harder than he would have thought. Maybe it was because he'd known him for so long, or perhaps it was because Willy was trying to do the right thing. But inside, Bass knew it was because Willy had trusted in Bass to protect him, and now he was dead. Bass was strong enough to set aside most of his regrets. It was necessary in this business if you were going to make a difference. And Willy wasn't an innocent either. He certainly knew the risks of the business he chose. Still, even with all that, Bass couldn't help but feel like he failed. He reaffirmed for himself right then that he'd see to it the Mexican paid.

Bass left the Doc's office and went back to the Jail. He wanted to report what had happened to Arguello and have another talk with young Lonny Dahl. When he got to the Marshal's office, he noticed several horses tied to the hitch rail in front. He tied off Emma, walked up the steps to the boardwalk, and went inside. Arguello was sitting at his desk, and around him stood three able-bodied men, all heeled and talking with Arguello.

4:30 p.m. November 6th, 1888
City Marshals Office
Matamoras at Salinas Ave.
Laredo, Texas

"Marshal Bass, good, I'm glad you've returned. I've found us some help. I think you know Ray Wilke from the livery. The young man with the long hair is Gus Freeman. He's a drover and sometime bronc buster who's worked for me off and on. The next one was a deputy here before Matt Cole dismissed him. He's Norm Hacket. Norm's the best man with a handgun I've ever seen. I've just gone over what we're up against, and maybe you can add to it."

"All right. Boys, My name is Frank Bass. I'm a U.S. Deputy Marshal. Ray there and I have met but you other two are new to me. I wanna thank you for pitching in here. Marshal Arguello is a good man and his recommendation means a lot.

We're after several men out at the Tierra Blanca for murder and cattle rustling from the King Ranch. The short version is that some weeks ago, a group of five or six outlaws stole twenty-four head of Longhorn cattle from the King Ranch, and in the process of bringin' 'em back to Atwill, a U.S. Deputy Marshal was killed when he tried to stop them. His name was Howard Gosling. Maybe some a you mighta known him. Most folks liked him. Harold had a posse with him, and all but one of them was killed.

I believe the man that pulled the trigger on Howard is named Cherry Lennox. I arrested him a week or so ago, and in the process, I shot him in the leg. He's cuffed to his bed at Doc Gately's and thinks he's convinced me another man shot Harold.

That man was Bloody Ron Fox. I arrested him in Nuevo Laredo and took him to Doc's as well. He was shot through the shoulder. That night at Doc Gately's, Lennox got free of one of his cuffs and was able to give Fox a high dose of morphine, so much it killed him. That told me for certain that Lennox is our trigger man.

Now, I've also arrested the last man in that group of outlaws. His name is Lonny Dahl. He's in a cell in the back and I'm about to go talk to him.

Any questions?" Ray Wilke asked. "Geezes, Marshal, sounds like you got everybody involved. Can't we just go out and arrest Atwill?"

"Good question. I wanted to be sure we have a witness that will say Atwill organized the whole thing. 'Makes him accountable for the murders of Harold Gosling and the rest of the posse men. The ringleader of the group was an outlaw named Dan Bogan. He was killed by one of Atwill's men just after they turned over the stolen herd. I believe Atwill assumed the others would head off to Mexico and never be found. Killing Bogan distanced him from the crime." Bass hung his head and said, "I also smuggled Atwill's foreman, Willy Banes, off the ranch. He's a man I've known for some time. 'Known for brand forgery. Unfortunately, he's been killed too. I have a deposition from him and from the one posse man that escaped. I plan to talk to the boy in the cell back yonder today."

Norm Hacket, who was quiet through it all, finally asked, "Marshal Bass? What is it exactly you want us to do for you?"

"Another good question. I'd like you boys to accompany me and Marshal Arguello out to the Tierra Blanca for the purpose of arresting Landon Atwill. He's likely got some help out there, so we'll have to be careful." Bass paused again to gather his thoughts, "There's one other thing. Atwill has a small Mexican-looking fella workin for him. I believe he killed Matt Cole and Willy Banes, the man I said I'd protect. There may also be an injured outlaw named Tom Horn staying with Atwill. They have some history together. I will be taking care of these two men personally. None of you will have any responsibility for their apprehension. Am I clear?" Each man understood what Bass was saying, and each nodded silently.

"Fine then. Now, I want to talk to the young Mr. Dahl. After that, I'll come up with a plan of action. You'll all be deputized by me and will draw federal deputy wage. It also means if anything happens to you while we're doin this thing, your families will be provided for. Now, excuse me. Let's meet up tonight at the Arbuckle Hotel at around 7:00 p.m."

Arguello handed Bass the keys to Dahl's cell, and the four men went about their business, presumably to get some supper. Bass went back to talk to Lonny Dahl.

"Lonny? Wake up son. I wanna have a talk." Bass unlocked the cell and walked in. he sat on the cot opposite Dahl. "Lonny? You seem like a good kid. How'd you get mixed up with guys like Dan Bogan and Bloody Ron Fox?" The boy looked younger, sitting alone in the cell. "It was my Pa. He said if I wanted to be a man, I should go with Dan Bogan. They was friends, and Dan was supposed to show me the ropes of cattle rustling. So when he left our farm, I went with him."

"What's your Pa's name?"

"Pa's name is Tagin. I use my Ma's name, Dahl."

"Your Pa is Pete Tagin?"

"Yeah. He comes by our farm every so often when he needs money or a stake. Ma and my three brothers been workin the farm since he took off years ago. I left to make my fortune, but I spent most a what we was paid on Eugenia."

"So, did you ever get money from Landon Atwill?"

"No, never did. He had some kinda funny little Mexican workin for him, and he paid us. Never got no money from Mr. Atwill."

"I see. So...you and Dan Bogan and a few others just decided to go out and steal cows to sell to Landon Atwill, right?"

"Well, yeah. And then we was paid."

"I'm curious. How did Bogan know where the cows were?"

"Oh. Cause Mr. Atwill told him where they was and about how many to take." Bass sat up straight. He wondered why he hadn't asked that question of anyone before.

"How do you know Atwill told him?"

"'Cause I was with Dan at the time. See, Dan was gonna show how to deal with rich guys like Atwill, so we went to his house, and he told Dan to take only the cows he wanted."

"And did you hear him say that?"

"Well, yeah. I was right there."

"What else was talked about at that meeting?"

"Ah...the price. Mr. Atwill said he'd pay Dan six hundred dollars to bring the cattle to the ranch. Dan said okay."

"All right. You've been most helpful. Now I'd like to ask about the shooting at San Ygnacio Bridge. Can you tell me who shot first?"

"Sure, it was Cherry Lennox. He was sittin his horse right up front a me and shot the lawman with his rifle. Then he shot someone else. Then they were all shootin, and I seen one posse man ride off. Oh yeah,... and while they was shootin'? I saw Dan shoot one of the Mexican vaqueros dead. I think it was cause the Mexican couldn't calm his horse. Then, the other one run off. I guess ascared he'd get it too."

"Very good, Lon. Now, I want you to answer the next question truthfully. You've given me enough information to talk to the judge for you but I have to ask. "Who did you shoot?"

" Me?" The boy looked at the floor and said, "I didn't shoot nobody...I dropped my gun when my horse spooked."

"Okay, Lon. I'm gonna put in a good word for you with Judge Staton. Don't mean you'll get off, you know. You was there stealin' cows just like the rest. But he may go easier on you for what you've told me." The boy nodded, continuing to stare at the floor. Bass got up and locked the cell. He walked out and sat with Arguello, who had just poured a cup of coffee.

"The boy gave us all we need. His story rings true and puts Atwill as the leader—the one who hired Bogan. Lonny's a direct witness, and I wanna make sure that what happened to Willy Banes doesn't happen to him. So I believe I'll be stayin here at the jail tonight. I'm gonna ask you to meet the others at the hotel at 7:00 p.m. and bring them back here. Right now, I need to see the judge about a warrant, so I gotta get to the courthouse before he leaves."

4:45 p.m. November 6th, 1888
Laredo City Hall
San Eduardo Street

Laredo, Texas

"Judge Staton, I'm glad I caught you. I wonder if I might impose on you for an arrest warrant."

Jim Staton, the sixty-year-old senior jurist for the tri-county area, was closing the books on his day. It had been a long and boring one, filled with paperwork, motions, stays, and scheduling conflicts. He was more than ready to head home to his wife Edna, a bourbon next to the fire, and his supper. *Now, an out-of-town Federal Marshal wants me to stay so he can make an arrest on his own schedule. Aw, hell with it, 'might as well.*

"Alright, Marshal, what's the cause." The old man pushed back a shock of his thick grey hair and sat at his desk.

"Suspicion of murdering a Federal Marshal and his posse and cattle theft, sir."

"A capital charge, interesting. Who's the suspect?"

"Landon Atwill." The judge dropped his pen, smudging the document he'd just taken from his drawer.

"Atwill? From the Tierra Blanca? You're charging him?'

"I am, sir." Judge Staton took out a fresh form.

"What's your just cause, Marshal? Can't be arresting wealthy citizens without good reason, you know?"

"Oh, I know that Judge. I have a witness who was present when Atwill ordered the theft and was also present when Howard Gosling and four other sworn deputies were killed." The judge continued to watch Bass after he'd finished and finally said. "Who's your witness?"

"One of the outlaws that Atwill hired."

"You really think his testimony will hold up against the kind of lawyer Atwill will hire? Bass nodded.

"When coupled with the sworn depositions you and I have taken...yes, I do."

The judge pulled another blank warrant page from his drawer, filled in the name and charge, and said, "Frank, I'm making this general enough that you can include others as you deem necessary, and I'll date it once you're finished. Hell, we'll figure it all out in court anyway. And…I wish you luck, son." Staton signed the page and handed it to Bass.

"Thank you, sir, 'plan to take action on this fairly soon." Bass put his hat back on and left the judge's office.

5:30 p.m. November 6th, 1888
City Marshals Office
Matamoras at Salinas Ave.
Laredo, Texas

Desmond Arguello was lighting the lamps out in front when Bass reined up at the jail.

"Figured I'd better hang around till you got back, just in case that Mexican somehow got wind of our prisoner." Bass dismounted and answered.

"He sure seems to keep himself informed. I figure he knew Matt Cole's routine pretty well and when he'd be alone. Also, sure, Matt knew all about the shooting and cattle rustling. That's probably what got him killed. But I have no idea how that Mexican knew about Willy Banes. I don't believe we were seen leaving the ranch, and I was awfully secretive with him when we got to town. I felt pretty good about leaving Willy on his own, hell he was more scared he'd be seen than I was."

"Weren't you afraid he'd run out on you?"

"Nah, though now I kinda wish he had. Why don't you go have somethin to eat and then stop by the hotel to bring the men back here? If you think of it, ask them at the café to send over somethin' for the two of us."

"Will do, Frank."

7:00 p.m. November 6th, 1888
City Marshals Office
Matamoras at Salinas Ave.
Laredo, Texas

All five men sat around Arguello's desk except for Gus Freeman, who sat on the floor propped against the cell room wall. Bass began.

"I went to see Judge Staton this afternoon and told him we'd need an arrest warrant for Atwill. He worded it so we could arrest anyone else we had a reason to suspect was in on it.

Now, I know it's likely that Atwill has some protection out there, but I'm really only interested in taking down Atwill. 'Course, if during the arrest process we discover someone deserving of attention, we'll oblige." Norm Hacket asked, "Are you pretty sure of the five hands, or are you just guessing?"

"Well, I've been out watching the place for a few days, and on one day, I followed Atwill and five guys out to the place where they got the stolen cows hidden. I never saw more'n six or seven men out and about in the ranch yard. Let's remember that the Tierra Blanca has a legitimate herd somewhere, too, and I'm guessing Atwill has a good number of hands watching 'em."

Arguello asked, "Can we make our arrests without alerting the whole ranch, do ya think?"

"Glad you asked 'cause what I'm thinkin is we go in the early morning, say 4:30 a.m. or so before the sun's up. We know where everybody will be at that hour. My plan is to get into the house and take Atwill first. Head a the snake kinda thing. I figure that may slow down his bodyguard little Mexican enough that we can disable him easy enough.

The unknown here is the other outlaw, I believe is there. Tom Horn. He ain't involved with Atwill's plan but may start shootin just cause he hears somethin. 'Course that wakes everybody up, but like I say, if we have Atwill, the others will likely back down. So that's my plan. Any questions?" Norm Hacket asked, "Yeah. When do we do this?"

"Okay. I'm thinkin mornin' after tomorrow. That'll give me one more chance to watch the ranch from a distance. I can also re-count gunhands. So everybody play it close to the vest tomorrow and get some rest. We'll meet here at 3:30 a.m. the next mornin.'"

Twenty-Five

11:15 a.m. November 7ᵗʰ, 1888
A Position of Cover
Hillside on Eagle Pass Road
North of Laredo, Texas.

Bass took up his usual position about two hundred or so feet from the Tierra Blanca yard. There was some activity at the corral. Bass could see horses were being saddle broke, and that always attracted a crowd. He spotted a thin man with his foot in some kind of cast watching the action, but he never turned for Bass to get a look at his face. The assumption was that it was Horn, and Bass continued his observations. He began thinking of his own place and remembered he now had a kind of watchdog who seemed particularly protective of Lil. He'd never had a dog before, primarily because he was away so much and couldn't take care of a house pet. There were the usual feral cats around his place and Paulo's that performed their function well, but he'd never had a dog.

Naturally, he began to scan for any indication of a ranch dog on the premises, and after getting bleary-eyed starin' through the lenses, he determined there was none. This was a relief because any dog in the house would have to be dealt with, and Bass didn't care to shoot innocent critters just for doin' their job.

A few more minutes and, Bass saw the small Mexican man come from the house and talk to Horn, who had turned and was now identifiable. Then, they both returned to the house together. Bass decided to stay for a while longer, and when the bronco breaking stopped and the men returned to their cots in the bunkhouse, Bass decided he'd seen enough. He found Emma, climbed aboard, and pointed her head back to town.

5:00 p.m. November 7ᵗʰ, 1888
City Marshals Office
Matamoros at Salinas Ave.
Laredo, Texas

Des Arguello was talking with Lonny Dahl and sharing stories about Lon's father, Pete Tagin. "So, does your old man ever come around anymore?"

"Yeah, sometimes, just to say 'hey.' He used to hit Ma up for money whenever he came by, but you know, lately, the last year or so, when he comes back, it's to give her money. 'Don't know where he gets it, and Ma don't ask. She just says thank you and takes it."

Arguello was listening and said. "Doubt it's honest money, knowin' your Pa. When I knew him, he could charm 'skin off a snake. And sweet talk the women? I mean, they fell all over themselves for a chance at him. 'Course he'd be older now, so that may not hold true no more, but my, my. Some of us would just stay close to pick up on his leavin's."

"I know, that's what Ma always says, too. She don't know why he keeps comin' back, but he does." Bass listened to a moment of their talk and then walked in.

"Des? We planned on an early start. 'Like to have Ray Wilke sit the jail and watch over our star witness while we're gone. He's older, and we may have to be quick on our feet. I know a bit about him too and would feel more comfortable knowin he's here."

"Alright, Frank. I'll tell him... he ain't gonna like it, but I'll tell him.

I'll check in with the others, too, remind 'em of the time. Is there anything special you'll want 'em to have?"

"No. They'll know what to bring. We're gonna need a dark lantern, 'hopin' you got one."

"I do. In the shed out back."

"You go on then, check in with the boys, and get some rest. I'll see you all at 3:30 tomorrow mornin.'"

Bass waited 'til Des. Arguello had left to go about locking the back door and closing down the shutters. He checked on Emma in the small barn in back and then entered the jail through the front door and locked it behind him.

He chucked more wood in the stove and put coffee on to boil, then settled into the chair behind the desk. He briefly thought about sending a wire home, telling Sally that his business was nearly through. He thought better of it, though. He was afraid it might jinx their play.

3:15 a.m. November 8th, 1888
City Marshals Office
Matamoros at Salinas Ave.
Laredo, Texas

Ray Wilke was the first to arrive. He knocked on the door using a forceful blow of the side of his hand, and when Bass opened the door, Wilke strode in stiffly and sat in the chair at the desk. Bass closed the door, knowing what prompted Wilke's brusque arrival, and sat across from him at the desk.

Wilke spoke first.

"I'm as good as any of 'em, you know?"

"I think you're better than any of 'em. 'Why I want you here watchin' the kid back there. You know there's a fair chance that the five of us won't be comin back. I still need someone to produce our witness for court if Atwill gets the better of us. 'Never thought for a moment you were less than the others. Thought you'd be more useful here."

Wilke sat up straighter in his chair. "I know I'm older, 'might not be able to get around quick as I'd like."

"And here at the jail, you don't need to. But you'll be alone. And if Atwill and the others do for us, I'll need your courage to stand 'em off. Understand?"

"I do." Wilke looked Bass in the eye and said, "Won't let you down."

The sound of horses being reined up outside caused them both to stand up. One by one, the three men walked into the jail office, making elbow room scarce.

"Boys, grab what you need from the gun rack there; spare shells are in the drawer below. Des? Would you mind fetchin' along two dark lanterns?"

Arguello left the room with an oil lamp to retrieve the dark lanterns stored in the shed next to the barn. While he was gone, Bass said,

"Coffee's hot on the stove. What's the moon like? Last night, it was crescent." Gus Freeman said, "Tis. Waxing maybe. Sure won't give us away... but won't help neither."

Des Arguello returned with two dark lanterns and filled each from a quart jar as Bass began to draw the layout of the Tierra Blanca yard on the desk. When he finished, he began.

"Okay, boys, jump in if you see somethin' I miss. I figure we go in through the main gate, no reason not to. Besides, to the south, the cover is too heavy to get through in the dark, and to the north, along the road, we'd have to go up a good quarter mile to find a place to cross. I know, I've done it."

Now, we'll leave the horses on the south side and go into the main house right here at this backdoor. Alright. I want you, Gus, and Norm to take up a position here, outside the bunkhouse. I believe there's only the one door, but if there's one in the back, and they start to run, you'll be able to see 'em from here. I'm guessin' if they run out, it'll be because of a shot from inside, so they'll be armed and headin' either for the house or the corral. If they head for the corral, let 'em go. But if they come for the house, don't hesitate. Lay down whatever fire you need to.

Now me and Des here, we'll go inside and roust out Atwill and the Mexican. I'll find Tom Horn myself if he's still there. The two of us will cuff the prisoners and carry them across our saddles to get back to town. Once we're on the road, Gus and Norm, you can skedaddle yourselves."

Norm made a suggestion. "Since we're more or less independent of you boys, maybe me and Gus should leave our horses at the gate so we don't have to run all that way back to the house."

Bass nodded. And said,

"Fine with me. And you two might wanna think about headin north and comin' back to town across the San Ygnacio Bridge. I know it's longer, but if you're followed, they might not think to follow in that direction.

"So, there it is. Everybody clear? I guess I don't have to say this'll likely be, kill or be killed...so watch yourselves, boys. Ray? We already talked. None of what we do tonight works without we have Lon Dahl." Ray Wilke nodded his affirmation.

Bass left to saddle Emma and as he rode back around to the front of the jail, all three of the others were waiting. Bass led the way out of town, west along Matamoros and then north on Eagle Pass Road. It was clear and cold at that hour. The thin light of the moon behind them cast faint shadows of their movements, and the steam billowed from their horses' nostrils as they canted their way toward the Tierra Blanca gate.

As Bass rode, he decided to carry one of his Walker Colts along with the .44 Army in his holster. It occurred to him that if shooting started, and he was afraid it would, having a small canon in his hand might be a difference-maker. In any event, he didn't see how it could hurt.

He knew the others were probably thinking of family loved ones at home. He specifically hadn't asked about family connections when they met for that reason. The fear of leaving the people you love could sometimes interfere with judgment. Bass recalled from experience that knowing who had family to care for usually affected his thinking, too. He became protective and made slanted decisions.

If a man had a young family at home, Bass didn't want to know about it.

It took forty-five minutes, by Bass's Elgin, to reach the Tierra Blanca. He held up his arm, signaling a halt while he and Des Arguello lit the dark lanterns.

Once done, he said softly, "Everybody check your weapons. We're gonna walk 'em in from here. In the still darkness, the squeaking of saddle leather and the metallic clicking of firearms and horseshoes seemed deafening. Bass knew it could not be heard for any distance, but he still wished for complete silence.

Single file, they led their horses through the arched gate of the ranch, and as they passed under, Gus and Norm split off for their position near the bunkhouse. Once they'd settled into their spot, they could hear horses in the corral two hundred feet away as they became restless. Norm whispered, "They can smell our nags."

Gus nodded. "Not much to be done about it." Both men readied their Winchester rifles, settled into cover near the south side of the bunkhouse, and waited for the action they hoped wouldn't come.

Bass and Arguello had left their horses tied off at a hitch at the south end of the veranda, where they couldn't be seen from the bunkhouse. They each carried a dark lantern and took the long way around the house to the back door. Bass figured it would be the furthest from wherever Atwill was sleeping. He pressed slowly down on the latch until it stopped. The door was locked from the inside. Not uncommon, though some ranches leave an access to the house available at all hours.

Using his knife, he slid the blade between the door and the jam until it reached the hilt. He pushed on the hilt, hoping to lift the latch bar high enough that the door would swing free. The lock was too tight, however, and the latch bar didn't budge. He jiggled the handle a few times and tried again. Still no luck. Next, he took a roll of bandaging tape from his pocket and created a crisscross pattern on the glass window above the handle. He held onto one end of the tape and used his elbow to break the glass. The blow produced a thudding sound along with a cracking, like sheet ice breaking, but the tape kept the window glass from falling and shattering on the floor.

Bass was able to reach inside, lift the locking ring off the latch, and open the door. Both men went inside and closed the door behind them. Bass led the way, opening the lantern shade slightly, just enough so that he could keep from stumbling over furniture. With Arguello behind, they slowly and quietly checked each room until they came to a hallway with double doors at the end. Obviously, this would be a bedroom. They'd already passed what looked like an office.

Bass closed the lantern and very quietly worked the latch. As he swung the door open, Atwill struck a match to light an oil lamp on a table next to where he was sitting. He held a pistol in his right hand, and it was pointed at Bass's middle.

"Good morning, Marshal Bass. Welcome again to Tierra Blanca. This time, you won't have to sit on that hill across the road." Bass turned to look at Desmond Arguello. His pistol was pointed at Bass as well. "Sorry, Frank, business is business, ya know. And, like I said, Atwill has more money than fleas on a hound. Move over there in the corner where I can see you better."

Bass moved slowly, his hands held up away from his sides and turned to face both men standing in the lamplight. "Des. I shoulda known. Damn. It was you that tipped the little Mexican off about Willy Banes wasn't it? Sure it was. You're the only one I told about it."

"That's right, Frank, and poor old Matt Cole, too. Mateo is an amazing man. In fact, I told him you had Lennox and Fox over at Doc Gately's, but before he could act, Lennox took care of Fox for us."

Then Landon Atwill said, "He is particularly effective, don't you agree? Ah... please to put your handgun on the floor and kick it away. There's a good chap."

Bass did as he was told, and once he did, he lowered his arms to his sides.

"Yes, your Mateo is a dutiful employee. Where is he now, by the way?"

Atwill smiled and said,

"Why, he's on his way to the jail, of course. To dispatch that young man you found for me. And then he'll finish up with that mad dog Lennox fellow, though, as Marshal Arguello here said he did prove useful with 'Bloody' Ron Fox, didn't he?" Atwill was enjoying himself.

Bass asked.

"Did you put him up to that? Don't believe he'd be smart enough to figure things out for himself."

Atwill shook his head.

"Oh, don't sell Mr. Lennox, short Marshal. I believe he had you going for a while there, didn't he?"

Bass smiled wanly and said, "Yeah I guess he did, at that." Bass paused for a moment, looking from one man to the other. So what happens now? Do we wait for Mateo to return, or do you just shoot me here?"

Arguello stepped forward and said,

"Actually, Frank, there's someone waiting for you that asked to have that pleasure for himself. I'm sure you'll remember him from your trip to Denver. He doesn't get around very well, so he's waiting in another room for you. Now, if you please? Back through this doorway and then, second door on the left."

Bass's hands were by his side, and his canvas duster was open. He turned toward the door and stood between Arguello, who was backing down the hallway with his pistol still on Bass, and Atwill, who now stood next to the lamp. As Bass moved forward into the shadows of the hall, he moved his hand to the butt of his Walker Colt tucked into his belt. Once he was fully in the shadow, he drew the weapon and fired a fifty-caliber slug into Arguello's middle. The concussion from the blast lifted him from his feet and sent him sprawling on the floor to the end of the hallway. He was dead as the explosion still echoed throughout the house. Atwill was taken by surprise at the shot, and the concussion startled him just long enough for Bass to fire again. This time, the heavy slug took Atwill in the neck, severing his spine as it passed through and opened the carotid. The man bled out on the floor without being able to raise his hands to his wound or kick his legs in defiance.

Bass wasn't through. There was still the matter of the second door on the left. Bass wheeled in place, lowered his Walker, and saw the door open. A short-barreled shotgun muzzle appeared around the door and pointed down the hall, but Bass couldn't see the man that held it. The two barrels were fired at once, sending buckshot flying down the hallway in a spray of lethal pellets that crashed into the woodwork and partially caught Bass in the right leg. Bass pulled the trigger again on the Walker and sent a bullet, shattering the wooden door and knocking it off its hinges.

Almost deaf now from the three explosions in close quarters and nearly blinded by the acrid smoke of the havoc he'd unleashed, Bass hobbled to the second doorway and saw Tom Horn on the floor, desperately crawling for a pistol that rested on the bed. Bass could see his mouth was open, but he could hear only muffled words. Horn's eyes were wide and pleading, reflecting the mortal terror of his situation. He turned onto his back, flailing with his arms in a desperate attempt to deflect the bullet he knew was coming. Bass could see the man crying,

"No! Stop! Please, No!" but Bass was finished with him. He pulled the trigger one last time and saw Horn's body bounce off the floor as it recoiled from the penetration of the slug. Horn's face was frozen in wild-eyed panic when he died.

Bass leaned against the wall and closed his eyes when he heard muffled rifle fire from outside. He tied his kerchief around his leg as a tourniquet, went back to pick up his Colt, and then hobbled to the back door. He stood for a moment, collecting his wits, and finally yelled through the door.

"Hold your fire! Hold your fire, all of you!" The shooting stopped, and Bass yelled again across the yard, "It's over! It's all over in here! Atwill is dead! There's no one to pay you!

Pack up your gear and leave! We won't shoot! Go on, now. We won't shoot!"

Bass then looked to see the deputies he'd set to watch the bunkhouse. "Boys?! Gus, Norm! Go on home, boys. It's all over in here now. Go on home and come see me in the morning!" He saw the two figures stand and walk quickly to the horses.

The adrenalin was starting to pass now, and Bass's leg throbbed painfully. He had no idea how many pellets he'd taken or how much blood he'd lost, but he did know he had to get back to the jail as quickly as possible. He limped to where Emma stood waiting with Arguello's horse and hoisted himself into the saddle. He knew the Mexican had a lengthy jump on him, so he spurred Emma into a gallop right away. He had no idea what time it was. All he hoped was that it wasn't too late for Lonny Dahl.

As he passed Arguello's Livery and turned on Matamoros, he was in a cold sweat and fighting off shock from blood loss. Still, he continued. He rode toward the jail and could see lamps burning from the inside, but he also knew that didn't mean anything. By this time, Ray Wilke and Lonny Dahl were probably dead on the floor, their throats slit like Willy Banes. The town was still quiet, and Bass could see the eastern sky beginning to lighten.

He reined up outside the jail; 'no point in trying to be quiet anymore. His only hope was that he'd find the Mexican killer still in the building. He had difficulty lifting his right leg over the saddle to dismount, but eventually, both feet were on the ground, and his Walker Colt was in his hand. He stopped at the front door and listened. Nothing, just as he feared. He daren't wait any longer, so he pushed the latch handle and stepped inside, pistol at the ready.

"Oh, hey, Marshal. Where's the other boys?" Ray Wilke was sitting in the desk chair reading a paper, just as they'd left him.

Bass stood with his pistol, looking worn, pale, and about to drop. He asked,

"Ray? 'You all right? How's the kid, how's Lonny?"

"We're fine, Marshal. Ah, had a visit from that little Mexican fella earlier."

Bass was animated again.

"Yes. Yes, that's what I mean. What happened to him?" Ray spoke matter of factly.

"Well, I caught him sneakin' around out back. The horses gave him away. Anyhow, we scuffled a bit, and, damndest thing, he fell on his knife, yes sir, cut his own throat from ear to ear. He's still out back, 'didn't want to drag him inside, make a mess like that."

Bass still looked confused as he set his Walker on the desk. He was ghostly white and was sweating again. That's when Wilke asked,

"What happened to you? By God, Frank, your leg's bleeding. You stay here. I'll fetch Doc Gately. You can tell me what happened out to Tierra Blanca when we get back."

Once Wilke had closed the door behind him, Bass's world began to spin. He toppled forward, catching himself on the desk, and then he collapsed to the floor.

Twenty-Six

9:15 a.m. November 8th, 1888
City Marshals Office
Matamoros at Salinas Ave.
Laredo, Texas

Bass woke up on a cot in a jail cell. Sunlight was streaming through the door to the office, and he could hear voices talking. He recognized one as Doc Gately, so he called out, "Hey, Doc? You out there?"

Gately came into the room and said, "Well, big surprise...You're shot in the leg. How do you feel?"

Bass didn't open his eyes.

"Groggy. Feel like I could sleep for a week."

Ray Wilke came in at that point. "How is he, Doc?"

'You gonna have to take off the leg, like you said?" Bass opened his eyes and looked at Wilke.

"That ain't funny, Ray." Wilke smiled, looking at Bass.

"Aw, c'mon. It's a little funny. Gallows humor, ya know?"

The Doc asked, "Speakin' of gallows, what the hell happened out there last night? Did you arrest anybody? Or did ya just shoot 'em all?"

"That ain't funny either, Doc, though yeah, I did shoot 'em all.

Arguello was in on it with Atwill. That's how one of my witnesses got it. Mexican did him in."

"So I take it then that Atwill and Des Arguello ain't comin back?"

"Not unless they're carried. Oh Ray, remember the guy that shot me and my horse?"

"Yeah, you get him too?" Bass grinned slightly.

"Did. Serves him right, shootin' my horse."

Doc picked eleven number 8 shot pellets from Bass's right leg before using astringent and bandaging. "Good thing it was bird shot, won't hardly even leave a scar."

Gus Freeman and Norm Hacket both stopped by later in the day to hear the story of what happened inside Atwill's house. They both had trouble believing that Arguello had sided with Atwill. Bass thanked them both and promised them the usual seventy-five dollars each for their help. Of course, there was nothing usual about the payment. Bass always rewarded courage.

Bass went back to the hotel late in the morning and put Emma away with instructions for a good feed of oats if they had any. He stopped at the bar and bought a pint of Old Overholt rye whiskey and a newspaper before slowly climbing the stairs to his room. Once there, he poured himself a large glass of the rye, swallowed most of it down, and settled on the bed to read the paper. He fell asleep before finishing the headlines.

Bass woke up the next morning at 7:00 a.m., went down to the dining room for breakfast, and then hobbled over to City Hall to see Judge James Staton. He told the whole story yet again and made a couple of recommendations.

"Judge, since the matter of cattle theft and murder has been pretty much resolved, I'm gonna recommend that we release Lonny Dahl. He's already identified Lennox as the man who pulled the trigger on Harold Gosling, and we have Lennox in custody at Doc Gately's."

"Uh-uh. Frank, I must point out that the boy was present for the theft. Even if he didn't personally kill Harold, he's still an accessory."

"I understand that, judge, and of course, you know the law better'n me, but the boy was urged to join that gang by his own father, Pete Tagin. You probly heard a him. Family's dirt poor. Even Cherry Lennox said the boy wasn't much more than a nuisance. I believe lockin' him away at Huntsville with a bunch of hardened convicts would only make a green young man another hardened convict."

"Well, there's truth to what you say, and I'm not without compassion. I know Peter Tagin by reputation, as you say, and he is a cracker-jack scoundrel. I'll think on it. 'Best I can do."

"That's fine, just fine, Judge. 'Couldn't ask for better. Now, one more thing. I'd like to recommend Ray Wilke for the job of Town Marshal. He already proved himself in dealin' with Atwill's Mexican friend, and since Arguello's Livery is out of business, at least for a while, he's out of a job. 'Works out all the way around."

"I agree. It does seem to make sense. I'll bring it up with the mayor tomorrow at the Governance Meeting. Is there anything else you'd like to suggest to make our little community run more smoothly?" Bass grinned back at the Judge.

"No, Judge, that's all I have ... for now. Actually, I'm just about to fetch my horse and go down to the Railroad Office and buy a ticket home."

"Well, in that case, Marshal Bass, safe travels." The judge stood and shook Bass's hand.

Bass rode eight blocks west to the Railroad Ticket Office on Santa Isabelle Street near the Rio and tied Emma to the hitch post in front. When he limped inside, he was aware that the few customers that were waiting in line had noticed him. They nodded and smiled. One lady even curtsied quickly, tilting her head and smiling coyly. Bass tipped his hat to all, though he was confused and more than a little self-conscious.

When it was his turn at the booth, the clerk welcomed him by name. "Marshal Bass, how can I help you today?"

Bass hesitated, trying to recall if he'd met the man while in town, and finally said, "A ticket to El Paso for tomorrow, please. It'll be for me and passage for my horse, too?"

"Yes, sir, the *Rio Flyer* it is. 'Departs tomorrow morning at 7:45 a.m. 'Arrives the next morning at 6:00 a.m. Water and meal stops en route. Now, what kind of accommodations would you like?"

"Hmm? Oh, don't matter. I guess I can sit up in the bar like I did comin' down."

"Nonsense, Marshal. We can't have the hero of the Tierra Blanca sitting up all night. I'm going to upgrade you to a drawing room, sir. No extra charge. That'll be forty-nine dollars, sir, uh, no charge for your fine horse. Our pleasure, sir." Bass looked at the clerk with a quizzical expression. He was grateful, of course, but didn't understand first how word had gotten out and second why folks were so appreciative.

He paid the forty-nine dollars and shook hands with the clerk through the bars of the cage,

"Well, thank you very much for your kindness. It's a long trip, and I'll certainly be more comfortable. Oh, and my horse thanks you, too."

Bass tucked the tickets into his coat pocket and climbed back on Emma for the ride back to the hotel to pack and advise the clerk he would be leaving in the morning and to prepare his bill. When he arrived after tying off Emma, he noticed the lady reporter sitting on the hotel steps.

"Well, Miss Perez. It's nice to see you this mornin'. I expect you're here to collect on my promise, true?"

"Exactly, Marshal Bass. And I plan to quote you extensively."

"Well, I don't know I'll make for such good readin', but come with me, and we'll have some lunch. I'll give you your story."

Margaretta Perez and Bass settled into a corner table, and each ordered a whiskey when the waitress stopped by. Perez started by asking,

"So, Marshal, your work here is done? I noticed you limping coming in, where you hurt badly?"

"Oh, no, not really. A few pellets from a shotgun up at Atwill's place is all. And yes, I'm set to leave for home tomorrow morning. 'Been gone too long. My baby girl is standing on her own, probably walkin' all about our place by the time I get home."

"You have a little girl? I didn't know that. What's her name?"

"Lillianne. After her Grandmom."

Perez smiled, "That's sweet. Tell me, how does your wife feel about you being away so much?"

"She tolerates it. She knew what I did for a living when we met. In fact, she asked me to help her on an investigation. That's how we met. It worked out well, and we're doin fine. Off the record, she's gonna have another little one in springtime. Maybe a boy this time."

"It seems like you have it all under control then. Was there anything about this latest arrest that had you fooled?"

"Ah, actually, I didn't know that Des Arguello was involved with Atwill until the very end. Other than that, it came down pretty much as I suspected. There was a wild card in there that caused a problem, but that worked out, too."

"A wild card? How so?"

"A fella I arrested in Denver a few months back came lookin for me, but like I said, it worked itself out for the best."

"I guess so. The story about how you defeated Landon Atwill hasn't even hit the papers yet, and you're already the town's hero. Atwill was a nemesis to most everyone in town and the root of most of the crime hereabouts. Can you tell me anything about how you resolved his criminal ways?"

"Well, ah, sure, I guess. I was in a position where I had to shoot him and Des Arguello. Both had me at bay, but I found an opportunity. I was prepared to arrest Atwill, you know, and had Judge Staton issue a warrant. Just never got to use it cause of Arguello switchin' sides."

"And your wild card?"

"Well, that was the shotgun. 'Had no choice there either. 'Career outlaw… won't be missed."

Well, it sounds to me like the people of Laredo are well served. We have a new town marshal, I hear."

"Oh? The mayor approved it, then. Good, good. Ray Wilke is an honest man and very capable."

"And now there is to be a trial, according to the mayor. A murder trial for the suspects in the Harold Gosling killing along with his deputies. Will you be here for that?"

"Oh no. I'm not needed for that. Judge Staton has my report as well as affidavits from others involved. I suspect justice will be served proper without my presence."

They took a break from the question-and-answer conversation to eat lunch. Beefsteak and eggs for Bass and soup and a ham sandwich for Margaretta. When they had finished, Margaretta asked one last question.

"Marshal Bass, you have almost singlehandedly purged our town of corruption and what used to be the rampant crime done by known criminals crossing the Río without fear of retribution. I imagine you feel pretty good about yourself right now."

Bass took a moment to think back on his time in Laredo and finally said, "Well, I thank you for those fine words, Miss Perez, but I made a whole bunch of mistakes, too. Misjudging Des Arguello was one, but I also lost two prisoners in the mix, and that wild card outlaw I mentioned, well, he killed two innocent citizens as well. So I guess to answer your question I'd say yes and no. There always seems to be a trade-off when tryin to correct things."

They were both silent for a moment, and then Bass finished his second whiskey and said,

"Now, if you'll excuse me, Miss, I have a few things left to do." They rose at the same time, preparing to go their separate ways. Margaretta paid for lunch.

Bass's last task during his stay was to say farewell to Ray Wilke and advise him to pay Gus Freeman and Norm Hacket the seventy-five dollars he had promised and to send the bill to his office in El Paso.

He also said goodbye to Lonny Dahl, mentioning that he'd already talked to the judge on his behalf. He said, "If things work out for you, look me up in El Paso. Might be able to find work for you."

Finally, he took a last ride down to the Post Office, where he sent three telegrams.

The sun was warm, and a slight breeze had come up so he wrote out his messages at the window on the boardwalk.

First to Sally.

My Love. All wrapped up here. 'Heading home. I've sure missed my ladies. See you Sunday. love Frederick

Next, he pulled out the original wire he'd gotten from the governor. It had the name of the King Ranch Manager, and Bass wanted to let them know their cattle were available to retrieve.

Richard Kleberg – King Ranch, San Fernando Creek, Texas Mr. Kleberg, your cows are safe and ready to drive back home.

The outlaws have all been dealt with.

Town Marshal Wilke in Laredo will assist.

-U.S. Deputy Marshal Frank Bass

It was a long message, but it had to be sent. Bass figured if Kleberg had any questions, Ray Wilke could answer them. He then sent one last message, this one to Bart Mariany.

Bart- back Sunday. Horn is Dead.

– Bass.

End

The KING RANCH

The Rancho Santa Gertrudis (the King Ranch) was established in south Texas in 1853 by Riverboat Captain Richard King and a retired Texas Ranger named Gideon K. Lewis in the area known today as Wild Horse Desert. Originally a Spanish Land Grant, it is the largest working ranch in the country, with a total square mile area the size of Rhode Island. It was originally established as a cow camp along Santa Gertrudis Creek, which encompassed roughly 24 miles. Over time, the ranch grew through various partnerships and purchases, reaching its present total of 1,289 square miles.

Their original brand, *LK (Lewis and King),* is still used today, but the Running W, which is said to represent the horns of a Longhorn, was registered in 1869 and is most recognized today. The Ranch owns around twenty-eight registered brands.

Early in the twentieth century, King Ranch developed The Santa Gertrudis Breed, which was a cross between Brahman bulls (7/8ths purity) and purebred shorthorn cows. In 1923, a bull calf was born, and it became the founding sire of the Santa Gertrudis breed. These distinctive 'red cows' have become the standard for the King Ranch.

The Ranch also is involved in American Quarter-Horse breeding and sales. Every Quarter-Horse bred on the Ranch is descended from 'Old Sorrel, ' the Foundation Stallion of King Ranch. The expertise in breeding Quarter-Horses was carried over into Thorough-Bred Race Horses, and the Ranch's breed improvement program produced **ASSAULT,** the Triple Crown winner, in 1950. The Ranch's colt **MIDDLEGROUND** won both the Kentucky Derby and the Belmont Stakes. BOLD VENTURE (the 1936 Kentucky Derby and Preakness winner) sired these two colts out of thorough-bred mares acquired as part of the Quarter-horse breeding program.

Today, the King Ranch Headquarters is located in Kingsville, Texas. It is open to the public, and tours can be arranged via their website.

Oh, one last thing. I know I killed off Tom Horn in the second book of the series, **The Skills of Ezra Lacey,** *But he was just such a bad guy I figured, hell, I'll do it again.*

-Will Astrike

Acknowledgments

First, as always, I want to thank my wife, Sheryl, who is my first proofer and most ardent critic.

Also, I thank my writing group in Ashland, Oregon, for their encouragement and good-natured tolerance of my foolishness. They know who they are, so I will not mention them by name.

And finally, I want to thank my new friend Dan H. from Texas who has helped immeasurably in the editing of this book.

About the Author

Will Astrike is a retired western historian. He lives with his wife, Sheryl, in Oregon

He can be reached through his website at

www.westernauthor.net

Read more at https://www.westernauthor.net.

www.ingramcontent.com/pod-product-compliance
Lightning Source LLC
Chambersburg PA
CBHW060524160726
47991CB00001B/170